"Men like you are selfish," she continued, her voice trembling.

"You think your stupid beliefs give you the right to take whatever you want. But you're wrong. What you believe is wrong. And you're not going to win."

Her chest heaved. Her eyes stung, but she blinked back the tears, refusing to give him the satisfaction of seeing her cry. She would not show any weakness around this man.

His eyes turned even blacker. He closed the distance between them, but she held her ground, refusing to budge. "Stay in the hut, Nadira. Don't try to escape."

"Or what?" she taunted. "You'll kill me?" She let out a high-pitched laugh.

His big hands gripped her shoulders. He gave her a shake, fueling her temper even more.

But then his mouth was on hers. She froze, utterly shocked, the feel of him slaying her senses—his warm, hard lips, the scrape of his sandpapered jaw, the strength in his massive hands. A thought bubbled up, that she needed to resist this, but it vanished like smoke in the wind.

Buried Secrets: Three murder witnesses, one deadly conspiracy.

Dear Reader,

When most people think of cosmetic surgery, they think of facelifts and fillers, implants or liposuction—procedures designed to enhance a person's beauty and youth. But there is another side to plastic surgery, the healing side, restoring features disfigured by accidents, violence or disease.

The heroine of *Seduced by His Target,* Nadine Seymour is just such a plastic surgeon. She specializes in reconstructive work on battered women. Coming from an abusive background, Nadine understands the value corrective surgery can have, not just in making these victimized women beautiful again, but in helping repair their broken lives.

But Nadine has wounds of her own, deep ones she has avoided for fifteen years. Now, when her past finally catches up to her, she must stand her ground and confront her enemies, including a lethal warrior who is everything she most fears...and desires.

This is the last installment of the Buried Secrets trilogy. It has been quite an adventure watching these three courageous runaways confront their pasts, face down their biggest fears and earn the happy endings they deserve. I hope you've enjoyed their stories as much as I have.

Happy reading!

Gail Barrett

SEDUCED BY HIS TARGET

—

Gail Barrett

HARLEQUIN® ROMANTIC SUSPENSE

To John, one of the good guys.

Recycling programs
for this product may
not exist in your area.

ISBN-13: 978-0-373-27851-0

SEDUCED BY HIS TARGET

Copyright © 2013 by Gail Ellen Barrett

Printed in U.S.A.

HARLEQUIN®
www.Harlequin.com

Books by Gail Barrett

Harlequin Romantic Suspense

Cowboy Under Siege #1672
**High-Risk Reunion* #1682
**High-Stakes Affair* #1697
***Fatal Exposure* #1757
***A Kiss to Die For* #1766
***Seduced by His Target* #1781

Silhouette Romantic Suspense

Facing the Fire #1414
Heart of a Thief #1514
To Protect a Princess #1538
His 7-Day Fiancée #1560
The Royal Affair #1601
Meltdown #1610

Silhouette Special Edition

Where He Belongs #1722

*The Crusaders
**Stealth Knights
***Buried Secrets

Other titles by this author available
in ebook format.

GAIL BARRETT

always knew she'd be a writer. Who else would spend her childhood grinding sparkling rocks into fairy dust and convincing her friends it was real? Or daydream her way through elementary school, spend high school reading philosophy and playing the bagpipes, then head off to Spain during college to live the writer's life? After four years, she straggled back home—broke, but fluent in Spanish. She became a teacher, earned a master's degree in linguistics, married a coast-guard officer and had two sons.

But she never lost the desire to write. Then one day she discovered a Silhouette Intimate Moments novel in a bookstore—and knew she was destined to write romance. Her books have won numerous awards, including a National Readers' Choice Award and Romance Writers of America's prestigious Golden Heart Award.

Gail currently lives in western Maryland. Readers can contact her through her website, www.gailbarrett.com.

I'd like to thank my brother, Ken Archer, for helping me with the financial details of this story, and my critique partner, Karen Anders, for her expertise and support. Thank you both!

Chapter 1

It was the perfect day for a kidnapping.

Steel-gray clouds hovered over the mountains, obscuring their escape route. Thunder rumbled in the distance, promising to mask any cries for help. The local farmers, exhausted after a brutal day spent toiling in the Peruvian highlands, had taken shelter in their drab mud huts, oblivious to the terrorists preparing to pounce.

Gazing through his binoculars, Rasheed Davar lay flat on his belly in a tuft of *chiliwua* grass, studying the American medical team milling around their camp below. "Which one is the target?"

The terrorist beside him lowered his binoculars, his silver tooth gleaming in the dwindling light. "She's not here yet."

She? Rasheed shifted, a sliver of uneasiness stirring

inside him, but he clamped down hard on the doubt. He couldn't react, couldn't show any hesitation or concern. Too many lives depended on this mission's success—including his.

Schooling his expression into indifference, he thumbed the focus on his binoculars and continued to survey the camp. A young blond woman fed kindling into the campfire. A gray-haired man sat beside her, stirring something in a metal pot. Both wore scrubs, typical attire for the volunteer medical teams that traveled through the remote villages in the Andes Mountains doing humanitarian work. Another woman, a brunette in a bulky parka, knelt on a tarp laden with pharmaceutical supplies, sorting and packing them into various bags. On the periphery of the camp, beyond a cluster of dome-shaped tents, a brown-skinned man, his *chullo* hat and poncho marking him as a Peruvian native, tended the tethered mules.

"So what's the plan?" Rasheed asked.

The terrorist looked at him again. Known only as Amir, he had cold, flat eyes as black as death, and promising as much. Rasheed had met hundreds of men like him during the years he'd lived in the mountains of Jaziirastan, working his way through the training camps. Ruthless. Callous. Inured to all human feelings except one—sheer, unbridled hate. Men who would kill in a heartbeat, whose goal was the annihilation of anyone who didn't submit to their way of life. Zealots who destroyed innocents with utter disinterest, murdering women and children with no remorse.

Like Rasheed's pregnant wife.

"We'll wait for the woman to show up," Amir told him in his native Jaziirastani. "As soon as we identify her tent, we'll rejoin Manzoor. We'll move in tonight when the rain hits. Manzoor and I'll stand guard. You'll grab the woman. Just make sure you get the right one."

"I'll get her," he promised. He had no choice. He had to play his part.

But why did they want a prisoner? This crack terror cell, the Rising Light's most elite contingent, had come to Peru for one reason only—to join up with the South American drug cartel that would ferry them into the United States. Or so Rasheed had thought. This surprise detour to capture an American doctor didn't make sense.

But he didn't dare question their plans. Neither Amir nor Manzoor, their small cell's leader, trusted him completely, even though he'd been careful not to cause any doubt. He'd paid his dues. He'd spent years proving his loyalty as he rose through the Rising Light's ranks. And thanks to his Jaziirastani parents—and the CIA's most talented forgers—he had the linguistic skills and documents to pass as a native of that land. Whether the terrorists suspected him of being a traitor or were withholding information out of their usual paranoia, Rasheed didn't know. But he needed to show them the blind obedience they expected to keep from tipping them off.

"We'll exit that way," Amir continued, pointing toward a slot between the hills. "We'll need to move fast. God willing, we'll have success."

Rasheed gave the expected response. But his idea of success didn't match Amir's. He'd only celebrate when he'd thwarted the upcoming attack and brought down the terrorists' kingpin, the financier who'd murdered his wife.

Thunder drummed across the steep terrain. The wind bore down, sweeping through the wheat-colored clumps of grass, bringing with it the threat of rain. Then a movement on the trail below them caught his attention, and he aimed his binoculars that way, careful to keep the lens from reflecting the waning light. Two people, a man and a woman, came into view, both carting backpacks, both wearing jackets over their surgical scrubs.

Rasheed's pulse began to speed up.

The man led the way. He was tall, thin, probably in his mid-thirties, with a long, narrow face and a large hooked nose. He had a short, scraggly beard, and blisters on his nose and ears, thanks to the scorching, high-altitude sun.

The woman walked beside him, her head bent, her face hidden beneath her wide-brimmed hat. Rasheed stayed stone-still, keeping his binoculars trained on her as she hiked along. Then suddenly, she raised her head and glanced around, as if sensing his scrutiny, and he finally caught a glimpse of her face.

His breath made a hitch. His heart stumbled through several beats. "That's the target?" he blurted out, unable to conceal his disbelief.

"That's her."

She was beautiful. Strikingly so with high, sculpted cheekbones, delicately winged black brows and a full, lush mouth in her tawny face. Her skin was satin smooth, her lips a tempting pink. She wore her long black hair in a single braid, but the wind had worked the shorter strands loose, sending them dancing around her face. She moved with an athletic grace, hinting at a slender build beneath her coat. But it was her remarkable face that held him spellbound, making it damned near impossible to breathe.

Then she turned her head, staring straight into the binoculars, and everything inside him stilled. Her eyes were green, the cool, silvery-green of desert sagebrush or ancient olive trees. The pale color was unexpected, captivating, provoking something instinctive inside him—the primitive male urge to possess.

His ancestors would have raided for her, started wars over her, killed for her. She had the rare kind of beauty coveted by sheikhs and kings.

"Who is she?" he asked, aware he was taking a risk. Questions aroused suspicions. And he'd worked too hard to infiltrate this terror cell to blow his cover now.

But this woman…

"She looks Middle Eastern," he added as an excuse.

Amir grunted. "She's Jaziirastani."

Jaziirastani? Why were they kidnapping a woman from their own country? His curiosity mounted, but Rasheed knew better than to ask. He had to bide his time, displaying the blind compliance the terrorists expected while somehow ferreting out their plans.

The target hiked across the clearing toward the tents, her movements graceful despite her pack. She dropped off the unwieldy backpack with the woman organizing the supplies and lingered for a moment to chat. He studied the tilt of her head, the elegant way she moved her hands, still wondering who she could be. Then she continued to a large, gray-and-blue tent beneath a tree. She disappeared inside, emerging a few minutes later wearing jeans instead of scrubs, and started back across the camp toward the fire.

Amir caught his eye. His checkered kaffiyeh headscarf flapped in the wind. "We have the information we need. She's in the farthest tent. Let's go." He started scooting backward through the grass.

Rasheed hesitated, shooting the medical group another look as they went about their tasks, heedless of the raid that was about to shatter their night. If only he could warn them. They'd come here with noble intentions, doing their part to mitigate the misery of the impoverished farmers' lives. And they didn't deserve the fear they were about to suffer during the attack.

But he couldn't risk it. He couldn't do anything to blow his cover now, not when this mission's success lay squarely in his hands. Because whatever these terrorists had planned, whatever the reason they'd hired a drug cartel to smuggle them into the United States, this thing was huge, rumored to rival 9/11 in scope. And it was up to him to discover their plot and stop them, no matter what it took.

The sky grew dim. Thunder grumbled again, rolling up the valley and reverberating against the terraced hills. The medical team members halted their activities and looked up. The clouds were drawing closer, their tombstone-colored bottoms growing more ominous as they dragged rain across the jagged peaks. The mules picketed beside the tents began to stir.

Aware of Amir's impatience, Rasheed spared the Jaziirastani woman a final glance. No, he couldn't warn them. He couldn't risk interfering in the attack. All he could do was try to protect them the best he could while keeping his goal in sight.

If there was one thing Nadine Seymour would never understand, it was man's propensity for violence. No matter where she'd traveled or worked—whether in glitzy New York City, in her father's native land of Jaziirastan, or here, in the isolated mountain villages of Peru where thatch-roofed huts clung precariously to the craggy hillsides—she'd come across the same defeated women, their bodies battered and bruised, their eyes filled with hopelessness and despair.

She would never understand it. Never accept it. And she sure as hell would never put herself in a position to experience it firsthand.

"So how did it go today?"

Her lower back aching, her head throbbing from the scarcity of oxygen at fourteen thousand feet, she lowered herself beside the campfire and warmed her hands. She glanced at Henry, taking in his kind blue eyes, his sparse gray hair sticking up in disarray, the white whiskers emerging on his jaw. A retired general practitioner in his late sixties, he'd helped organize this trek along the ancient Inca trade routes to the tiny hamlets scattered throughout the peaks—places where there was no electricity, no running water, no medical service or phones. Just unrelenting misery and abuse.

"The same as always," she said, releasing a sigh. "Parasites, basal cells, some battered women and kids."

"Did many people show up?"

"Yeah, we missed you." Their small team—two doctors, two nurses, a pharmacist and an interpreter who doubled as their cook, mule tender and guide—had been traveling in the Andes with Medical Help International, a private charitable organization, for over a month now, in areas so remote some villagers had never seen foreigners before. But despite the isolation, word of their impending arrival had spread, and people had straggled into their makeshift clinic all day, standing patiently in line for hours, and paying with whatever they could—food, blankets, coins, even an occasional chicken or bird. Twelve hours later, the last few patients had finally left, their prescription drugs tucked into their *unkuña* carrying cloths, hiking in their tiretread sandals back to their potato farms and alpaca herds hidden in the ravines creasing the hills.

"The violence is always the worst." Her voice hardened at the thought. These people had a tough enough time simply trying to survive. Not only did they battle poverty—including a disheartening lack of basic amenities—but they faced danger from the drug runners smuggling coca north into Brazil and Colombia, destined for the markets in the United States. They didn't need the added terror of domestic abuse. "I'd like to find someplace it doesn't exist for once."

Henry's eyes softened. "I'm not going to argue with that, but your impression might be a little off."

"I know." As a plastic surgeon in New York City, she specialized in reconstructive work. And while she saw her share of accident victims and cancer survivors, she'd also seen far too many faces destroyed by fists— just as she had growing up.

Setting that depressing memory aside, she summoned a smile. "I'm just tired, I guess." They'd spent weeks on the trail, sleeping in tents, hiking into villages so high she could hardly breathe. Sometimes they saved a life. That hope kept them going, making them feel they were doing some good, even if their efforts never seemed like enough. But sometimes the suffering overwhelmed her, despite her attempts to stay upbeat.

"I'm sorry I couldn't help," Henry said.

She cast the elderly doctor another glance, unable to miss the wistfulness in his voice. "Don't be silly." Henry was suffering from a moderate case of altitude sickness, or *soroche* as the locals called it, which had kept him confined to the camp. Except for Manny, their native interpreter, they'd all suffered headaches and fatigue as they'd crossed the slopes. But Henry's case had been the worst, dangerously so.

"How's your head?" she asked.

"Better."

"Have you been chewing the coca leaves?"

"Yes, Doctor Seymour." He slid her a cheeky smile.

She didn't smile back. They still had several more hamlets—at an even higher elevation—to reach before they headed down to a safer altitude. "You sure you want to continue?"

"Of course."

"What's your reading on the pulse oximeter?"

"Nearly eighty."

"Eighty? It should be back in the nineties by now. The high nineties." Cerebral edema, swelling of the brain caused by a lack of oxygen, wasn't a joke. Hikers died from it every year—which Henry knew. "Tell me your name and birth date."

Henry sighed. "I'm not confused, no more than I usually am. My pulse is normal. My gait's steady. My appetite is coming back. Don't worry. I'll tell you if it gets any worse."

Assuming he was lucid enough to notice. "You'd better." Not only was the trail about to get steeper, but they were entering an area notorious for drug smugglers. Hopefully, their organization's scouts were right, and the drug cartel had moved out due to the rainy season about to begin. But the team still had to move quickly and keep their wits about them if they hoped to survive unscathed.

"I'm monitoring it," Henry assured her. "And I *am* getting better. I just need another day to rest. I'll be jogging up the trail in no time."

She studied his face. He was still too pale and drawn, but maybe he'd improved a bit. Still, she'd been on these trips with him before. She knew how stubborn he could be. How generous. He would never want to slow them down and deny a villager their services— even if it killed him to soldier on.

A rumble of thunder caught her attention, and she looked up. Still worried, she studied the storm clouds crawling over the peaks, their slab-gray bottoms laden with rain. Lovely. By the time they set out in the morning, they'd be trudging through mud. She just hoped their tents didn't wash away before then. "I'd better help Lauren secure the supplies."

Henry started to rise with her, but she held up her hand. "Stop right there. You're going to sit here and have another cup of coca tea. And chew a few leaves while you're at it. Doctor's orders." She smiled at Henry's salute.

Hurrying now, she started toward the tarp where the pharmacist had spread out their medical supplies, reorganizing them for the following day. But halfway across the clearing, that odd feeling returned, the same creepy sensation that had plagued her earlier, as if someone had her in his sights. She came to a stop and glanced around, scanning the steep hills surrounding the camp, the long, yellow grass waving in the wind, the lone hawk riding the thermals in the gloomy sky.

Her heart still beating fast, she shifted her gaze to the camp itself—the tents grouped to one side, their native interpreter, Manny, tending the mules nearby. The pharmacist rushed to bundle up their medications while the two nurses carted the finished packs to the supply tent to keep them dry.

Nothing was wrong. No one was watching her. She was imagining that ripple of danger, the shock of remembered fear.

With effort, she shook the feeling aside. She was being ridiculous. No one could have found her here. How much more isolated could she get? She was tired, that was all. She just needed a hot meal, a warm sleeping bag and a good night's rest to feel like herself again.

The wind whipped down, splattering icy raindrops over her cheeks. *So much for comfort.* Still, she could bear it. She'd faced far worse conditions than a freezing rainstorm during the years she'd lived on the streets.

But as she continued toward the pharmacist, the doubts came back full force. No matter where she was, no matter how much time had passed, she could never be completely safe. And she couldn't afford to forget that—because if her enemies ever caught up with her, she'd be dead.

The uneasy feeling was back.

Nadine lay motionless in her sleeping bag several hours later, her breathing shallow, her gaze glued on the walls of her pitch-black tent. The rain bludgeoned the roof. The wind gusted and moaned, buffeting the nylon sides and tearing at the meager stakes. Above the storm, a mule made a plaintive *haw* while thunder crashed and shook the ground.

Something had woken her up. But there was no way she could have heard anything above the raging storm. And yet, the feeling of danger consumed her, the sensation that something bad was about to occur.

Knowing better than to ignore her instincts, she sat up. The pharmacist, Lauren, lay sleeping beside her. Anne, one of the nurses on the trip, snored on her other side. Nadine visualized the small camp's layout—the men's red tent, the smaller supply tent where Manny slept, enjoying his privacy. He was the only one who traveled armed.

The mule brayed again, followed by something that sounded like a horse's neigh. Struck again by the feeling of wrongness, she held her breath, struggling to distinguish sounds in the seething storm. Surely she'd imagined the horse. No one would venture out on a night like this.

Not quite convinced, she dressed quickly in her sweater and jeans. She tugged on her boots and laced them, then took hold of the flashlight and lowered herself back onto the sleeping bag. Of course, she was overreacting. Sure, they were traveling through an area prone to drug smugglers, men who carried on a lucrative side business kidnapping foreigners for cash. But they were south of the coca fields. MHI, the agency that organized the trip, had monitored the situation carefully and hadn't spotted any drug cartel activity in months.

And there was no way her family could have caught up with her out here. She'd fled her home—and the marriage her Jaziirastani father had arranged—over fifteen years ago. And while they'd promised retaliation, vowing to kill her to avenge their slighted honor, they couldn't possibly have found her, not after all this time. She'd changed her name. She'd created a fictitious identity, complete with documentation, including a passport so authentic she routinely sailed through United States immigration points without a hitch. Even the most dogged investigator couldn't connect her to Nadira al Kahtani, the terrified girl she'd once been.

A man shouted near the tent. Startled, she sat bolt upright again. *Manny.* He'd probably heard the mules and gone outside to calm them down. Maybe he needed her help. If those mules got loose, they'd have to chase them all over the mountains to find them, wasting valuable time.

Making a quick decision, she pulled on her hat and coat. She didn't relish getting soaked, but she couldn't shirk her responsibilities. They all had to work together to make this trip a success. And Henry couldn't offer much assistance in his weakened state.

She picked up the flashlight and flicked it on. Careful not to disturb her tent-mates, she crawled over her sleeping bag to the storage area near the door.

Suddenly, the flap whipped back. Startled, she glanced up, catching sight of a man's dark face. He hurtled inside in a burst of cold and rain, knocking the wind from her lungs as he slammed her down.

Chapter 2

Rasheed sprawled over the writhing woman, struggling to get her under control. He didn't want to hurt her. He didn't want to involve the other women in the tent and risk their capture, too. But his target bucked and squirmed beneath him, yanking his hair, raking her nails down his cheek, making it difficult to hold on. Then she dug her thumbs into his eyes.

He reared back in the nick of time. *Damn.* Whoever this woman was, she knew how to fight. Fed up, he grabbed hold of her arms and dragged her outside the tent into the blustery storm.

Rain lashed his face. The wind clawed at his hair and clothes. The woman managed to jerk one hand free and lunged toward him, jabbing her finger into his armpit, sending pain shuddering through his nerves, despite his coat. He swore, but didn't let go.

Instead, he tackled her to the ground then flipped her over and sat atop her, using his weight to hold her down. But she trapped his feet against her side and knocked his arms loose in a move so quick it caught him unprepared. Then she rolled him over and tried to stand.

His respect for her grew, even as his training kicked in. He still didn't want to harm her. But damn it, he had to play his part. And frankly, she was better off with him than the real terrorists, who'd probably kill her if she tried to resist. Using brute force, he took her down again, ignoring her yelp of pain.

Knowing he had to hurry, that too much could go wrong if he drew this out, he whipped out a scarf and secured her wrists behind her back as she thrashed and struggled to rise. Thunder boomed. Lightning crackled in the sky, illuminating the woman's furious green eyes. His breath sawing, he wrapped another scarf around her mouth, muffling her angry cries.

Then he stood. Breathing heavily, he pulled her upright. She took a quick step back, intending to run, but he went in low and scooped her up. Then he slung her over his back in a fireman's carry and loped toward his waiting horse.

She squirmed, and he staggered off balance, nearly dropping her in the mud. The wind howled past. The skies seemed to open up, the rain bucketing down so hard he could barely see. He made it to the horse, then tossed her over the saddle, and started to untie the lead.

But she wriggled loose and fell. Lightning scissored the sky, followed by a vicious crack of thunder. Already spooked—and with a woman now crawling beneath his hooves—the gelding reared and tried to bolt.

Swearing, Rasheed dived at his captive and dragged her from beneath the trembling horse. He had no choice now. She'd get killed if she tried to run. And he couldn't reason with her. She'd never cooperate with a kidnapper, even if it was for her own good.

Wishing he could avoid it, he gripped her neck, bearing down on the pressure points. Short seconds later, she slumped, unconscious, to the ground. He spared a moment to soothe the gelding, then picked up the woman and draped her over the pommel, positioning her so she wouldn't fall.

"Easy," he told the prancing horse. Still trying to catch his breath, he unhitched the lead and sprang into the saddle, adjusting his prisoner across his thighs.

Lightning erupted in a staccato burst, revealing the billowing sheets of rain cleaving the night. Rasheed glanced at the camp, taking in the chaotic scene. One man lay on the ground. Another chased the mules as they galloped off. The tents flapped like sheets on a clothesline, their stakes torn loose by the savage storm.

He sent a fleeting wish for the medical team's safety, hoping they'd be all right.

He was less certain about the spitfire in his lap.

Holding on to his unconscious captive, he wheeled his gelding around. He spurred him into motion, cantering to the trailhead where the leader of the terror cell lay in wait. Then, with the thunderstorm raging around him, he raced off into the night.

Nadine regained consciousness bit by bit. Her forehead throbbed. Her throat felt bruised and raw. Every inch of her body ached, from her incredibly sore ribs to the fire scorching through her shoulder blades. And she couldn't seem to move her arms.

Someone had kidnapped her. The realization flooded through her in a rush. Henry. Lauren. Manny. Oh, God. Where were they? Panicked, she wrenched open her eyes. Then she blinked, struggling to orient herself and make out shapes in the inky night. Flames from a campfire flickered several yards off. The rain had stopped, but moisture clung to the air, so she doubted much time had passed. More impressions began to emerge from the darkness—the low rocks slanting above her, the trickle of nearby water, the chill from the stone floor seeping into her bones. She was in a cave, her hands bound, her back propped against the wall.

She'd dressed before the attack, so she still wore her jacket and jeans. But she'd lost her cap, and her wet hair clung to her neck and cheeks, adding to the cold. Her arms were completely numb.

She wriggled her icy fingers, then pulled on her restraint, unable to loosen the knot. At least her kidnappers had removed her gag, enabling her to breathe.

But who had captured her and why?

She turned her head, focusing on the campfire outside the cave. Three men sat around it, a row of boulders at their backs. To the right were several horses, their saddlebags piled nearby. To the left was a sheer rock wall. Smoke from the campfire rose in lazy wisps, then dissipated in the pitch-black air.

Trying not to attract their attention, she studied the men again. One lay on his side, asleep. Beside him, a man wearing a white turban cleaned his weapons and whistled an off-key tune. The closest man sat facing the campfire, his back to the cave, his collar-length black hair gleaming like obsidian in the wavering light.

They all had jet-black hair. The two she could see best had swarthy skin and beards. Were they Hispanic? Middle Eastern? Her heart swerved hard at the thought.

But that was ridiculous. They couldn't be Middle Eastern, despite the turban the one man wore. They had to be drug runners. Who else would be traveling through the Andes on horseback—and kidnapping foreigners, no less?

Besides, who these men were, or why they'd brought her here didn't matter right now. She had to concentrate on getting free.

Except…where were the other prisoners? Surely they hadn't only kidnapped her?

Frowning, she ran her gaze around the cave again. This time, she caught sight of a man lying prostrate in the shadows, and her heart missed several beats. *Henry.* She couldn't mistake his gray hair. And of all the people to kidnap…he was already suffering from altitude sickness. He couldn't take any more abuse.

But where was the rest of the team? Her uneasiness growing, she struggled to remember details about the attack. But all she recalled was a kaleidoscope of jumbled impressions—slashing rain, a heavily muscled man knocking her down, the scream of a frightened horse. The storm had been too fierce, the raid too fast. Maybe the other team members had gotten away.

And if they had, they'd immediately mount a rescue…or maybe not. They wouldn't know where the kidnappers had gone. The rain would have erased their tracks. And even assuming they did catch up, they couldn't take on a drug cartel. It would be suicidal to try, especially since Manny had the only gun. No, they'd head straight down the mountain to the nearest town and summon help.

Which meant she was on her own. She had to decide on a plan, then help Henry escape while they still had the advantage of surprise.

Assuming he was alive.

Her eyes swung back to their captors. The men continued to lounge around the campfire, still not looking her way. But they didn't need to keep watch. They'd blocked the mouth of the cave, trapping Henry and her inside.

Her hands bound, her movements awkward, she fought her way to her knees. Then she crept across the cold, stone ground toward Henry. Several difficult yards later, she reached his side.

"Henry," she whispered, kneeling beside him. He groaned, and she tried again. "Are you all right?"

His eyes fluttered open, and he clutched his head. "Nadine?" He sounded dazed. "What the hell...?"

"Shh. We've been kidnapped. How do you feel?"

"Awful. Like a mule stepped on my head."

She could imagine. "Can you loosen this scarf? My hands are tied."

Grimacing, he released his head. "I'll try."

"Hold on. Don't move." She swiveled around, leaning close enough for him to reach her wrists. Then she waited while he fumbled with the knots.

"It's wet. I can't... Wait. Here we go." A second later, the scarf slithered free.

Prickles stabbed her arms. She gasped at the rush of pain, then bit down hard on a moan. Hunching her shoulders, she rubbed her arms and hissed as the circulation began to return.

"Are you okay?" Henry whispered.

Still wincing, she sucked in a breath. "I'm fine." Better than he was, at any rate. Trying to ignore her discomfort, she turned to him again. "Come on. Sit up so I can check your head."

Scooting closer, she wrapped her arm around his waist. Then she slowly tugged him upright and leaned him against the wall. She slanted a quick glance at the men outside, but they weren't paying attention to them. *Yet.*

"I've got a penlight," Henry said. He reached into his jacket pocket and pulled it out.

"Wait." Nadine crawled around Henry, positioning herself between him and the cave's entrance in case their captors looked their way. Then she clicked on the tiny flashlight and trained it on his scalp. "You've got a knot and a nasty gash. Look at me." She angled the light toward his eyes. "Your pupils look good. Do you have any nausea? Dizziness?"

"Both. I probably have a concussion."

"Hopefully a mild one. Does anything hurt besides your head?"

He grimaced. "Isn't that enough?"

"Definitely." A concussion combined with altitude sickness would cause anyone tremendous pain, let alone a man his age.

She eyed his head again. "We really need to clean that cut. I don't suppose these guys have a first aid kit."

"Doubtful." He craned his neck to see the men outside the cave. "So who are they?"

"Good question." One she didn't have a clue how

to answer yet. "I'm guessing it's the drug cartel the agency warned us about."

"I thought they'd moved out of the area."

"That's what they said. Obviously, they were wrong."

Henry slumped back against the rock and closed his eyes. "So what are we going to do?"

"Get you to a hospital, for one thing." He needed medical attention at once—an oxygen tank, a CT scan and several days of bed rest, preferably at a lower altitude.

But how could they escape? Henry wouldn't last on foot. A jolting race down the mountain on horseback would make his concussion worse. And even if they could slip past their captors, where would they go? She had no idea where they were. She couldn't roam aimlessly around the Andes in the darkness with an injured man in tow.

But neither could she leave him behind.

Her gaze gravitated back to the men. She didn't want to bargain with their kidnappers. But what other choice did she have? And maybe they'd made a mistake. Maybe they'd captured the wrong people—and she could convince them to let them go.

"Stay here," she murmured to Henry. "Let me deal with this." Inhaling to gather her courage, she rose and walked to the entrance of the cave.

The captor with the turban stopped sharpening his knife at her approach. His gaze pinned hers, and she abruptly stopped, a stark chill scuttling through her nerves. His eyes looked cruel and utterly ruthless, as if every trace of humanity had disappeared from his soul. And she knew instinctively that this thug would kill her in a heartbeat without a qualm.

He muttered something she couldn't hear to the dozing man. That man roused himself and sat upright, and her disquiet edged up a notch. He had the same full beard and swarthy skin, but he was heavier, with a coarse, flat nose and fleshy lips. He also wore a scarf, the black-and-white-checkered kaffiyeh that the Arabs wore. His silver tooth winked in the light.

Shuddering, she crossed her arms, the impression that they were Middle Eastern growing stronger now. But even with their head coverings it didn't make sense. They *had* to belong to a drug cartel. She was in the mountains of Peru, not the Middle East.

But the way they continued to stare at her with something akin to hatred in their eyes…

Memories bubbled up, fragments from news reports she'd read—how Middle Eastern terrorists had formed partnerships with South American drug cartels who smuggled them into the United States.

Nonsense. She couldn't go off the deep end and let paranoia skew her thoughts. She squared her shoulders and raised her chin. *"Oiga,"* she said in Spanish. "Excuse me."

Neither man answered, and her belly made a little clutch. They had to understand Spanish. Unless they spoke an indigenous language, like Quechua or Aymara…

She racked her brains, scrambling to remember the handful of phrases she'd learned. *"Imainalla-kashanki.* Hello. Do you speak Spanish?"

The third man lumbered to his feet. He turned, and his gaze slammed into hers. And for a moment, she couldn't move. The intensity in his eyes held her riveted, cementing her in place. Startled, she took in his dark, slashing brows, his collar-length coal-black hair, his high, bold nose in his chiseled face. He was tall and lean, with broad shoulders tapering to a flat belly and muscled thighs. His mouth was hard, his onyx eyes unreadable, not providing any hints of his thoughts. But his hot black eyes simmered with intelligence, prompting another flurry of nerves.

This was the man who'd attacked her. She couldn't mistake him. The scratches she'd carved on his cheeks gave him away.

He wasn't exactly handsome. Taken individually, his features were too rough-hewn for that. But he was striking, incredibly so, from the sharp perception in his unwavering eyes to the day's growth of beard stubble darkening his jaw. He reminded her of a primitive warrior, an ancient desert sheikh.

A man she'd do well not to underestimate.

He skirted the fire and headed toward her, then stopped a few feet away. This close, she could see the straight, inky lashes fringing his eyes, the stark grooves bracketing his grim mouth, the sensual shape of his bottom lip. Her nails had barely missed his left eye, and one long scrape ran from the upper edge of his cheekbone into his beard stubble, adding to his ruthless look. He was half a head taller than she was, putting her at eye level with the hollow of his muscled throat. She tilted her head back to meet his eyes.

For several seconds, he didn't speak. Instead, he continued to study her, spurring her heart to an off-kilter beat. Then he lowered his gaze, letting it travel slowly over the length of her, causing her heart to race. His gaze flicked back to hers, the impact no less powerful this time. And she couldn't mistake the sexual awareness flitting through his eyes.

The answering warmth in her body shocked her. Appalled, she hugged her arms.

"What do you want?" he asked in English. *Flawless, American English.*

"You're American?"

"No." He didn't elaborate, but she angled her head, studying him with even more interest now. Few non-native speakers had an accent that perfect. He *must* have spent time in the States—which might make him sympathize with them.

"Listen," she began. "I don't know who you were after, but you must have made a mistake. I'm a doctor. So is Henry, the man I'm with. You must have confused us with someone else."

He folded his arms, the motion emphasizing the breadth of his muscled chest. "We didn't make a mistake."

Taken aback, she tried to recoup. "If you're after a ransom—"

"We're not."

Her heart skipped. *They had to be.* Ignoring his answer, she tried again. "I can get the money. I have a friend, a photographer. She can come up with whatever you want. Just take us to a town where I can contact her."

His black eyes continued to hold her. Firelight danced on his swarthy skin, emphasizing the harsh hollows of his granite face. "I told you. We don't want your money."

"But then…" She glanced at the other men. Their fixed stares further unnerved her, and she tightened her grip on her arms. And suddenly, visions spun through her mind of terrified captives paraded across the television screen, pleading desperately for their lives—and then slain. Did these men intend to *kill* them?

No. She quashed a burst of dread. She couldn't start imagining the worst. They probably planned to negotiate a prisoner swap, to force the Peruvian or American government to free a jailed criminal in exchange for them. FARC had used that tactic in Colombia for years. Maybe these men were doing the same.

But that brought dangers of its own. She couldn't risk the public exposure, no matter how much she wanted to get free. She'd spent too many years on the run, always moving, always changing her identity, carefully staying out of the limelight to evade the enemies dogging her. Not only was her powerful family hunting her down, but she had a gang executioner on her trail, a man who needed to ensure her silence after she'd chanced upon his crime. And if he ever figured out who she was, he wouldn't just go after her. He'd pursue the other two witnesses, her closest friends.

But as much as she wanted to bolt she couldn't worry about herself right now. She had to think of Henry, and get him to a hospital fast. She'd plot her own escape later, once she made sure he was safe.

She lifted her gaze to her kidnapper's, wishing she could read the thoughts behind those impenetrable black eyes. "Is there a reason you need two doctors? Does someone need medical help?"

"No."

"Because Henry's hurt. He has a concussion. Altitude sickness, too. He needs urgent medical care. We need to get him down the mountain to a hospital before his condition gets any worse."

His brows snapped into a frown. He glanced toward the cave behind her, a hint of uncertainty flitting through his eyes. Or had she imagined that? Just because he spoke English like a native didn't mean he had a heart.

But whether he sympathized with them or not didn't matter. She had to convince him to let Henry go.

"Henry has HACE," she continued. "High altitude cerebral edema. His brain is swelling, and the concussion is making it worse. If we don't get him to a lower altitude immediately, he could die."

The white-turbaned man by the campfire rose. Her kidnapper glanced his way, and suddenly, a shutter fell over his face, every trace of sympathy vanishing from his eyes. "Get back in the cave," he told her and turned away.

But she leaped out and grabbed his arm. "Wait."

He stopped. He slowly turned to face her, his gaze trained on hers. An electric jolt sizzled through her, the iron feel of his bulging biceps scorching her palm like a red-hot brand. Startled, she released her grip. What was *that*? Shaken at her odd reaction, she stepped back.

"Please." She inhaled to steady her nerves. "Henry and I… We're not important. No one cares if we disappear or not. And the organization we're with, Medical Help International, won't negotiate with you. We signed an agreement. They're not responsible for rescuing us if anything goes wrong."

"I told you, we don't want your money."

"Then what *do* you want?"

He didn't answer, and she tried again. "There's no

point in keeping Henry. You can't possibly need him. He's too sick. You have to let him go."

The white-turbaned man approached, fingering his gun. Nadine sucked in a breath, determined not to show any fear. But this man's dead eyes made her insides crawl.

"What's wrong?" he asked her kidnapper in Arabic, and her heart stopped cold. Oh, God. These men *were* Middle Eastern.

What were they doing here?

Her kidnapper turned to the turbaned man. "The man in the cave is hurt. She wants us to let him go."

Her lungs seized up. Dizziness barreled through her, and she feared she was going to heave. They weren't only speaking Arabic, but Jaziirastani, a dialect spoken only in her father's country.

The father who wanted her dead.

The man's hate-filled eyes burned into hers. "He's staying with us. Now shut up and get back in the cave."

Nausea roiled inside her. She couldn't seem to draw a breath. But she had to stay calm, *think* and get Henry out of this mess—before he ended up dead.

"I'm sorry," she said in English, trying her best to look confused. "I don't understand what you're saying. I don't speak your language."

"The hell you don't, *Nadira al Kahtani*. Now get back in the cave or I'll shoot your friend."

Her knees went weak. Shocked speechless, she staggered backward, then stumbled into the cave. She wobbled over to Henry and collapsed on the ground beside him, her carefully built world crashing apart.

"What happened?" he asked.

Too overwhelmed to answer, she pulled her legs to her chest, her entire body starting to shake.

They knew her name. They knew who she really was.

"Did you find out what they want?" he asked again.

She'd found out, all right. *They wanted her.*

After fifteen years on the run, her past had caught up with her. And this time it looked as if there was no way out.

Chapter 3

Rasheed couldn't believe it. Their captive was Nadira al Kahtani, the daughter of his prime suspect. *The daughter of the man who'd murdered his wife.*

Still struggling to process that bombshell, he adjusted the cinch on his gelding's saddle as the terrorists prepared to ride out. He'd known she was Middle Eastern. And he could see her as a member of the Jaziirastani royal family with her regal, spirited air. But Nadira al Kahtani? The daughter of the banker financing this terrorist mission? It didn't make any sense.

Incredulous at the revelation, he shuffled through his memories, trying to reconcile this stunning development with what he knew of the secretive clan. Yousef al Kahtani was a wealthy Jaziirastani banker who resided in Washington, D.C. The intelligence community had long suspected him of funneling money to the Rising Light terrorists and funding jihadist activity worldwide. But thanks to his generous campaign contributions, he also had power. And every time they got close to unraveling his murky activities, some high-level politician ran interference, stopping the investigation in its tracks.

Al Kahtani's wife had died over a decade ago. Aside from a son, Sultan, he had a daughter, Nadira, rumored to be both brilliant and beautiful, who'd disappeared shortly after her mother's death. In fact, she'd dropped off the grid so completely the CIA assumed she'd returned to her father's native country, where she'd either married or died.

Rasheed shot a glance at the woman sitting near the entrance to the cave. He skimmed the elegant lines of her profile, the feminine arch of her brows, and his pulse took another skip. Intel had definitely gotten the *beautiful* part right, especially with her startling green eyes. But where had she been for all these years? How had these terrorists found her when the CIA couldn't track her down? And if her father was financing this jihadist expedition, why would they capture her?

Growing even more confused now, he turned his attention to their extra supply horse and inspected the tack for frays. No matter what the explanation for the kidnapping, their cell leader, Manzoor, couldn't have plotted it on his own. He might be in charge of their crack contingent, but he didn't have the power to shape their agenda, only to carry out their attacks.

So who had authorized the woman's abduction? Why would they kidnap her now, en route to an important mission—a mission rumored to be so catastrophic it had the intelligence community running scared? And if al Kahtani wasn't funding the upcoming attack, who was?

Unable to come up with an answer, Rasheed grabbed the horses' reins and led them to the cave. But there was one thing he did know—everything about this kidnapping felt off. His instincts were clamoring hard. And he had to watch his back. Yousef al Kahtani was no fool. He'd evaded prosecution for years, running a financial operation so labyrinthine even the CIA couldn't sort it out. And this could all be an elaborate ruse. Al Kahtani could have sent his daughter here to investigate *him.* He'd penetrated Rasheed's cover once before—and killed his wife to warn him off.

Now he might be using his daughter to strike again.

The woman rose at his approach. She straightened her spine and faced him—her chin canted high, her hands balled into fists, her gorgeous eyes challenging his—a show of feistiness he'd come to expect after the way she'd fought him off. But as he drew to a stop beside her, he caught a myriad of other emotions crowding her eyes—worry, uncertainty, *fear.*

He frowned. The fear could be an act, a way to gain his sympathy and test where his loyalty lay. But could she actually make her face go pale on command?

And if she *wasn't* pretending, if she wasn't in cahoots with her father, and she really was an innocent victim in this attack, then why had they kidnapped her? What did she know about their plans?

He came to a stop, resolved. Whatever the answer, he had to find out. Thousands of American lives hung in the balance, depending on his success.

"Henry's getting worse," she announced. "We need to get him to a hospital right now."

Rasheed shifted his attention to the injured doctor and inwardly groaned. She was right. The poor guy looked like the epitome of misery with his thin shoulders bowed, his hair sticking up in snowy clumps, his hands cradling his bloody head.

But what could he do to help? He didn't have the authority to let him go. And showing even a hint of sympathy would invite the terrorists' attention, increasing their suspicions of him.

Cursing this complication, he reached into his saddlebag and handed her a pouch of leaves. "Here. Try these."

Her jaw sagged. "Coca leaves? Are you kidding? He doesn't have a tension headache. He has a concussion. I told you. This is serious, life threatening. He needs oxygen and a CT scan."

And *he* had a cover to maintain. He couldn't afford to act out of character with so many lives on the line. Keeping his expression blank, he shrugged. "If you find an oxygen tank lying around, help yourself. In the meantime, you'll have to make do with that."

Her cheeks flushed. Her eyes darkened to forest-green, her indignation clear. And without warning that attraction leaped between them, that deep, sensual awareness he'd felt toward her from the start. And he had the damnedest urge to haul her against him, to turn that passion toward something more pleasurable—a kiss that would make them burn.

Stunned, he turned back to the horse. What the hell? Talk about the wrong woman! She was the daughter of a terrorist, his prime suspect, the man who'd ordered his wife's death. She couldn't get more off-limits than that.

Not that there was a *right* woman. He didn't have relationships anymore, not since his wife had died. He'd spent too many years in the terror training camps, too many years living amid the dregs of society to ever lead a normal life. That part of him was gone. And even if he could turn back time and be the man that he once was, he wouldn't do it. He refused to put a woman in jeopardy again.

Dragging his mind back to his mission—the *only* thing that mattered—he glanced at Henry again. "You know how to ride?"

The doctor looked up, confusion in his dazed eyes. "I went on a pony ride once as a kid."

Great. A regular Buffalo Bill. "How about you?" he asked Nadira.

Her eyes narrowed. "Why? Where are we going?"

Not bothering to answer, he motioned toward the extra horse. "You can ride the mare. Henry will ride with me."

"He can't ride. I told you, he has a concussion."

"Would he be better off on foot?"

"He'd be better off if you hadn't kidnapped him."

No kidding. And as soon as they reached a village, he'd try to convince the terrorists to leave him behind. But in the meantime…

He glanced at the men sitting astride their horses—their sharp gazes taking in every detail of the exchange—and hardened his voice. "Look. We're heading out. You can ride or walk—your choice. But either way, you're going to move. Both of you. *Now.*"

Nadira crossed her arms. Her full lips flattened into a mulish line. Rasheed held her gaze, knowing he couldn't afford to relent—not with the terrorists watching their moves. She'd pay too high a price if he did.

But Henry lurched to his feet, interrupting the standoff, and staggered his way. "Don't worry. I can ride."

Sure he could. The man could barely stand upright, let alone trot down a mountain trail. But without a helicopter to airlift him to a hospital, what other choice did he have?

With a sigh, he mounted his horse. He held out a hand to Henry, but his gaze went to Nadira again. "Help him up."

For a minute, he thought she'd refuse. She glanced at the steep rocks hemming them in, the two men waiting on the trail ahead, as if weighing her chance of escape. But then she moved to Henry's side.

"Put your foot in the stirrup," he told Henry.

The doctor grabbed his hand and complied. With Nadira's help, Rasheed pulled him into place behind him, wincing at his feeble moan. He just hoped the old man could hold on.

Nadira walked around the gelding to the supply horse, then vaulted into the saddle with practiced ease. He let go of the reins, and the mare pranced back. She expertly wheeled the horse around.

Then she paused, and her gaze collided with his. And for a moment time seemed suspended, her green eyes pinning him in place. A flush darkened her cheeks. Her black hair had escaped its braid, tumbling like silk across her slender back. She sat with a regal air astride the horse, the dawn-tinged mountains rising around her, her brilliant eyes defiant, pride etched in her royal lines.

She was mesmerizing. Gorgeous.

And she was the daughter of his enemy, the key to stopping this terror attack.

He hardened his resolve. "Let's go."

She shot him a glare, then nudged the mare into action and started down the rocky trail. Rasheed fell in behind her, his eyes on her swaying back. She was the key, all right. She just might have the answers he needed to unravel this case. And if so, he intended to get them.

Starting now.

By the time they finally stopped to rest five hours later, Nadine knew one thing. Henry wasn't going to make it, and it was all her fault.

She climbed down from her horse with a groan, muscles she hadn't used since childhood protesting with a vengeance now. They'd been working their way down the mountain for hours, the sun frying her scalp as it inched toward its midday pinnacle, the parched brown landscape gradually giving way to a vibrant green. Every time she'd glanced back, she'd glimpsed Henry barely clinging to their kidnapper, his face chalk-white, his eyes lolling back in his head. It was a miracle he hadn't passed out.

The gelding came to a stop beside her, and the kidnapper called Rasheed leaped off. Shaking aside her discomfort, Nadine hurried over to help Henry dismount.

But the kidnapper beat her to it, catching the injured doctor before he fell. "I've got him."

Henry tottered and leaned against him, the deathly pallor of his skin making her even more alarmed. She hugged Rasheed's heels as he half carried, half dragged

Henry into the shade of a sprawling tree and settled him against the trunk. Henry slumped back and closed his eyes.

Worried, she knelt on the ground beside him and checked his pulse. His forehead was clammy, his breathing too shallow and fast. The gash on his head had stopped bleeding, thank goodness, but he still sported that ugly knot.

Rasheed dropped the saddlebag at her feet. "How is he? Any improvement?"

"Improvement?" She tipped back her head and glared. "Look at him! I told you he couldn't ride."

His gaze shifted to the wounded man. He rubbed his scruffy jaw, an emotion that resembled sympathy ghosting through his dark eyes. And for a moment, she was tempted to believe that he was a good guy, that he cared about their safety and was actually on their side.

Shocked, she gave herself a mental shake. What was this? Stockholm syndrome? This man wasn't her friend. He was an outlaw, a criminal, the man who'd kidnapped her. Was she so desperate for an ally that she'd started imagining kindness where it didn't exist?

So what if he spoke English like an American? So what if he was gentle with Henry, and seemed sensitive to his plight? It was probably a ploy, a trick to make her more pliable, to convince her to cooperate. She had to stay on guard.

"He can rest while we eat." Rasheed motioned to the saddlebag he'd dropped. "There's water in there. Some dried food, too. There should be enough for all of us. Go ahead and get it out."

"What? You expect me to wait on you after all you've done?"

He shot her a level gaze. "Get out the food, Nadira."

"Nadine."

"What?"

"I'm Nadine, not Nadira." She hadn't gone by that name in years. And she had no intention of starting again now.

His eyes held hers for a heartbeat. The silence between them stretched. "Fine. Then, get out the food, *Nadine.* And don't leave this spot." Not waiting for an answer, he strode off.

Indignant, she scowled as he watered the horses, then joined the other men. He was delusional if he thought she'd cooperate with him. She was a prisoner, not his servant, and he could get his own damned food.

Still fuming, she turned her attention back to Henry. But one glance at the older doctor, and her anger instantly deflated, giving way to a rush of concern. His eyes were closed, his skin waxy in the midday light—definitely not a good sign. She removed her jacket, balled it up and wedged it behind his head.

Then she settled on the ground beside him, pulled her knees to her chest and tried to think. Her head ached. She was so thoroughly exhausted she wanted to curl up in a ball and sleep. And icy frissons of panic kept creeping through her nerves, the extent of her predicament impossible to ignore.

Her father had found her. How he'd done it in this remote location she didn't know. But he had to be behind her kidnapping. Nothing else made sense. And unless she escaped, he was going to make good on his promise to see her dead.

Even worse, she'd dragged Henry into this mess. Now his life was in danger because of her.

What was she going to do?

She rubbed her gritty eyes, sighing as the warm breeze tousled her loose hair. The temperatures had risen as they'd headed downhill, riding northeast toward the coca fields. She glanced at the sheer mountains jutting into the sky, the river wending through the valley miles below. In the distance, coca fields filled the ancient terraces, forming a multihued patchwork of green.

Knowing she had to come up with a solution, she looked at her captors again. They knelt in the shade beside the creek, going through the ritual of their midday prayers. A cold feeling took hold in her gut. They were the same type of men she'd grown up with, the men she'd fled her home to escape—zealots who preached a doctrine of hatred, bullies who used brutality to get their way. Men like her father, her brother. Men who treated women like property, who thought they had a divine right to control her destiny and would kill her if she didn't comply.

Her gaze narrowed on the white-turbaned man with the creepy eyes, the one they called Manzoor. He appeared to be their leader, given how the other men deferred to him. She could envision him consorting with her father. He had the same inhuman eyes.

The man with the silver tooth and checkered scarf was named Amir. He struck her as less intelligent, as more of an enforcer than a thinker, but she knew better than to sell him short. He had a sadistic look about him, as if he delighted in inflicting pain—like her heinous brother, Sultan.

She was less certain about Rasheed, the man who'd captured her. Her gaze lingered on him as he went through the prescribed motions of the midday prayer. He intrigued her; she'd give him that much. Every time she looked his way, her nerves went on full alert. But he was too earthy, too masculine with that beard stubble and muscled build—exactly the kind of man she took pains to avoid.

As if sensing her appraisal, he turned his head, his dark gaze fastening on hers. And for an instant she couldn't breathe, her heart embarking on a crazy sprint. She took in his shaggy, jet-black hair, the intelligence in his midnight eyes, the banked power in the way he moved. He'd removed his jacket when the weather warmed and pushed his sleeves to his elbows, exposing the dark hair sprinkling his corded arms.

The men all stood, and he looked away. She dragged in a breath, trying to figure out her baffling reaction to this man. He was obviously a criminal. Why else would he kidnap her? But she couldn't escape the impression that he was different somehow. She kept imagining those glimmers of sympathy, making her wonder if he might care.

She rolled her eyes in disgust. Talk about wishful thinking! She was grasping at straws, letting his undeniably virile looks influence her thinking and indulging in fantasies that could get her killed.

Besides, she didn't need his help. She'd relied on herself for years, surviving far worse dangers than this. And she was going to escape these men.

But she had to help Henry recover first. Her own stomach growling, she opened the flap on the saddlebag and rooted inside for food. She unearthed a container filled with some kind of jerky, several bags of dried fruit and nuts and a cache of coca leaves. She set the food on a towel with a bottle of water, then gently nudged Henry's arm. "Henry, wake up. You need to eat."

He opened his eyes with a groan. "What?"

"Come on. You haven't eaten in hours."

Grimacing, he sat up straighter and glanced around. "Where are we?"

"I don't know. We've been heading north toward the border with Colombia." She handed him the water bottle. "We've descended quite a bit, though, so you should start feeling better before too long."

"I hope so. My head…"

Nadine peered into his bloodshot eyes. "Your pupils look normal. How's your vision?"

"Better. Clear. And the ringing in my ears has stopped. But I'm tired. And this blasted headache…"

"Try to eat something, and then you can take a nap." She pulled the towel closer, making it easier for him to reach.

"I don't suppose you have any painkillers?"

"No, just the coca leaves."

Henry grunted. "Looks like I'll get some firsthand experience with folk medicine this trip."

"I'd rather get you to a hospital." Not that she discounted the coca leaves. A natural analgesic, the locals had used them for centuries to treat everything from broken bones and malaria to asthma and fatigue. But Henry needed more medical care than that.

Nibbling a slice of jerky, she turned her mind back to their main problem: how to escape. Their medical team would alert the authorities, of course. But they'd been too high in the mountains to reach civilization for at least another day. And until they did, until the government could mobilize their forces and send out someone to search for them, she and Henry were on their own.

But Henry couldn't hike. He'd never survive a flight on horseback with the kidnappers in full pursuit. And even if they had the supplies, even if they wanted to hide out in the mountains until their kidnappers gave up and left, Henry didn't have the luxury of time. So unless a miracle occurred, they were out of luck. She'd have to wait until they reached a town where they could find a car.

She glanced at Henry again. He'd collapsed against the tree trunk, already asleep, a half-eaten slice of jerky in his hand. Hoping the nap would do him good, she returned her attention to the three men concluding their prayers. A minute later Rasheed broke away from the group and headed her way.

Her heart began to drum. She dropped her gaze, feigning fascination with her jerky as he joined her at the tree. He lowered himself to the ground beside Henry and reached for the bags of food, and she struggled to stay aloof—but he was too blatantly male to ignore. She took in the impressive breadth of his shoulders, the thick tendons roping his tanned arms, and her pulse beat faster yet.

Rasheed's gaze tangled with hers. Her nerves made a little hum. He studied her with the clear sexual interest she'd come to expect from men. But his expression seemed more thoughtful, more assessing, as if she were a mystery he was trying to solve.

"So what kind of doctor are you?" he asked, his deep voice rumbling in the quiet air.

"A good enough one to know that Henry needs help."

He glanced at the sleeping doctor, then back to her. "I meant, do you have a specialty?"

"Why? What difference does it make?"

"None at all."

Averting her gaze, she hugged her knees. She didn't want to talk to her captor. She didn't trust this attempt at civility, this sudden desire to act nice. It was probably a good cop, bad cop routine he'd worked out with the other men, a way to make her malleable.

But if there was any chance he'd intercede on Henry's behalf, it wouldn't hurt to cooperate—up to a point. "I'm a plastic surgeon."

His dark brows rose. "Is there a need for that out here?"

"There's a need for it everywhere people suffer abuse." She shot him a pointed look. "Men like to inflict pain. Women and children pay the price."

Rasheed looked away—but not before she caught an emotion stealing through his eyes, a hint of something bleak.

His reaction threw her for a loop. She wasn't sure what she'd expected—a snarky remark about BOTOX or maybe a shrugged dismissal, reactions she'd experienced often enough. But for a second, Rasheed had looked…haunted, as if she'd triggered a memory that caused him pain.

Was that why he'd become a terrorist? Had he suffered a personal loss, experiencing a pain so devastating that he'd gone rogue, and lashed back at society? He didn't seem the terrorist type—he treated Henry with a basic kindness that seemed at odds with his violent life. And she should know. She'd seen the real deal—men like her brother with his ingrained cruelty. And try as she might, she couldn't quite see Rasheed that way.

So maybe he'd started out as a good guy and then gone off the rails. Or maybe he'd been brainwashed into extremism, an idealistic young man searching for meaning who'd fallen victim to a radical ideology.

She didn't care. *She couldn't.* This man was a criminal. His life, his past, whatever private suffering he'd endured didn't matter to her. She had to keep her focus on where it belonged—getting Henry free.

He downed a handful of nuts, then packed up the remaining food. "We're leaving in a few minutes."

"Already? We just got here." She glanced at Henry in alarm. "Can't we let him rest for a while? He needs to sleep."

"Sorry."

"But—"

"We can't." His voice rang with finality. He took out a couple of empty water bottles and a packet of purification tablets, and set them on the grass. "Go fill these up in the stream."

"What? You think I'm your servant now?"

"No, I think you need the water. I've got enough for myself. But if you and Henry want to go without..." He got to his feet with a shrug. Then he picked up the saddlebag and strode off.

She opened her mouth to protest. But damned if he wasn't right. She had to take care of Henry, even if it meant following this man's orders—for now. Still scowling, she gathered the bottles and rose.

But as she worked her way through the bushes and undergrowth toward the mountain stream, more doubts spun through her mind. She wasn't prone to illusions. She didn't indulge in useless fantasies. She was good at reading people—she'd had to be to survive the years she'd spent on the streets. So why did Rasheed seem so different to her? Was it merely wishful thinking? Was it an aftereffect of the kidnapping, a result of the trauma she'd been through? Or was there a chance that she was right, and he actually cared about them?

She didn't know. And until she was sure, she had to watch her step. Rasheed was smart. She hadn't misjudged the intelligence in his penetrating black eyes. She couldn't afford to make a mistake with Henry's life at stake—not to mention her own.

When she reached the creek, she headed upstream to a spot where the water ran clear and fast. She knelt and filled the bottles, adding the purification tablets to make it safe. That done, she took a minute to wash her hands and face, letting the cold, clean water soothe her nerves.

Behind her, a chinchilla scurried through the grass. Birds twittered in a nearby shrub. The warm breeze rustled the trees, the tranquil scene at odds with the nightmare her life had become. With effort, she shook off a wave of longing—for her team, for the inner peace she'd taken for granted only a day ago. Trying to keep her focus on the present, she collected the bottles and headed back along the path through the trees.

But a man blocked her way.

Amir.

She abruptly came to a stop. Every muscle in her body tensed. She took in his big, beefy hands, the power in his massive arms, the hatred simmering in his narrowed eyes. And she knew with an absolute certainty that he intended to do her harm.

He tossed a saddlebag in the path. "Fill up my water bottles now," he ordered in Jaziirastani.

A swarm of uneasiness seized her. She did not want to deal with this man. He looked as cruel as her brother, Sultan, a monster who delighted in inflicting pain. And captive or not, she had no intention of being this sadist's slave. "Forget it."

He went dead still. "What did you say?"

"I said no, I won't do it. I'm not going to wait on you."

His eyes blazed with an odd excitement. He took several quick steps toward her, and adrenaline pumped through her veins. She spun on her heels, and started to run, but he was faster than she'd believed. He grabbed hold of her hair and yanked her backward, sending fiery pain slashing through her scalp. Gasping, she dropped her supplies.

But she didn't intend to submit. Calling on all her street skills, she whipped around and lunged toward him, ignoring the sharp pain flaying her head. Then she rammed her knee into his groin with all her might. He bellowed with rage and staggered back.

But he was still too fast. His huge fist came out of nowhere, slamming into her face. The force lifted her off her feet, and she crashed to the ground, pain exploding behind her eyes. She let out an anguished cry.

He strode over and kicked her ribs. Agony knifed through her, knocking the breath from her lungs. She curled into a ball and wheezed.

"Leave her alone."

Her jaw throbbed. The coppery taste of blood filled

her mouth. She panted and gasped, trying to inhale around the fire torturing her ribs, and managed to push herself to her knees.

Rasheed now faced Amir. He stood on the path between them, his legs planted wide, his hands balled into fists. Tension rolled off his powerful frame.

"Get out of my way," Amir told him. "This isn't your business."

"The hell it isn't. I kidnapped this woman. She's under my protection now."

"She's not your prisoner. She belongs to us all. And she can do our work until we're done with her."

"Not unless I say so. *I* decide what she can do. And you won't put a hand on her."

Amir's eyes flared. A blade appeared in his hand, and Nadine's already ragged breath came to a halt. *A knife fight.* She'd witnessed one in Oakland once—and once had been enough.

"You're challenging me?" Amir's tone was deadly now.

"I caught her," Rasheed repeated. "So I control what she does. The man, too. No one touches them or gives them orders except me."

Amir stared at Rasheed, pure loathing in his eyes. Nadine tried to suppress a shudder, but failed. Rasheed had just made an enemy.

Because of her.

Neither man moved. Testosterone crackled in the air. Fearing the bloodbath that was about to break out, Nadine began to creep backward, not wanting to get caught in the deadly fight.

But then Manzoor's voice barked out from behind the trees. "Where is everyone? Let's go!"

Amir's eyes narrowed. Several heartbeats later, he slid the knife back into its sheath. "We aren't finished. We'll deal with the woman later. But be careful, brother. You might not want to close your eyes at night." He turned on his heel and stalked off.

Nadine didn't move. She kept her gaze on the bushes, her heart still galloping through her chest, terrified that he'd come back. But then Rasheed turned around and took her arm, and helped her to her feet.

"Are you all right?" he asked.

All right? Her jaw felt cracked. Her ribs burned so badly she could hardly breathe. Even her hair follicles ached. And without warning, tears sprang into her eyes, the horror of the attack beginning to sink in. Mortified by her show of weakness, she hurried to wipe them away.

But Rasheed stepped close and grasped her chin. His eyes stayed grim, but his hands were surprisingly gentle as he turned her head from side to side to inspect her face.

"You're bleeding." His voice came out gruff. His thumb stroked her bottom lip, the feathery touch quickening her pulse.

And then his eyes met hers. Her pulse skidded off beat. And for a long moment she gazed into that hypnotic blackness, conscious of his calloused fingers skimming her jaw, the heat radiating from his golden skin, the sheer maleness of him as he towered above her, solid and strong.

He looked lethal. Almost feral. Every inch the war-

rior—the kind of man she'd always feared. And yet…
standing in his embrace with his big hand cradling her
jaw, his wide shoulders sheltering her from the world,
she felt completely safe.

Which didn't make a whit of sense.

"I…I'm fine," she managed to whisper.

His eyes stayed locked on hers. Something seemed
to pass between them, something she couldn't name.
Then he dropped his gaze to her mouth, and for one
wild moment, her heart went completely berserk. And a
myriad of emotions roiled inside her—relief, gratitude.
Desire.

He blinked and lowered his hand. "Come on. We
need to go." He turned and strode through the trees.

Shaken, she watched him leave. What had just happened? Had he been intending to *kiss* her? And had
she been about to let him? Had she completely lost
her mind?

Stunned at her behavior, she gathered the water bottles from where she'd dropped them and returned to
the gurgling stream. She was glad he'd defended her.
She couldn't bear the thought of that creep, Amir, putting his hands on her.

But why had he done it? He had no reason to come
to her aid. Was he merely defending his male pride
and claiming her as his property—or something more?

Thoroughly confused now, she knelt on the bank
and splashed cold water on her battered face. She had
to proceed with care. Rasheed might have come to her
rescue this time, but he was still the one who'd kidnapped her. She couldn't trust him. She couldn't let

herself care about him. She couldn't fool herself about who—or what—he was.

And she definitely couldn't desire him.

Now she just had to convince her treacherous body of that.

Chapter 4

Rasheed rode down the trail a short time later, still incredulous at what he'd done. He'd stupidly challenged Amir. He'd nearly blown his cover and given himself away. He'd jeopardized five years of painstaking work, five years spent laboring in the training camps and insinuating himself into the Rising Light hierarchy to stop these murderous thugs. He'd endangered the success of this critical mission, putting the fate of thousands of innocent civilians in doubt.

All because of this insane attraction to his captive, a woman he couldn't trust.

He shifted in his saddle, trying not to jostle the injured doctor collapsed like deadweight against his back. He eyed Nadira—Nadine, he silently corrected—ahead of him on the trail, her slender shoulders slumped, her slim hips swaying as the mare descended the rocky slope, and knew he'd had no choice. He'd had to intercede. The sight of Amir putting his hands on her had razed his self-control. There'd been no damned way he could stand aside and let him hit her, even on the off chance that it was all a ploy. It went against everything he believed in and who he was.

The problem was that he'd done far worse than defend her. He'd done more than nearly give in to the urge to kiss her and slake his body's long-dormant needs. He'd come dangerously close to letting her penetrate something inside him, allowing her mesmerizing eyes to crack open the lid on his buried emotions—and tempting him to care.

And that was a danger he couldn't afford. His work ruled his life now. He couldn't go back, couldn't resurrect the man that he once was, no matter how much she appealed to him. That part of him was dead.

To be safe, he had to maintain his distance from her, especially if she was here at her father's request. Although frankly, the more time he spent around her, the harder that was to believe. Her fierce resistance to any orders, her rush to protect Henry at any cost—even her refusal to use her Jaziirastani birth name—suggested that she was exactly what she seemed: a victim in this affair. Then again, these terrorists were shrewd. He wouldn't put anything past them in their quest to root out a traitor, especially on a mission this big.

The gelding lurched, and Rasheed adjusted his grip on the doctor's wrists, trying to keep him from falling off. Regardless of his doubts about Nadine, there was one thing he knew for sure. Henry had nothing to do with the upcoming attack. He was an unlucky bystander, an unfortunate do-gooder whose admirable intentions had placed him in the terrorists' path. Now Rasheed had to convince these men to leave him behind—or Henry might pay for that generosity with his life.

The horses continued plodding downhill. The creak of the leather saddles, the muffled thud of their hooves broke the silence of the mountain air. Mulling over his course of action, Rasheed glanced at the sheer peaks towering overhead, the rows of cultivated coca now encroaching on the wilderness. A hawk soared silently past, the predator a stark reminder that he had to proceed with care. Manzoor was astute. If he wanted to persuade him to release Henry, he had to be careful not to tip him off.

Manzoor reached a clearing a moment later and drew his horse to a halt. The group straggled to a stop beside him, the buzz of insects loud in the air. Nadine slid off her horse without a word, dropped the reins and staggered off, seeking the privacy of the nearby shrubs.

The other men swung down. Rasheed inhaled and steeled his nerves. This was it. It was time to make his move. He knew he was taking a risk. These terrorists would perceive any concern as weakness—or worse. But he had to do something about Henry. And he had to do it now, before Nadine came back and overheard.

"We have a problem," he told Manzoor, who was taking a map from his saddlebag. He waited until the leader looked up, then gestured toward the doctor sleeping against his back. "This man isn't going to make it. His condition is getting worse."

Manzoor unfolded the map and shrugged. "The woman is a doctor. Let her deal with him."

"She tried to, but he's too sick. The ride is making him worse. We need to leave him behind."

"We can't." Clearly dismissing the subject, Manzoor turned his attention to the map.

Rasheed slid a glance at Amir. The terrorist stared back, his eyes simmering with resentment, and Rasheed bit back a curse. He didn't want to give Amir another reason to suspect him, but for Henry's sake, he had to persist.

"He's too weak to ride anymore," he continued. "He keeps passing out. He can't be that important to our plans."

Manzoor raised his head. Annoyance flickered in his black eyes. "He's not important. But the woman won't try to escape while he's along, so he stays."

Rasheed couldn't argue with his logic. Nadine obviously cared about the older man. And using him to control her was a surefire way to keep her in line. "I understand that. But I'm telling you, he can't hold on."

"So let him fall," Amir cut in. "That will teach him to pay attention."

"A fall will kill him."

"So? Why do you care?"

"I *don't* care." Rasheed chose his words with caution, aware that he was walking a tightrope, and that a slipup would invite more suspicion of him. "He doesn't matter to me. But I do care about the success of our mission. And the doctor's a complication we don't need. He's only slowing us down."

Manzoor's gaze went to the sleeping man. "We only need him until we reach Buena Fortuna. We'll dispose of him there."

Rasheed's heart skipped a beat. *Dispose* could only

mean one thing. If the concussion didn't kill Henry before they reached the town, Manzoor would. He wouldn't leave any witnesses behind.

And it made sense. According to his intelligence briefings, Buena Fortuna was the town where the drug plane would pick them up. The plane would fly them to the staging area on San Gabriel, a small, private island controlled by the drug cartel off Colombia's Caribbean coast. There they'd make their final plans before entering the United States. And it was Rasheed's last chance to meet with the undercover operative who'd infiltrated the cartel and tell him what he'd learned.

Except he hadn't learned anything of value yet.

"How far is it to Buena Fortuna?" he asked.

Manzoor looked at the map. "Twenty-five miles. We'll reach it in the morning if we push through."

Twenty-five miles! *Hell.* It was way too soon. He needed more time than that to question Nadine and find out what she knew.

Keeping his voice indifferent, he perservered. "He won't make it that far. I say we spend the night in a village to let him rest."

But Manzoor only shook his head. "No, we will ride through the night. We don't have time to waste."

Rasheed curbed his frustration, knowing he had to back off. "You're in charge. But the horses are worn-out. They'll collapse before then. And the man won't do us any good if he dies along the way."

Manzoor only grunted in reply.

Rasheed pulled out his canteen and drank, but his thoughts continued to spin. What a mess. He had to get Henry to safety before his usefulness ended and Manzoor had him killed—assuming the doctor didn't die before then. And yet, he also needed information about this case, vital information that only Nadine could provide. And as soon as he spirited Henry to safety, she'd try to leave.

But could he justify delaying Henry's rescue for the mission's sake? And what about Nadine? If she was as innocent as he strongly suspected, didn't he have an obligation to help her escape? But could he really trust her? What if he misjudged her? Could he risk making a mistake of that magnitude?

The branches of the dense shrubs moved. Nadine emerged a second later, her head down, her long, black hair spilling over her arms. She walked straight to the mare, her movements stiff, her discolored jaw bearing the imprint of Amir's fist. Then she glanced at him, her eyes shooting daggers, and his hopes sank.

She'd heard. She now knew they intended to kill Henry when they reached the town. And if he'd learned anything about this woman, it was that she'd never capitulate. She was going to do something reckless to get her companion free.

Swearing at his predicament, he tightened his grip on the reins. He had to stop her. He couldn't let her risk her life. But if he interfered—even to protect her— she'd trust him even less.

She mounted the mare, her expression hostile— whether from anger or pain, he didn't know. But he did know one thing. He'd just made this complicated situation even worse. He had to help the injured doctor. He couldn't tip off the terrorists and ruin his chance to stop the attack. He also had to contend with Amir, a man clearly gunning for revenge.

More importantly, he had to get close to Nadine and

find out more about the terrorists' plans. And he had to do that without giving in to the attraction simmering between them like a cauldron ready to blow.

But if she was the innocent he believed, he'd just guaranteed that she wouldn't trust him. And yet, if there was any chance she was in league with these terrorists, he couldn't trust *her*.

So which was she—her father's accomplice or a victim?

With time running out, he had to decide on an answer fast.

The kidnappers were going to kill Henry. She had to get him to safety quickly. And she couldn't trust Rasheed to help.

That horrible realization had plagued Nadine as they rode down the mountain for the past few hours, fording streams and traversing coca farms, moving relentlessly closer to Buena Fortuna, the town where Henry would die.

That near kiss hadn't meant anything to Rasheed. The compassion in his eyes wasn't real. It had only been an illusion, a pathetic fantasy forged by her desperate mind. She was completely on her own here. And even though Manzoor had finally relented, agreeing to stop for the night in this mountain village, she only had hours, maybe a day at most, to help Henry escape.

And she still didn't know how.

Trying not to panic, she knelt in the hard-packed dirt beside Henry in a hut the terrorists had commandeered. He lay on a sleeping pallet made of straw, an alpaca wool blanket pulled up to his neck, his face almost as gray as the whiskers covering his chin. The wooden door was ajar, the rustles of nocturnal creatures and chirp of crickets filling the night. The thatched roof formed a peak overhead.

"I'm sorry to cause you so much trouble," he murmured. "I'm a total pain in the ass."

She studied him in the lantern's glow. Dark circles underscored his eyes. The pale light wavered, casting shadows over his face, emphasizing the gaunt hollows of his cheeks. "Don't be ridiculous. You're not a pain."

"You could escape without me. I'm slowing you down."

"No, you're not. Now stop worrying about it."

His tired blue eyes met hers. "I'm serious, Nadine. Take one of the horses and ride for help. It's the only chance we have."

Her heart skipped. Had he overheard the terrorists' plan to kill him? But no, they'd been speaking in Jaziirastani. He couldn't have understood. *Thank God.*

Because the last thing he needed was a worry like that. She refused to even tell him why the men had kidnapped them. He needed all his strength to get well.

"Would you leave without me?" she countered. When he grimaced, she gave him a pointed look. "Exactly. And I'm not leaving without you, either. We're in this thing together. Now just concentrate on resting and getting stronger. I'll think about it tonight, and tomorrow we'll make our plans."

He reached out and squeezed her hand. A faint smile reached his eyes, edging out the pain. "You're a good friend, Nadine."

Hardly. She'd gotten him into this disaster. He'd been kidnapped because of her. And now his fate was in her hands.

The wooden door creaked, and she turned her head. An old woman came through the door, lugging a pot of food. Barely five feet tall, she wore a thick wool cardigan sweater, several layers of skirts, and the usual tire tread sandals on her swollen feet. Her face was weathered and brown, her hip-length braids threaded with gray, her age somewhere between forty and ninety, impossible to discern.

Nadine rose, towering over the tiny woman, and helped her set the pot on the wooden crate serving as a table beside the bed. *"Gracias,"* Nadine told her. The woman smiled, revealing gaps in her stained teeth, and murmured something in return. The farmers spoke a variant of Quechua, not Spanish, making communication hard.

Not that they needed words. The terrorists' guns had made their meaning clear.

But Nadine still wished she could thank her properly. The terrorists had forced the villagers from their beds and demanded food. And while she was glad for Henry's sake, their strong-arm tactics made her cringe.

"You'd better get some rest," Henry urged her. "I'll be okay here."

"You sure?"

"I'm just glad to get off that damned horse. When we get out of these mountains, I'm never riding again."

If he got out of these mountains. He might not survive unless she came up with an escape plan fast.

But he was right. A hot meal and a good night's sleep would help him more than anything she could do right now. She eyed the steaming stew, the mouthwatering scent of chicken reminding her that she hadn't had a decent meal in days.

"All right," she said. "But promise me you'll drink more tea."

"I will. I'll even chew those disgusting leaves if you insist."

"I do." She crossed the dirt floor to the door, then summoned a smile she didn't feel. "Don't worry, Henry. I promise I'll get us out of this mess." She refused to fail this man.

She ducked through the low doorway and stepped outside. Then she paused and peered into the darkness, surprised her ever-present guard wasn't hovering nearby. But the men had pegged her correctly. They knew she wouldn't leave without Henry. And in his weakened condition, he couldn't go far.

But there *had* to be a way to escape. Still thinking that over, she started down the moonlit path between the huts. Calling the settlement a village was an exaggeration. It consisted of half a dozen mud huts perched on the edge of the mountain, surrounded by coca plants. She passed a chicken coop and shed, heard the grunt of a rooting pig. But there was no sign of a road, no other way out that she could see, only this narrow dirt trail through the terraced fields.

She glanced at the low-growing trees silvered with moonlight and sighed. She didn't blame these farmers for cultivating coca. They lived in houses without windows or lights, with no running water, no schools for their children or health care, just barely scraping by. The profit in coca lay further up the chain with the drug cartels. These poor people were just trying to eke out a living, growing a product that met an insatiable foreign demand.

A minute later she reached the edge of the hamlet.

She spotted the horses grazing beside the path, the three captors talking in a moonlit field, and turned around. Not wanting to draw their attention—or worse, reveal that she was plotting an escape route—she followed the scent of wood smoke to the cooking fire instead.

The farmers fell silent as she approached. Too ravenous to care about their disapproval, she beelined to the soup pot, salivating at the tempting scent. A woman filled a large pottery bowl with rice, then dumped a ladleful of stew over top and handed it to her. Nadine shot her a smile of thanks, wove through the sullen men to a log and sat.

The stew was amazing—thick and hot, a delicious blend of potatoes, chicken and peppers, and bursting with seasonings. She'd devoured half the bowl before she could force herself to slow down.

But then Rasheed appeared in the line. He headed her way a moment later, carrying his own big bowl of stew. She tensed as he sat beside her, his nearness scattering her pulse. And suddenly she was far too conscious of his hard thigh resting close to hers, the glint of firelight in his jet-black hair, the warmth emanating from his big frame.

Disgusted at her reaction, she scowled. What was it with this man? So what if he was attractive? So what if he'd saved her from Amir? He wasn't her ally. She'd overheard what he'd said to the other men, how they planned to dispose of Henry when they reached the town. And while he'd suggested resting overnight, he hadn't done it out of kindness. He only wanted to expedite their trip so he could hand her over to her father—the man who wanted her dead.

And the disappointment she'd felt when she'd heard his words was beyond absurd. She couldn't build this man up into some kind of savior just because he'd rescued her. He was still violent. He'd nearly engaged in a knife fight with Amir. If he really cared, if he had any real compassion inside him, he'd let them go.

He turned his head, and his dark gaze stalled on hers. And for an instant she imagined she saw it again, that glimmer of sympathy in his dark eyes.

Which only proved she was losing her mind.

"How's your face?" he asked.

"It hurts. What do you think?"

His gaze roamed over her jaw, his scrutiny somehow sensual, and her heart fumbled several beats. "I'm sorry," he said.

"Yeah, right." She couldn't keep the sarcasm from her voice.

He angled his head to meet her eyes. "I am sorry. I don't want to see you hurt."

"Sure. That's why you kidnapped me."

His strong jaw flexed. "I've got a job to do. It's not something I can talk about. But I don't wish you any harm."

"Then let us go."

"I can't." Regret tinged his voice—and damned if he didn't sound sincere.

She lowered her gaze to her stew, but her appetite had deserted her. And suddenly, she was so tired, so incredibly confused. Who was this man? Why was he bothering to be nice to her? He'd protected her from Amir, risking his life on her behalf. But he'd also captured her and was planning Henry's death. So which was the real man—the kidnapper or the protector? Did he care, or was he playing some kind of twisted mind game to amuse himself?

She closed her eyes, too tired to figure it out. And for the first time, despair spiraled through her, the terrible dread that she might not survive.

No. She refused to think that way. She'd been in dangerous situations before, and she'd always made it out alive. But what if she didn't this time? What if she couldn't save Henry? What if that dear doctor died because of her?

There *had* to be a way to escape. She had to put her mind to it and come up with a plan, no matter how impossible it seemed. She wasn't going to let these people win.

Forcing herself to think, she focused on the half a dozen farmers standing around the fire, drinking *pisco* and coca tea. These men made their living producing coca. They harvested the leaves and converted them to paste, which they sold in the nearest town. To make the paste they needed chemicals, gallons of it— kerosene, gasoline, ammonia—which wouldn't be easy to transport on these mountain trails.

Unless they had a truck...

That thought gave her pause. She hadn't seen any signs of a vehicle. She hadn't even seen a proper road. But if they had one, they'd probably park it near the pit where they made the paste.

Her hopes ticked up. She racked her brains, trying to remember what she'd heard about making paste. First they harvested the leaves and dried them. Then they put them in a *pozo,* or pit, and added water and kerosene. To avoid hauling water, they'd probably build the pit near a stream.

And if she could find that pit, she could find whatever vehicle they used to transport the chemicals—hopefully, a car or truck.

She stole a glance at Rasheed. He watched her with steady eyes, and her pulse increased its beat. She'd never fool him. He'd never let her out of his sight. Unless… She rose.

"Where are you going?" he asked.

She gestured toward the path behind the cooking fire. She'd seen enough villagers come and go while she'd been eating to figure out where it led. "The ditch—or whatever it is they use. Why? Do you want to come with me?"

His gaze stayed on hers for a heartbeat. A long second later, he shook his head. "No, go ahead. But Nadine…don't try anything rash."

Not bothering to answer, she returned her bowl to the bucket by the fire. Then she started down the moonlit path leading away from the huts, trying to act nonchalant. But she didn't have much time. She had to locate the coca pit and hurry back before Rasheed grew suspicious and came to investigate.

The stench told her when she'd reached the right place. But a sudden crackle in the underbrush caught her attention, bringing her to a stop. She held her breath and listened hard, scouring the darkness around the path. Nothing. Probably some nocturnal animal hunting for food.

Still, in case one of the kidnappers was lurking nearby, she slipped behind the wooden screen and used the ditch. Then she took another, narrower path through the woods, following the sound of a rushing stream.

Seconds later, she reached the creek. She washed

her hands, the icy water a shock to her nerves. The stream itself wasn't wide, maybe ten feet across, but it probably flowed straight from the snowcapped peaks. She rose and glanced around, not sure which way to go. But if she were dumping toxic chemicals into the river, she would choose a spot downstream.

Clicking on Henry's penlight, she headed along the bank. She picked her way through the bushes and rocks, tripping over branches and rotting logs. But several minutes later she stopped. There was still no sign of a pit. For all she knew it could be miles in the other direction. And she was running out of time. If she didn't head back soon, Rasheed would divine her plan.

Deciding to keep going to the next bend, she continued hiking downstream. The creek twisted and curved, and then she spotted another path, probably leading straight from the coca fields. Her excitement mounting, she picked up her pace. And then she saw it—the pit where they made the paste.

It was literally a hole in the ground lined with a plastic tarp. They'd built a lean-to around it to protect it—a crude, wooden structure with a metal roof. Various supplies were piled outside—barrels containing chemicals, coils of plastic tubing, wooden poles to stir the paste. Hardly a high-tech operation, but it sufficed.

She continued past the pit, and her heart made another leap. *A pickup truck.* So she'd been right! And there was the road—a rutted tractor trail disappearing into the woods. She could sneak out later with Henry and hightail it to the nearest town.

Thrilled at her discovery, she hurried to the truck. It had a flat rear tire, rusty doors and barrels piled in the bed. But she didn't care. As long as it ran, she would drive it on the rims.

Assuming she could find the key.

She shone the penlight through the window and looked inside. No key. *Damn.* One of the villagers must have it. But maybe Henry knew how to hot-wire an engine. She'd go straight to his hut and ask.

But then a twig crackled behind her. Her heart lurching, she whirled around. More branches snapped, and panic jolted her into gear. Someone was following her. Scared now, she darted up the path leading through the coca fields.

But the moon was too bright, the trees too low to conceal her for long. Afraid her pursuer would see her, she ducked behind a cluster of bushes and hid.

The crashing sound grew closer. Her pulse racing, she peered through the branches at the path. A man came into view, and her breath stopped cold. *Amir.*

He paused a few feet away. Then he slowly turned, checking the brush nearby. She held herself dead still, praying he wouldn't notice her. Even in the darkness, he gave her the creeps—his big body vibrating with menace, hatred simmering from him in waves.

She'd grown up around men like him. She'd seen her father batter her mother. She watched her brother bully her gentle sister-in-law into meekness with his vicious fists. But Nadine didn't cower to anyone. She'd learned to stand up for herself early on. She refused to let anyone dictate her life or rob her of her precious dreams, no matter how hard they tried to intimidate her.

But she still had to evade Amir.

He turned and headed back toward the creek. She waited for several more seconds, then rose and stepped toward the path. Without warning, a man grabbed her from behind, his big hand muffling her startled cry. Then he dragged her behind the bushes again.

"Quiet," he whispered in her ear.

Rasheed.

Stunned, she obeyed. His rock-hard body held her immobile. His steely arm banded her waist. And questions spun through her mind. Where had he come from? Why on earth would he help her hide? A split second later, Amir came back into view, and her heart went into a freefall. If Rasheed hadn't stopped her, she would have walked right into a trap.

Amir stood on the moonlit path. Endless minutes ticked past. Then he swore and whirled around, heading toward the creek again.

For a minute, neither moved. She stayed frozen in Rasheed's iron arms, struggling to think. But she was far too conscious of his callused palm grazing her mouth, his ragged breath rasping in her ear, the concrete angles and ridges of his muscled body wedged against her back.

Then he released his hold on her and stood. "Come on," he murmured, pulling her to her feet. "But be quiet."

Keeping his hand on her forearm, he dragged her along the path toward the huts. She stumbled behind him, the quick pace making her breathless as she tried to keep up. They cut through the grove of trees, finally reaching the hut closest to the chicken coop. He pulled her through the door and let her go.

A second later, a kerosene lantern stuttered to life. He set it on a wooden crate, and a halo of light revealed the room. Beside the crate was a cane-backed chair.

A straw pallet lay in one corner, a stack of dishes and tools in another. Clothes hung from pegs on the walls.

Rasheed swung around to face her, and for the first time, she got a close look at his face in the dim light. The fury in his eyes took her aback.

"What the hell do you think you were you doing?" he demanded.

"I… Nothing."

"You were trying to escape."

"No, I wasn't. I was just—"

"For God's sake, Nadine. Don't you know how dangerous that was? That man, Amir. Don't you know what he'd do if he'd caught you there?"

"Of course I know. He hit me, didn't he?" Her jaw still throbbed as proof.

His eyes blazed even hotter. A muscle leaped in his granite jaw. "That was nothing. A man like that… If he'd caught you…" His voice was close to a shout. "I warned you not to do anything dumb."

Her own temper flared. "Dumb? What's so dumb about trying to escape? What do you expect me to do? Just sit here like a helpless lump?"

"I expect you to listen to me."

"Listen to you? After you kidnapped me?"

"You don't understand." Exhaling roughly, he shoved his hand through his hair. "It's not just you and Henry. The villagers… If you escape, they're going to take the blame."

Her mouth went slack. She stared at him, so angry she could hardly speak. "You'd hurt them? You'd punish those poor people if I left?"

He didn't answer. He didn't need to. The proof was in his eyes.

And that was the final straw. He'd grabbed her from her tent. He'd tied her up and knocked her unconscious, hauling her across the mountain in the pouring rain. She was filthy and tired. Every part of her body ached. And if that wasn't enough, at the end of this journey both she and Henry were going to die.

"You people are something else," she choked out. "Dragging those poor farmers into this. They're just minding their own business and trying to get by. And Henry—he's a good, kind man who was trying to make a difference in the world. But you don't care about them, do you? It doesn't bother you to have their deaths on your hands."

A flush climbed up his face. His jaw tightened to steel. And a warning sounded in her mind, the realization that she ought to be careful, that maybe she'd misjudged him since he'd rescued her from Amir. But she'd been pushed too far for restraint.

"Men like you are selfish," she continued, her voice trembling. "You think your stupid beliefs give you the right to take whatever you want. But you're wrong. What you believe is wrong. And you're not going to win."

Her chest heaved. Her eyes stung, but she blinked back the tears, refusing to give him the satisfaction of seeing her cry. She would not show any weakness around this man.

His eyes turned even blacker. He closed the distance between them, but she held her ground, refusing to budge. "Stay in the hut, Nadine. Don't try to escape."

"Or what?" she taunted. "You'll kill me?" She let out a high-pitched laugh.

His big hands gripped her shoulders. He gave her a shake, fueling her temper even more.

But then his mouth was on hers. She froze, utterly shocked, the feel of him slaying her senses—the warmth of his hard lips, the scrape of his sandpapery jaw, the strength in his massive hands. A thought sprang up, that she needed to resist this, but it vanished like smoke in the wind.

Pleasure jolted her veins. Her knees wobbled, threatening to collapse. Sensations collided inside her, bursts of heat and need, and a raw, primal delirium more acute than anything she'd ever experienced, wiping every coherent thought from her head. Her body swayed into his, the intensity of her response overwhelming, sending thrills skipping and swirling through her veins.

But just as abruptly, he broke away. Breathing hard, she stared into his eyes. They were hot, hungry, furious.

Oh, God. What had she done? *She'd just kissed her enemy.* She'd responded to him with total abandon, with a frenzy she couldn't contain. Even now she wanted those big, rough hands on every part of her. She spun around, appalled.

"I'm warning you," he rasped from behind her. "Don't try to leave."

It took her several seconds to find her voice. "Or what?"

"Just don't, Nadine."

The door thudded closed. Still breathing hard, she turned around. But Rasheed was gone.

Chapter 5

Why had Rasheed kissed her?

That question still ricocheted through Nadine's mind the next day as they resumed their trek down the mountain, following a river toward the valley below. She'd spent half the night tossing and turning, reliving every thrilling moment of that shocking kiss, until she'd finally surrendered to exhaustion and slept. And even now, when she should be plotting an escape plan, when they'd nearly reached the town of Buena Fortuna, where Henry's journey would come to a deadly end, that blasted kiss kept derailing her thoughts. His intriguing scent, the rough insistence of his mouth, the glorious feel of his steel-hard muscles pressed against her… The memories kept inundating her senses, making it impossible to concentrate.

She doubted it had meant anything important to

him. He'd probably suffered a fleeting lapse, succumbing to a heat-of-the-moment impulse prompted by their argument. But the question that really plagued her was why she'd kissed him back.

Twisting in the saddle, she aimed a quick glance back his way. He sat astride his horse, one lean hand gripping the reins, the other holding Henry in place. He looked like a Wild West outlaw with those inscrutable black eyes, the stubble coating his rugged jaw, the hard angles of his lethal frame.

The thing that really perplexed her was that she didn't usually go for men like him. Aside from the glaring fact that he was a criminal, that he was consorting with men who intended to kill her, he was too overtly masculine for her tastes. She preferred less physical, more cerebral men.

But maybe the kidnapping had peeled away her defenses. Maybe her instincts had taken over, and she'd clung to him out of a primitive, survival-of-the-fittest type of need.

She rolled her eyes. He was *fit,* all right—the most virile man she'd ever seen.

Regardless, she couldn't deny that his kiss had set off a delirium of sensual awareness—which only compounded her doubts. Could she really have responded that way to a *terrorist?* Even given the abnormal situation, could a criminal cause that insane need? And if he wasn't a terrorist, then who was he? Why had he rescued her, twice? And what job did he have to do? Did he mean delivering her to her father…or something else?

She turned back to the trail with a sigh. At this point, it didn't matter. She had to forget the kiss, forget the hormones tossing her equilibrium on end, and focus on helping Henry escape—before they reached Buena Fortuna and his time ran out.

A moment later, they reached a ridge, and Manzoor brought his horse to a stop. Nadine followed suit and dismounted while the men headed to a grassy space to pray. With a groan, she stretched her legs, then joined Henry at a boulder overlooking the valley below.

"How are you doing?" she asked him.

His faded blue eyes met hers. "Better. My head still hurts, but the altitude sickness is gone. At least I'm not gasping for breath every time I walk a couple of feet."

"Your color's good. Your lips aren't blue anymore." Which meant his blood oxygen was probably close to normal again. The lower altitude had definitely helped.

But he still looked exhausted with those dark circles rimming his bloodshot eyes. And he had to avoid sudden movements or he'd make his concussion worse. Frowning, she settled beside him on the rock, her anxiety kicking up even more. Because the real question was, if his life hung in the balance, could he find the strength to run?

"It looks like we're almost to a town," Henry said, gesturing toward the valley with his canteen.

"It's called Buena Fortuna." Worried, she turned her gaze to the town below. "The men said we were heading there."

The small town lay at the bottom of the cordillera along a tributary of the river they'd been following all day. The slopes closest to the town were bare. Mud slides had washed away the deforested topsoil, leaving ugly brown scabs covering the hills.

The town itself was a frontier settlement, a jumping-off place for people heading into the jungle, a small trading hub where farmers hauled their coca paste and sold it to the drug cartel. The mountainous coca-growing region lay to its west. Brazil was to the east, Colombia to the north. Just outside of town was an air-strip, a coffee-colored slash carved out of the jungle, a simple dirt runway with half a dozen warehouses sprawled nearby. The planes picked up the paste and flew it to Colombia to the cocaine processing labs.

Aside from the airstrip, the town didn't consist of much, only a few unpaved roads lined with wooden shacks. The bulk of the buildings hugged the river snaking through the valley floor, its sluggish water the same muddy brown as the anacondas lurking in the jungle nearby.

"So what's the plan?" Henry asked, meeting her gaze.

She shot a quick glance back at their captors, but they were still busy doing their prayers. "We need to make a break for it when we reach the town."

His gray eyebrows gathered into a frown. "You don't think we can reason with them? I thought they wanted a ransom."

She hesitated, not wanting to confess the truth, that these men were going to kill him because of her. Knowing Henry, he'd try to do something heroic to help her, sacrificing himself to keep her safe. "That's what I thought at first, but I heard… I got the impression they might harm us when we reach the town."

"That doesn't make sense. Why did they kidnap us then?"

"You're right. It doesn't make any sense." And nei-ther did the hope she couldn't quite extinguish, that

Rasheed might still turn out to be a good guy and come to their aid. Exasperated, she pushed him out of her mind. "But even if they don't hurt us, once we get into the jungle it's going to be harder to escape. We could get lost and wander around for weeks. This could be our only chance."

Henry's gaze held hers, his blue eyes thoughtful now. "Is there something you're not telling me? I get the impression that there's more to this kidnapping than you've let on."

"Of course not." She tried to sound convincing. "I'm just saying that we need to escape when we reach the town."

"All right." His eyes still doubtful, he looked toward the valley again. "You think we can find someone to help us?"

"I doubt it. The drug cartel probably controls the town. Most of the people probably work for them. And the ones who don't will be too afraid to help."

"So what do you suggest?"

Considering that, she studied the town. She couldn't see a highway leading out of the jungle. People arrived mainly by plane or boat. And since the drug smugglers operated the airplanes…

"We need to get on a boat."

"How? I don't have any money, do you?"

"No," she admitted, her own doubts mounting. "Maybe we can stow away."

A soft thud sounded behind her. Tensing, she jerked around. *Rasheed.* He stood with his hands braced on his hips, his piercing gaze skewering hers. "It's time to go."

Uneasy, she bit her lip. Had he overheard them?

Would he try to stop them if he had? She tried to read his expression, but as usual, she couldn't glean any clues.

"So soon?" She hedged. "Can't we stay here and rest a little longer?" She needed more time to plan.

"No. We need to go."

The other men headed toward them, the purpose in their steps impossible to miss. This was it—the moment of truth. Her time was finally up. In a few short hours they'd reach Buena Fortuna, and she'd have one chance, one shot to help Henry escape.

And if she failed, her friend would die.

By the time they arrived at Buena Fortuna three hours later, Nadine's stomach was in total rebellion, her nerves wound so tightly she wanted to retch. She scanned the murky river gliding past, the hodgepodge of boats thronging its shore—rafts, canoes, thatch-roofed vessels piled high with cargo of every sort. Wooden huts crowded the banks, perched haphazardly on logs, as if they'd washed ashore during a flood and gotten marooned in the debris.

They crossed the wooden bridge into town, the stench of rotting garbage strong in the air. Barefoot children stared at them from the buildings' shadows. Women washing clothes in the river shot them furtive glances, then turned away, confirming what Nadine had guessed. People minded their own business in a lawless town like this. No one would stick his neck out on their behalf—not when the price for interfering could be death.

Manzoor took the lead, steering their group down the main street through town, scattering chickens and a litter of pigs. They rode past fishermen selling piranhas and *paiche,* peasants squatting beside plastic tarps laden with jungle fruit. And with every step, Nadine became more convinced that the river was their only way out. They'd have to sneak aboard a boat, hide amidst the cargo and pray it got underway before the terrorists realized where they'd gone.

But they had to get away from their captors first.

She glanced at Rasheed riding on her right, Manzoor on the horse ahead, his white turban bright in the sun. Amir hugged her other side, riding so close that his horse kept jostling hers. They'd hemmed her in once they'd crossed the bridge, as if anticipating that she'd try to run.

Several minutes later, they arrived at the airstrip on the jungle side of town. She skimmed the deserted runway, the metal warehouses baking in the sweltering heat, and her nerves neared the breaking point. No one was around to see them. No one would hear a cry for help. She and Henry were on their own.

"Get down," Manzoor ordered, dismounting.

Trying to keep a lid on her rising panic, Nadine slid off her horse. What if she'd waited too long? What if they couldn't escape? Henry's death would be her fault.

"Over here." Manzoor strode to a metal shed and opened the door. She hesitated, searching frantically for another option, but Amir rammed his gun into her back. Her throat dry, she followed Henry across the dirt-packed lot.

"Get inside. Both of you," he ordered.

Her palms began to sweat. She shot a pleading glance back at Rasheed, but his face was still expressionless, his eyes remote. *So much for rescuing her.*

Feeling ridiculously disappointed, she followed Henry into the shed. Manzoor shut the door and threw the bolt.

For a moment she couldn't breathe. She stood in the stifling hut, perspiration running down her back, desperation threatening to do her in. Why hadn't Rasheed helped her? Why hadn't he come to her aid this one last time? How could he stand by and do nothing as an innocent man got killed?

She pulled herself back to reality, knowing she couldn't waste energy on wishful thoughts. Their survival was up to her now. She had to get them out of this mess.

Blotting the sweat stinging her eyes, she glanced around. The shed had a metal floor, a corrugated tin roof and a small, filthy window beside the door. She walked over, rubbed the dirt from the glass with her sleeve and peeked outside.

She couldn't see the men—only their horses—but she could hear them arguing nearby. She pressed her ear to the glass, catching words in Jaziirastani: horses, stable, gunshots, shed. Her throat clammed up, her worst fears materialized. They were arguing about where to kill Henry—and this shed was the perfect spot.

Then Rasheed and Manzoor came into view, leading the horses across the lot. Halfway across it Rasheed paused, his gaze meeting hers through the dirty glass. And for one wild moment, she wondered if he was trying to communicate with her. Was he encouraging her to escape? Warning her not to leave? Apologizing for abandoning her? But then he turned and walked away.

Her heart plummeted, any lingering hopes she had

for a rescue shattered now. It was up to her to save Henry's life.

But how? She could never overpower Amir. She raised her hand to her bruised jaw, proof of his speed and strength. She'd have to rely on her wits.

Determined, she turned to Henry. He stood as if lost, wobbling precariously on his feet. Even in the dim light she could tell he was feebler than he'd let on.

"Okay, listen," she said, trying to project an air of confidence she didn't feel. "They've left one man to guard us, the one they call Amir. I'm going to convince him to take me over to that warehouse." She pointed through the glass. "He'll probably lock the door as soon as I go out and leave you inside. Do you think you can climb out this window while we're gone?"

Perking up, Henry walked over and examined the latch. "I think so. The latch looks weak. Do you think we should risk it, though? If we make them mad…"

"We have to." She swallowed hard, knowing it was time to reveal the truth. "They're going to kill us, Henry. I just overheard what they said. We don't have any choice now. We need to get to the river and sneak aboard a boat."

His face blanched, but he managed a nod. "All right. I can do it."

"Good. As soon as you get out, run to the back of that building over there." She pointed through the glass at another warehouse. "I'll catch up in a minute." She paused. "But Henry…if anything happens to me, if we get separated, promise me you'll go to the river and leave."

Alarm flitted through his eyes. "I'm not leaving without you."

"You have to."

"But—"

"I'm serious, Henry. This is our only chance to get free. You have to get out of here."

"All right. But only if you promise to do the same."

"I promise," she lied. She was *not* leaving this man behind. She gave him a hug, praying he had the strength he'd need. "Good luck."

Gathering her own courage, she banged on the door. "Hello. I need to get out." Amir didn't answer, and she slammed her fist on the door again. "It's urgent. Open up."

The bolt rattled loose. The door opened a crack and Amir filled the door frame, his checkered scarf drooping around his neck. Sweat glistened on his dark face. "What do you want?"

"I need to go to the toilet."

"That's not my problem." He started to shut the door.

She wedged her foot into the space, keeping it open, her mind racing over what to do. She couldn't play on this man's sympathy. He didn't have it in him to care. But everyone had a weak spot, even a brainless goon like him. She hazarded a guess at his. "It certainly is going to be your problem if my father finds out the way you've treated me."

"He won't care."

He was right, but he might not know that for sure. "Then you don't know him very well, do you? He doesn't tolerate anyone mistreating his family, and you've already hit me once. When he hears about this, how you denied me basic hygiene…"

She managed to shrug. "Of course, it's your neck. If you want to take a chance on ticking him off, go ahead. But I wouldn't want to get on his wrong side if I were you."

Doubt flickered in his eyes. His shiny forehead creasing, he glanced at the empty warehouses, obviously trying to decide. "All right. But the man stays here."

She slipped outside into the afternoon sunlight. He locked the door behind her, caging Henry inside. Inhaling, she glanced around, then headed across the lot.

Amir hugged her heels. "Where are you going?"

"Into that building over there. It looks open. And it's big enough to have a bathroom."

"We have to stay near the shed."

"Stay here if you want," she tossed over her shoulder. She didn't break her stride. "But I'm looking for a toilet. It's an emergency." She doubted he would shoot her. If she knew her father, he'd order the men to bring her in alive. He'd want the satisfaction of exacting revenge himself. But she had to hurry and get Amir far enough from the shed so he wouldn't see Henry leave.

The terrorist stayed close behind her, as she'd hoped. She ducked into the empty building, then zigzagged through the deserted aisles to the rear door at a rapid pace. Exiting on the back side, she scanned the piles of boards and concrete, then walked to the end of the building and stopped.

She turned to Amir again. "There's a place around the corner I can use. But it's kind of open, and I need my privacy."

Amir crossed his massive arms. His gaze narrowed, and she held her breath, convinced he'd see through her flimsy ploy. "All right," he finally agreed, proving he wasn't the brains in this affair. "You've got one minute."

"That's all I need." Giddy with relief, she scooted around the corner, then ran flat out to the opposite building, spotting Henry staggering her way. *They were free!* Now she just prayed they could escape Amir and the other men.

Catching up, she took his arm, then pulled him between the buildings and out of sight. "Okay," she whispered. "We need to get to the river fast. We have to run."

Still hanging on to his arm, she urged him into a jog. She towed him down a couple of side streets, sweat streaming down her scalp and jaw, terrified they'd be seen. But she realized instantly that she had a major problem; Henry couldn't keep up. He slowed and stumbled behind her, his breathing growing more labored until he finally lurched to a stop. Wheezing like a steam engine, he grasped his head. "I can't do it."

"Just a little farther," she begged. "We're nearly to the river now."

"I can't. I'm sorry. It hurts too much. You'll have to go without me."

The hell she would. Her anxiety rising, she whirled around, desperate for a way to help him, and spotted a delivery cart parked nearby. She dashed over to the foot-propelled vehicle, tossed out a sack of potatoes and climbed aboard, ignoring a shout from inside the hut. "Come on. Get in. I'll drive you."

Henry tottered over and collapsed in the cart. Glancing back, she caught sight of Amir running toward them, shoving people out of his way.

Her pulse took flight, veering toward full-blown

panic now. "Hold on. He's after us!" She jerked the cart
into motion, then pedaled with all her might, bumping
down the unpaved road. Her breath sawed. Her lungs
burned with the effort to propel the cart through the
muddy ruts with Henry weighing it down. But then
the road began sloping downhill. They steadily picked
up speed. She swerved through a couple of alleys, still
angling toward the river. The smell of fish grew strong
in the air.

Then buzzards came into view, circling the garbage rotting along the bank. She came to a stop in
the crowded street and scanned the boats, searching
for a place for Henry to hide. She zeroed in on a long,
wooden vessel loaded with crates, its outboard engine
running as the driver prepared to depart. The driver
stepped ashore a second later, shouted to a man working on another boat and entered a riverside shack.

She leaped down and helped Henry out of the cart.
"That boat over there. The one with the thatched roof.
Go pick up a crate and take it onboard. Then hide un-
derneath the tarp."

"I can't leave you here."

"Don't worry. I'll be right behind you in another
boat."

"But—"

"There's no time. He's after us. You've got to go."

Henry's worried blue eyes held hers. And suddenly,
a swarm of emotions brimmed inside her, words she
wanted to say. But they didn't have time for a long
farewell.

"All right," he said, relenting. "But be careful."

"I will. Don't worry. Now get on board that boat."

He hobbled down the bank. Luckily, no one looked

his way. He paused to pick up an empty crate, then climbed onto the boat as if he had every right to be aboard. At the last minute, he turned back and lifted his hand, and her heart made a little clutch. Then he disappeared beneath the tarp.

Her throat turned thick and she swallowed hard, suddenly feeling bereft. It felt odd to be parting company with Henry after all that they'd been through. And for the first time since this ordeal began, she was on her own. But she had to make sure he survived.

Needing to divert Amir, to make certain he didn't notice Henry, she abandoned the cart and set off on foot, darting into the open road. She looked back, waited a second until she knew he'd spotted her, then sprinted past a row of huts.

A minute later, she swiveled around and spared another glance back at the cargo boat. The vessel puttered into the center of the slow-moving river, then started gaining speed, heading downstream with Henry stowed aboard.

She let out a shaky breath. She had no idea where the boat was going, or how Henry would get back to civilization when it eventually put to shore, but at least he was safe from the terrorists.

Now she had to worry about herself.

She started running again, knowing this was her last chance to get away. If she didn't escape now, if Amir and the other men caught her, they would turn her over to her father, and she'd be dead.

The road came to an end. She turned and started uphill, away from the river, hoping to circle back. But suddenly Manzoor came into view above her, heading her way.

She slammed to a halt. Her panic surging, she detoured into an alley between two buildings and ran back toward the river again. But the alley ended abruptly with a barricade, and she skidded to another stop.

She peered over the wooden barrier. Twenty feet below her was a pile of rocks. She spun around, searching for options, but then Rasheed appeared at the alley entrance, barring her way.

Her heart missed several beats. She glanced behind her at the rocks again—but she'd never survive the jump.

"Nadine!" he called. "Come this way." He started walking toward her, a gun in his left hand. And a terrible sense of betrayal seized her—because despite the kidnapping, despite his association with the other criminals, she'd wanted to trust this man. Some insane part of her had tempted her to believe that he was different, that his kiss had meant something important, that he wasn't as bad as he pretended to be.

"Let me pass," she begged.

"I can't." His voice was strained. "Not now. You have to come with me."

She grabbed hold of the barricade and looked down. She'd never make it. The rocks were too far away. She'd break a leg or worse if she tried to leap. But that was better than facing certain death at her father's hands.

"Don't do it," he warned. "Don't jump." Her gaze flew back to his. He was only a few yards away now, walking steadily closer, his eyes intent on hers. "You won't survive it. And I'm not going to hurt you. I'll help you. You can trust me to keep you safe."

Could she? Should she? She searched his eyes, wanting to believe in his sincerity. And her mind flashed back to the gentle way he'd treated Henry, how he'd protected her from Amir. But if she guessed wrong...

"I promise you, Nadine. I won't let anyone hurt you."

She had to decide. Manzoor waited on the hill above her. Amir was on the bank below. It was either jump onto the rocks or trust Rasheed—and take a leap of a different sort.

She sucked in a breath, knowing her fate rested on her choice. Her legs unsteady, hoping with every fiber of her being that she wouldn't regret it, she let go of the railing and walked to Rasheed.

"Don't say anything," Rasheed murmured, relief barreling through him as he seized her arm. "Just play along until we're away from the others." He had to make this look convincing or he'd blow his cover for sure. He'd had a hard enough time distracting Manzoor, keeping him from reaching the river before Henry escaped in the boat. He couldn't ruin everything now.

He pulled Nadine back down the alley into view. "I've got her," he called to Manzoor, who was watching from the hill above. "We'll meet you at the airstrip."

"Make sure she doesn't get away," the leader called back.

"Don't worry. She won't. You can depend on me." Needing privacy, he glanced around. He spotted an abandoned building beyond the hill, out of Manzoor's direct line of sight. Making a show of being rough, he dragged Nadine behind the building, then hustled her through the door. They were alone for now.

Nadine jerked her arm free, panting hard. Her

cheeks were flushed. Her eyes sparked at his in the light seeping through the cracks between the boards. "What do you want? Why won't you let me go?"

"I can't." God knew, he wanted to. But the truth was that he needed her help. And she was far safer in his hands than in Manzoor's.

"Please." Her voice trembled, the fear seeping through her bravado gutting his heart. "You have to help me. This is my only chance to get away. My father… He's going to kill me if you turn me in."

"What?" He stared at her, unable to mask his surprise. "What do you mean he's going to kill you?"

She frowned, confusion filling her eyes. "Don't you know?"

"Know what?"

"But…" She gave her head a shake. "If you don't know what he's doing, then why did you kidnap me?"

"I was following orders. I told you. I have a job to do."

Her eyes searched his. "But you know who my father is?"

"Yeah." He knew, all right. Yousef al Kahtani was the man financing this operation, the man who'd ordered Rasheed's wife's death.

"He's been looking for me for years," she said. "He wants to kill me. That's why I ran away from home."

Rasheed's mind spun. *Hell.* He hadn't expected this at all. "You ran away?"

"Yes, when I was seventeen."

That accounted for where she'd gone, and it explained why the terrorists had captured her now. Her father must have discovered her whereabouts and ordered them to bring her in. And, if it was true, then she really was a victim in this affair. That fear she'd exhibited was real.

Still, he had to be sure. "Why would your father want to hurt you?"

"Because of his *honor*." Her mouth flattened, her voice ringing with disgust. "He arranged a marriage for me when I was a teenager. To a distant cousin, an older man who has a higher standing in the royal family. But I refused and ran away."

An honor killing. He'd heard of those, of course. The archaic practice still happened far too often in tribal cultures in the Middle East. And he could imagine Nadine's value as a bride with her bewitching eyes. Her father could aim sky-high.

"And you've stayed hidden during all this time?" he asked, still not completely convinced.

"That's right."

"How?"

"At first I stayed on the move. Later I created a new identity. That's how I got through medical school without him finding me."

Taken aback by her story, he studied her in a different light. If she was being forthright, that had been some feat. She'd disappeared so effectively that even the intelligence community believed she'd died.

"And you seriously think he'll kill you?"

"I know he will. His honor is at stake. The cousin I was supposed to marry is the ambassador to the U.S. now. He isn't the kind of man who'd forget. Neither is my father."

Rasheed couldn't argue that. When al Kahtani had caught wind of Rasheed's investigation, he'd ordered the terrorists to kill his wife. He wouldn't blink at murdering a daughter who'd impinged his honor.

"And it's not just me," she continued, rubbing her arms. "My friends are in danger, too."

He frowned. "Why would he go after them?"

"He wouldn't. But after I ran away, when I was living on the streets in Baltimore, I witnessed a crime. A gang execution. Well, one of my friends saw it, one of the girls I hung around with. I was just standing nearby. But the killer has been after us all this time. And if he finds me, if I appear in public and he recognizes me, he might be able to find them, too."

"Christ." Rasheed ran his hand down his face. This was getting more complicated by the second.

And her revelation changed everything. If she was telling the truth—and he strongly suspected she was—he now held the fate of an innocent woman in his hands, the one thing he'd vowed he'd never do again.

"Please." Her green eyes pleaded with his. "You have to let me go. If you don't, I'm going to die."

Swearing, he spun on his heels, then paced across the room and back, his steps echoing on the wooden floor. His conscience demanded that he let her go. He had no right to hold her captive when her life could be at risk.

But he *couldn't* let her escape. Not only would he blow his cover, but he needed her help. He urgently needed information about her father to have any hope of stopping the attack. If he gave up now, if he aborted this crucial mission, thousands of people could die.

He stopped and faced her again, the desperation in her eyes erasing any doubt. She was innocent. There wasn't a chance in hell she was working with her father. And he couldn't deliver her to her death.

Unless she volunteered to stay...

His conscience balked. He'd already caused one woman's death. He'd dragged his wife into danger she'd never asked for, and she'd paid the ultimate price. Did he now have the right to involve another vulnerable victim, to ask Nadine to give up her chance at freedom to help bring her family down? Would she really work against them if he did?

It was time to find out.

Chapter 6

Rasheed knew he was flirting with danger. Revealing his covert status could jeopardize the investigation, potentially imperiling thousands of innocent lives—not to mention his own. But he couldn't see much choice. He had to tell her who he was.

"All right, listen," he said. "The truth is that I'm working undercover."

Seconds dragged past. Her eyes stayed fastened on his. "Undercover?" she finally said. "You're saying you're…some kind of agent? Like with the CIA?"

"That's right. I'm investigating Amir and Manzoor. They belong to an elite contingent of the Rising Light, a Jaziirastani terror group. Right now they're on a mission, heading into the United States. I infiltrated their cell to find out what that mission is. I didn't know they were going to kidnap you. But now that they have, I need your help."

"*My* help?" She sounded even more surprised. "I'm a plastic surgeon. How can I possibly help you?"

Hoping he hadn't misjudged her, he started pacing again. A dog barked outside. The sunlight slanting through the gaps in the wallboards made stripes across the wooden floor. He returned to Nadine and stopped. "We think your father is the Rising Light's chief financier. We've been investigating his link to them for years. The money travels a convoluted route from his bank in Virginia—Jannah Capital—to a Jaziirastani charity that supports this jihadist group."

"What makes you think that?"

"A few years after 9/11, when tighter financial regulations went into effect, we started noticing anomalies in his bank—high-volume transactions, unexplained deposits, multiple accounts transferring funds into the same account overseas. They sent me to one of the bank's subsidiaries, First Bangladesh, to check it out. I worked there for about a year, trying to follow the money trail, watching how the transfers came in and where they went. But I kept hitting dead ends. They disguise the transactions well. So I decided to go into the field instead." He'd had no choice after al Kahtani got wind of his investigation, blowing his cover at the bank to shreds.

"That's when I joined the Rising Light. I decided to approach the investigation from the other end, to try to uncover the people involved and see if I could make the connection back to him."

Her forehead creased, her eyes turning troubled now. Realizing she wasn't convinced yet, he went on.

"It took me a while to gain their confidence." Carrying out acts too repugnant to recall. "But I eventually worked my way up their ranks. Then, about six months ago, I got wind that they had something major in the works. I'd paid my dues, and they trusted me by then, so they agreed to let me in. That's why I'm here, to find out what they're up to and stop the attack." And connect the plot to al Kahtani, the bastard who killed his wife.

"What are they going to attack?" she asked, sounding numb.

"That's just it. We still don't know. They compartmentalize their information. That's standard tradecraft behavior. No one person has all the facts, except your father and maybe Manzoor. But whatever they're planning, it's going to be big. Internet chatter's heating up. Governments everywhere are on high alert. We think it's on the scale of 9/11."

She pressed her hand to her throat. "And the plane you're catching?"

"It's taking us to San Gabriel, the island the drug cartel owns. The cartel is going to fly us into the States on one of their drug smuggling runs. The Rising Light hired them to sneak us in. The CIA is going to facilitate the flight, to make sure we can land." And hopefully arrest the terrorists, assuming he'd unearthed enough evidence to pin on them by then.

"And you really think my father's involved in this?"

"I know he is. All our sources tell us so. But I can't prove it yet. He's too damned smart. He's got a firewall around him no one can penetrate."

He plowed his hand through his hair. "Look. I know I don't have a right to ask you this. And if you say no,

I understand. I'll get you to the river. I'll help you get on a boat and escape. But I'd like your help."

"But I still don't see what I can do."

"Stay a captive for a while longer, just until we reach the island. Fill me in on what you know about your family."

"But I don't know anything about them. I haven't seen or talked to them in fifteen years."

"You might be surprised. Any details you can give me, any bit of background information might trigger a clue. I'm desperate, Nadine. Thousands of people could die if we don't stop this attack."

Her face paled. She hugged her arms, her eyes filled with fear. "And my father? What if he catches me?"

"It won't get that far. I promise. There's another agent embedded on the island. We'll help you get away. I only need you to stay with me for a day or two, just long enough for you to brief me on what you know, and then we'll get you out."

More doubts clouded her eyes. She nibbled her lush bottom lip, her indecision clear. He knew he was asking a lot. She'd spent nearly half her life on the run from her powerful family. Asking her to trade her freedom—and risk her life—was too damned much.

She lifted her eyes to his. "When is the attack?"

"As soon we get to the United States, I think. We don't have much time."

She swallowed, the movement visible in her slender throat. But then she raised her chin. "All right. I'll do it."

His breath caught. "You're sure?"

She exhaled, the sound soft in the quiet room. "My father has tortured me long enough. I can't keep running forever. And if there's a chance I can help put a stop to this…"

Staggered by her courage, he moved in close. The afternoon sunlight sifted through the slats, painting silver highlights in her midnight hair. "I'll protect you, Nadine. I'll do everything I can to keep you safe. But I can't lie. There's no way to predict exactly what's going to happen. There's always a risk involved."

"I know that."

"And if you want to back out, if you don't want to chance it, I understand. I can still help you get away. You don't have to agree."

"Yes, I do." A haunted look darkened her eyes. "I've built a life now. I have friends, a career. I don't want to keep starting over every time he catches up. He's an evil man, Rasheed. Someone has to stop him before more innocent people get hurt. So if I can do my part…"

His eyes stayed on hers, her courage impressing him like hell. Unable to resist, he reached out and tucked a strand of hair behind her ear, the silky feel accelerating his pulse.

And suddenly, for the first time, he really saw her. He saw more than her dazzling green eyes, more than her heart-stopping face and tempting curves. He saw a woman with courage and strength, who was willing to put her life on the line to protect others from a violent fate.

This was the woman who'd defied Amir. The woman who'd been willing to barter her own freedom to get Henry the care he required. The woman who spent her life healing battered women, using her medical skills to ease their pain. And this was the woman who'd fled her home as a teenager, willing to brave the dangers of street life to pursue her precious dreams.

His throat thick, he traced her jaw, the purple bruise standing out in stark relief, proof of the violence she'd endured. He couldn't deny her physical appeal. She had an uncommon beauty, a combination of sultriness and passion that had attracted him from the start.

But her spirit impressed him even more. She didn't have to lead this kind of existence. It would have been much easier for her to give in to her father's wishes, marry a member of the Jaziirastani royal family and submit to the traditional role they'd prescribed. Or she could have cashed in on her exotic beauty, garnering fame and money as a model or a movie star. Even now, she could earn a fortune as a plastic surgeon catering to wealthy celebrities desperate to recapture their fading youth. Instead, she dedicated her life to helping the people the rest of society overlooked.

Her altruism affecting him deeply, he threaded his hand through her glossy hair. He skimmed the graceful line of her throat, the tilt of her gray-green eyes. Her full lips were parting in a sensual invitation he was hard-pressed to withstand.

And damned if he didn't want to kiss her again.

His mind clamored an instant warning, that he was making a mistake. This case was complicated enough. He couldn't get involved with a woman under his protection, not with so many lives at risk. Giving in to the impulse before had been bad enough, threatening to blow his objectivity sky-high. But now…

Now her spirit drew him like a beacon, torching a need in his jaded soul. Reminding him of a distant time when he'd been a different man, a man with honor and pride and ideals.

Unable to stop himself, he shifted closer, his palm bracketing her jaw. Her pulse raced under his thumb. Her breath hitched, the soft sound luring him in. Their gazes tangled, then locked, heat pulsing between them, that attraction he'd felt from the second he'd met her building steadily out of control.

And then her eyes fluttered closed, her lashes like soot against her pale cheekbones, her lips an invitation a better man would resist.

He was no longer that man.

He lowered his mouth to hers. Her sigh made his heart drum, her amazing warmth inflaming his blood. He took her lips in a blaze of possession, the velvety feel of her jolting every buried part of him back to life.

The scent of her inundated his senses, her soft curves driving him insane. He sank into the kiss, giving vent to the urges mounting inside him, to the clamors he couldn't contain.

And she kissed him back. Her gentle hands clung to his shoulders. Her moist tongue dueled with his. Growling, he widened his stance and pulled her against him, needing the intimate contact, planting his hands on her rounded hips. Her answering moan shuddered through him like a shockwave, and reality began fading away.

He wanted her. Badly. He trembled with the need to touch her, to lose himself in her sultry warmth. To pretend the past hadn't happened. To forget the danger lurking nearby, to be worthy and whole again.

But it *had* happened. He couldn't erase his mistakes—or forget the man he'd become.

And this wasn't the time or place. The terrorists

were waiting for him at the airstrip. He had an attack to stop. He'd spent too many years working toward this moment, sacrificing everything he'd once cared for, to lose sight of the mission now.

Shaking from the effort, he pulled away. His breath sawed in the silence. His pulse thundered out of control. He tucked her head to his shoulder and held her against him, absorbing the shivers racking her slender frame. Then he tipped his head back and closed his eyes, his frenzied heart working overtime.

Dumb, dumb, dumb. He had no business touching Nadine, no matter what she made him feel. Even if she weren't the daughter of his target, even if he wanted to be different, he'd spent too many years living amidst the bottom-feeders of society to ever lead a normal life. He didn't have it in him anymore.

And she was a woman in his care, a woman depending on him to keep her safe. He had to keep his wits about him, no matter how much she made him burn.

With difficulty, he pulled away. But the sight of her kiss-swollen lips, her incredible eyes blurred with desire, nearly obliterated his resolve.

"Listen, Nadine." His voice came out like gravel, and he cleared his throat. "I'm sorry about that. I shouldn't have… It was a mistake."

A flush climbed up her cheeks. Her gaze skidded away. "Right."

"It's the mission. We can't—"

"You don't have to explain. I understand."

"Do you?" He lifted her chin, forcing her gaze back to his. "This isn't a game. These men, Amir and Manzoor…they're ruthless. They'll kill us in a heartbeat. I've spent years training with them. I know how they think. They don't value life like we do. They think their reward comes after death. And they won't listen to excuses or reason. They won't forgive any mistakes.

"Right now, my cover is the only thing that protects you. I can't show any weakness. I can't reveal any concern about your welfare, or give them a reason to doubt my loyalty. Because if I slip up and they suspect I'm not what I've been pretending to be, we'll both die."

Her eyes stayed on his. She touched his face, the feathery feel of her soft fingers sparking eruptions inside his veins. "I said I understand. I grew up around men like them, remember?"

"I know." And without warning, he saw yet another side to this remarkable woman—the woman who'd fled her abusive home. She'd defied her powerful father. She'd gone on the run in pursuit of freedom, surviving despite the odds. Then she'd faced down a gang killer and outwitted not just her murderous family, but the CIA, staying hidden for fifteen years. She was courageous. Incredible.

A woman he feared he could care about too much.

Needing to create some mental distance, he stepped away. "We'd better go. They're going to be waiting for us at the airstrip. They'll get suspicious if we take too long."

He opened the door to the alley and looked out. Safe. *For the moment.*

Now he just had to keep her that way.

Nadine didn't know which decision was crazier—forfeiting her only chance at freedom or kissing Rasheed again.

She walked beside him down the dirt road leading to the airstrip, still trying to make sense of what she'd done. She had to stop her father. Even though the idea scared her, she was convinced of that. It was bad enough that he intended to kill her out of some sick, misguided belief. But she could not stand by and let him unleash a terrorist attack, extinguishing thousands of unsuspecting lives.

But kissing Rasheed…that had been total insanity. She couldn't begin to justify her reaction to him. He was exactly the kind of man she didn't want—secretive, dangerous, violent. Definitely not a long-term bet.

But the amazing way he'd kissed her… Shivering at the sensual memories, she slid a glance his way. She couldn't deny that he compelled her with that rock-hard physique and unkempt jaw. His rough good looks, his sheer, unbridled masculinity stirred something inside her, thrilling her in a way no other man ever had. And his revelation that he was a good guy, that he was working undercover to bring down the Rising Light terrorists had further penetrated her defenses, making him difficult to resist.

It was the bleakness shadowing his eyes, that glimpse of remembered pain that had really laid waste to her walls. She was a sucker for the underdog, and this man had a tortured soul—which was exactly why he was wrong for her. Because even if he'd kissed her senseless, even if he'd shaken up her preconceptions, making her feel totally, erotically alive, she couldn't deceive herself. Rasheed was a damaged man. Infiltrating that terror group had come at a cost. They would have tested him, making him do unspeakable things to prove his loyalty to their warped cause.

And he'd paid a price for that. She hadn't missed the desolation in his voice, the naked pain hollowing his eyes. Living outside the bounds of human decency— even with good intentions—had left its mark. Making him unpredictable. Unreliable. Wounded in ways that even a physician like her couldn't heal.

No matter how much he tempted her to try.

They turned the corner, entering the main dirt road through town, and Rasheed took hold of her arm. Knowing that this was it, that she had to play the part of the resisting prisoner in case the terrorists were lurking nearby, she intentionally dragged her heels. But her reluctance was far too real. Every survival instinct she possessed screamed at her to turn around, break free from this mess and run like the devil before her last chance for liberty disappeared.

"So tell me about your family," Rasheed said, his husky voice drawing her gaze.

"What do you want to know?"

"Let's start with the basics—who everyone is, the family dynamics, how they get along."

Struggling to focus on her family, she frowned. "Well, my mother died when I was a teenager. Aside from my father, there's just my brother, Sultan, and me. And his wife, Leila. He got married just before I left home. He's six years older than I am."

"He runs a real estate company?"

"That's right. He started off working in my father's bank after college. He got his degree in finance. Somewhere along the line he went into business for himself." She shrugged. "I don't know much about him now, except that he's successful and still lives at the family compound in McLean." She'd kept tabs on him, checking online as the years went by to make sure she didn't run into him.

Rasheed gave her a nod. "Go on."

A barefoot child darted past. She sidestepped to avoid him, and Rasheed loosened his grip on her arm. "My father pretty much ignored me until I was older. He doesn't have much use for girls. He only started paying attention to me when he decided to marry me off." She'd been a commodity to him then, something he could sell to enhance his prestige. "Sultan was his favorite, being a boy."

"How did you and your brother get along?"

She made a face. "We didn't. He's a bully. He bossed me around and made my life hell. My father encouraged him to torment me. He thought it made him a man."

Rasheed's strong jaw flexed. His eyes narrowed a fraction, taking on a deadly slant. "And your mother?"

Nadine exhaled, wistfulness whispering through her at the memory of her mom. "She was wonderful—kind, generous, courageous.... I don't know what I would have done without her. She braved my father's anger to make sure I had an education. She wanted me to have a life in America, to be someone in my own right and have the opportunities she never had. She died of cancer when I was sixteen."

"I'm sorry. That must have been hard."

She nodded, grateful for his sympathy. "It was. She was my ally. She brought me books, covered for me when I took part in academic things." Even taking beatings for it at times. "And she opened an account for me in another bank without my father catching on. She deposited money in it for years, putting away money in case I needed to escape. I withdrew it just before I ran away. I wouldn't have survived without it. I owe my life to her."

For a moment they didn't speak. They continued down the dirt road toward the airstrip, her thoughts lost to the memories, the tropical sun making her sweat.

"And your brother's wife?" he finally asked.

"Leila? What about her?"

"Any chance she could be involved in this?"

"I'd be shocked if she was. She's too meek." Naturally shy, her husband had further bullied her into submission with his cruelty. "But I didn't really know her that well. They got married around the time my mother died, about a year before I left home. And she didn't speak much Jaziirastani back then, just Farsi. She came from Iran.

"But my brother..." She suppressed a shudder at the thought of Sultan. "I wouldn't put anything past him. He was mean when I was a kid. Sadistic. He's probably worse now. And I told you, he and my father were always close. So if my father is involved in this, I'd bet money that Sultan is, too."

The airstrip came into view. Her heart began to jackhammer, her anxiety rising several rungs. A small plane now waited on the runway, stacks of coca paste lined up beside it. Several men she didn't recognize loaded the packages into the cargo hold.

Rasheed tugged her to a stop in the shadow of a building, out of view of the other men. And as she watched, he began to transform. The muscles of his face turned taut. His expression hardened, every trace of gentleness melting away. And suddenly, he looked exactly like a terrorist—dark, deadly, remote.

The kind of man she'd always feared.

"You're sure about this?" he asked.

She inhaled, wondering again if she'd lost her mind. "I'm sure."

His gaze burned into hers. His mouth turned even grimmer, the planes of his face like stone. "I'll do everything I can to protect you, Nadine. I promise."

"I trust you."

But gazing into his lethal eyes, the memory of that kiss still hovering between them, she was far less certain about her heart.

Had he made a mistake? Should he have risked bringing Nadine to the drug cartel's island? What if something unforeseen came up, and he couldn't get her back out?

Racked with doubts, Rasheed stared out the small plane's window four hours later as they prepared to land at San Gabriel Island off Colombia's Caribbean coast. His CIA handlers wouldn't have approved it. Involving an untested civilian in an operation of this magnitude presented too many uncertainties, no matter who or what she knew.

But he needed Nadine's help. He needed her insight into her family to help break this case open and stop the upcoming attack. It was the only hope he had.

Still, as the plane decreased in altitude, and the terrorists began stirring in the seats ahead, he couldn't halt his mounting unease. Because no matter how hard he tried to rationalize it, no matter how much he tried to convince himself that he'd done the right thing, his instincts warned him otherwise. Something was about to go wrong.

And he couldn't do a damned thing to stop it now.

The plane banked left. Rasheed stared out the oval window at the white sandy beaches beneath its wings. Beyond the shore was the turquoise water, ranging from bright aqua near the island to dark navy as the depth increased. He spotted the coral-colored mansion fronting the shore, the guest cottages tucked beneath the palm trees on either side, the sparkling, in-ground pool. He knew from his intelligence briefings that the cocaine processing labs were deeper in the jungled interior, conveniently out of sight—along with storage buildings and housing for the guards and staff.

The pilot made his final approach. He lowered the landing gear and raised the flaps, then dropped onto the paved runway with a gentle thump. The plane zipped along the manicured tarmac, splashing through puddles left by an earlier thunderstorm, and came to a stop near the end. While the engines powered down, a crew scurried up with a rolling staircase and opened the cabin door.

The terrorists all stood. Amir shot him a scowl, his eyes filled with undisguised resentment, and the foreboding inside Rasheed grew. The captives' escape had humiliated Amir, subjecting him to their leader's ridicule, and increasing his desire to see them dead.

Even more worried about Nadine's safety, he jerked his head at her. "Let's go." He kept his expression hard, his voice curt, knowing any sign of friendliness would alert Amir.

He waited for her to stand, then preceded her down the narrow aisle, stooping over slightly to keep from bumping his head. He ducked through the open hatch, his belly tightening as he stepped into the waning sunshine and went down the flight of steps.

The moist tropical air filled his lungs. A cool breeze rolled off the ocean, bringing with it the scent of salt. He scanned the coconut palms swaying in the breeze, the whitewashed hangars flanked by royal poinciana trees.

His mouth twisted at the irony. The island looked like a pricey tourist destination, an exclusive, high-end resort—and no wonder. The drug cartel generated billions of dollars trafficking cocaine, a fortune they used to influence police and politicians throughout the world. And this was their leader's domain. Everyone here was on his bankroll. His armed guards patrolled the grounds. No one came or went, or even entered the airspace around the island without permission from the cartel. Even the Policía Nacional stayed away.

Nadine came to a halt at his side. Rasheed grew tenser still, the nagging anxiety inside him increasing as several black sedans sped across the tarmac, their engines growling in the quiet air. They screeched to a stop, and two men emerged from the lead vehicle—the short one distinctly Hispanic, the taller man Middle Eastern. Both wore black suits, the weapons in their shoulder holsters creating a telltale bulge.

Then suddenly, Nadine went rigid beside him, her quick gasp putting him on alert. He shot her a glance, her shocked reaction provoking his instinctive need to protect.

"What is it?" he whispered, the foreboding he'd been fighting mushrooming into full-blown dread. What was wrong? Where was the danger? What the hell had made her so afraid?

Her gaze stayed stalled on the newcomers, every remaining scrap of color leaching from her face. "That man. The tall one on the left. That's my brother, Sultan."

Chapter 7

She'd just tumbled into a nightmare. Her worst fear, the situation she'd spent the past fifteen years trying to avoid had finally come to pass.

She was back in her family's power.

Nadine stared at the man striding toward her on the runway, the absolute horror of her predicament sinking in. She hadn't seen him since the day that she'd left home, pretending to head to the market, and fleeing for her life instead. But it was him. She could never forget the brother who had made her childhood hell.

She took in his powerful, planklike shoulders, the arrogance in his rapid strides. Sultan was older, of course, his waist and torso thicker, his jawline beginning to sag. As a boy, his handsome, teen-idol looks had masked his true nature, lending him a deceptive charm. But now... Now his black eyes blazed with cruelty. His lips formed a merciless slash. The years had stripped away all pretense of civility, revealing the sadistic man beneath.

His measured steps brought him closer. Pure panic took root inside her, triggering the desperate need to flee. Every survival instinct she possessed screamed at her to turn on her heels and run.

But there was nowhere to run. She couldn't escape. Her captors would gun her down before she'd made it a dozen feet. And she knew that was what he wanted, what he thrived on—that outward display of fear. Sultan was worse than any animal. He was a predator who took pleasure in his prey's terror, deriving a rush from the kill.

He came to a stop beside her. Summoning all her strength, she lifted her head, forcing herself to meet his gaze dead-on.

"Nadira." A perverse kind of excitement rang in his voice. "Did you think we'd given up on you?"

She clamped her lips to keep from answering. Any response, no matter how innocuous, would provide him with an excuse to lash out.

He took another step toward her. She inhaled, his woodsy oud oil cologne assaulting her senses, a smell she'd long ago come to loathe. "I told you we'd find you if you tried to run," he said. "I warned you that you couldn't escape."

Sweat trickled down her back. Her knees quivered badly as she battled to hold his gaze. But she was not going to buckle. No matter what he said, no matter how hard he tried to intimidate her, she was not going to reveal any fear. She was older now, stronger. She would not let him tyrannize her.

Irritation flickered in his eyes at her failure to respond. She knew it would fester inside him and fuel his hatred, making him more violent when he got her alone.

"I'll deal with you later," he warned, echoing her thoughts. He turned to the armed man at his side. "Take her to her quarters. I'll show these men to theirs."

The Hispanic man stepped forward. Short and powerfully built, he had dark olive skin, flat, unblinking eyes, a thick mustache and close-cropped hair. A snake tattoo writhed along his neck, adding to his menacing look. "This way," he said, his English heavily accented.

She swallowed hard, everything inside her rebelling at the command. But unable to see an alternative, she followed him to a sedan with dark tinted windows, trying her hardest to appear unfazed. He opened the rear passenger door and jerked his head. "Get in."

She took a step toward the car, but couldn't resist glancing back at Rasheed. He stood with his arms folded across his chest, his dark eyes carefully shuttered, obscuring any inkling of his thoughts. A pang of betrayal knifed through her, disillusionment that he hadn't helped.

But this wasn't his fault. He hadn't known Sultan would be waiting on the island. And what did she expect him to do? Pull out his gun and start shooting? Take on all these armed men alone? There was no way he could rescue her now. And unless he stayed in his undercover role, the men would kill him, too.

Besides, he'd warned her of the danger. She'd come here with her eyes wide-open. He hadn't deceived her about the risks.

She climbed into the car. The guard slammed the

door, locking her in. She stared straight out the tinted windshield, ice freezing inside her, knowing that nothing would save her now. She was at her brother's mercy.

And with every passing moment, her chance of survival was fading fast.

Nadine had never been the type to wait for help. She'd learned early on in her childhood that if she wanted to improve her circumstances, she had to do it herself. So why was she so desperate to see Rasheed?

Knowing she was acting ridiculous, she hung up her bath towel several hours later and combed out her freshly washed hair. It was futile to pin her hopes on some knight-in-shining-armor deliverance that would never come to pass. Even if he wanted to, Rasheed couldn't come to her aid. He had to protect his mission—a mission far more vital than rescuing her.

And obsessing about him wouldn't help. So what if he'd kissed her until her toes curled? So what if he'd turned out to be a good guy who wanted to bring her family down? Her brother's presence on the island had destroyed their plans. She was utterly on her own now. No matter what Rasheed had originally intended, she had to get out of this mess herself.

Determined to focus, to figure out some kind of escape plan, she crossed the room to the window and stared out. But the irony of her surroundings hit her hard. For the past six weeks she'd been camping in the mountains, sleeping on the hard ground and bathing in frigid streams. Now she'd landed in the pinnacle of luxury—a private cottage complete with polished marble floors, a king-size bed with a plush duvet and a bathroom straight from a decorating magazine. It had a minibar filled with snacks, a closet crammed with designer clothes in various sizes and nearly every comfort she could possibly require.

Except for one—her freedom. The iron bars on the windows proved that.

Sighing, she gazed out the window at the dusky night. Palm trees curved along the flagstone walkway. Bougainvillea climbed a trellis across the courtyard, their petals fluttering in the eastward breeze. She was in one of a series of tiny guest cottages tucked behind the main residence, just yards from the pristine beach. Aside from the bars on the windows, armed guards acted as sentries, ensuring her captivity.

She collapsed into the nearest armchair, still trying to formulate a plan. But realistically, what could she do? She was locked in a room on an island, miles from the Colombian mainland in the middle of a shark-infested sea. Even if she could sneak out of her prison, even if she could evade the drug cartel members patrolling the grounds, how could she possibly escape? She could hardly swim to land.

No, any way she looked at it, she was trapped.

A tapping sound came from the door. Her heart skipped, then sprinted hard, the air in her throat turning to dust. *Sultan.* Oh, God. He must have come to confront her. But would he bother to knock?

She rose and crossed the room, the slap of her borrowed sandals on the marble floor tiles sounding like a death knell in the quiet room. Bracing herself, she swung open the door. But instead of her brother, a woman wearing a black burka waited outside, holding a tray of food. "Dinner," she announced.

Nadine stared. The last person she'd expected to

find on the drug cartel's island was a woman dressed in full *hijab*. But something about the woman's voice seemed familiar, prodding a memory she couldn't quite conjure up.

She stepped back to let her in. "Thank you. Please put it on the table." Still trying to place that voice, she followed her into the kitchenette.

The woman set down the tray and lifted her veil. Nadine gaped at her, struggling to contain her shock. "Leila?"

She barely recognized her sister-in-law. Her complexion had turned sallow and pale. Her once-lustrous hair was lank and gray. Her cheeks were oddly flat and asymmetrical, the bone structure apparently diminished, thanks to repeated battering by her husband's fists. And she'd suffered damage to her facial nerves, causing a palsylike droop to the left side, making her lips appear deformed.

At thirty-six, she was only four years older than Nadine. She looked more than double that age.

"Hello, sister."

Nadine quickly inhaled, trying not to look aghast. But the change in her appearance made her reel. Leila had been a shy, pretty bride of twenty-one when she'd come to D.C. to marry Sultan. Within months, her reticence had turned to terror, her bruised body bearing the proof of his cruelty.

And now, fifteen years later…the years had aged her dreadfully, robbing her of her former beauty. Even her eyes looked dead, as if Sultan had beaten out every spark of life she'd once possessed.

And Nadine knew with a soul-deep certainty that if she had submitted to her father's dictates, if she'd gone through with the marriage he'd arranged, she would have ended up like Leila—broken, defeated, abused.

But why was Leila here? Her brother wasn't the type to treat his wife to a tropical vacation. Perhaps he'd wanted a servant along, someone to tend to his comfort and carry out his commands.

"Leila! What a surprise." She embraced her and gave her a kiss. "I didn't expect to find you here."

Leila smiled. Or at least, she tried to. One side of her mouth curved up, but the other stayed slack, turning the smile into a grimace instead.

"I'm having surgery. Didn't you know?"

"Surgery?" Nadine frowned. "What kind? Are you sick?"

"No, nothing like that. There's a famous plastic surgeon on the island. A world-renowned specialist." She lifted her hands to her face. "He's going to fix my cheeks and jaw."

Nadine blinked, certain she hadn't heard right. "A plastic surgeon? Here? Is there even a hospital?"

"Yes, of course. Sultan arranged it all."

Staggered by her announcement, Nadine sank into the nearest chair. Her brother had brought Leila here for cosmetic surgery. But why? This story didn't make any sense.

Not that there weren't good plastic surgeons in South America, even great ones. Cosmetic surgery was widely accepted in the region, and top doctors were in high demand. And it was possible the drug cartel kept one on staff. But there were also plenty of top-notch surgeons in the United States. And cost couldn't be an issue with the money her family had.

So why come here, to this remote Caribbean island to have work done?

More likely her brother feared an arrest. Any American surgeon with half a brain would figure out the cause of Leila's injuries and report him to the police. Of course Sultan would worry about himself.

"I'm not doing it out of vanity," Leila added. "I would never do that. But my looks have faded." She fixed her gaze on her clasped hands, a flush climbing up her sunken cheeks. "Sultan can barely tolerate being intimate with me when I have so many flaws. He insisted I have it done. And I want to please him."

Nadine's shock morphed into outrage. Her brother had battered his wife, causing permanent damage, and now demanded she have surgery to repair what he'd done? And all because he couldn't stand to look at her?

"Don't do it."

Leila's gaze shot up. "Why not?"

"You don't owe him anything, Leila. Don't subject yourself to surgery because of him."

"But I want to. I want to please him." She sounded mystified.

Nadine inhaled, struggling to calm herself. She wasn't going to change Leila's thinking. They'd been through this before, when she'd lived at home. Leila's subservience was too ingrained. She'd been raised to defer to her husband, and years spent acquiescing to an abusive monster had reinforced that trait.

"What exactly is the doctor going to do?" she asked instead.

"Implants, I think. To give my cheeks a better shape."

Nadine thought about that. Inserting implants wasn't

terribly risky if done right, but a lot could still go wrong. An infection could set in. A botched job could leave her even more deformed. And if the surgeon used counterfeit products, devices made from inferior materials, he could cause disfigurement or even death.

"Who's the surgeon?"

"I don't know. Sultan says he's famous, though."

But where had he trained? Who was the anesthesiologist? What kind of emergency equipment did the hospital have? "Tell me you at least had a physical and got cleared for surgery."

Leila shook her head. "Sultan said I didn't need one. He has arranged everything, and I trust his judgment."

Right. Trust the abuser. More anger flared inside her, along with disgust. "When is the operation?"

"Tomorrow."

"So soon?" She frowned. "Can't you delay it for a day or two? At least give me a chance to check things out. I'm a doctor now. I can make sure everything's okay."

"There's no need. I told you, Sultan has everything arranged. Now I have to go." She dropped her veil over her face and turned away.

Nadine scrambled to her feet. "Wait. Don't go yet. I wanted to ask you about my father." Leila didn't have any power in the family, and was loyal to her brother to boot. But she lived at the family compound. She'd seen visitors, deliveries, knew everyone's schedules now....

But Leila only hurried to the door. "I can't talk now. I'll see you tomorrow, after the surgery. I've already stayed too long." She slipped through the door and left.

For a moment, Nadine stood motionless, replaying their conversation in her mind. Leila was undergo-

ing cosmetic surgery at Sultan's request. There was a
plastic surgeon on the island, probably employed by
the drug cartel. And Leila was submitting to the pro-
cedure in an effort to please her husband, willingly
risking who-knew-what kind of dangers in a sick attempt to be a dutiful wife.

Still frowning, she crossed the room to the window
and looked out. She caught sight of Leila scurrying
down the path, her long, black robe flapping around
her ankles, her identity fully concealed.

Her face burned, anger warring with disgust. She
wasn't sure what made her madder—a brainwashed
woman like Leila or a culture that repressed women
and tolerated abuse.

And if she'd ever needed proof about men's penchant
for violence, her sister-in-law provided it in spades. Nadine would never understand it. Nor could she fathom
the thinking of victims like Leila, women brought up
to believe the abuse was normal—or worse, that it was
their fault. All she could do was mend the damage and
help these misguided women regain some dignity in
their downtrodden lives.

But she didn't have time to help Leila. She had her
own problems to deal with now. If she didn't escape
this island immediately, she would wind up dead.

But how could she forsake Leila? How could she
abandon her sister-in-law to an unknown surgeon's
hands? It went against her nature to turn her back
on a woman in need. At the very least she needed to
check out the hospital and make sure the equipment
was clean.

The hospital. Her mind raced. Leila had just provided her with the perfect excuse to leave her room.

And on the way, she could scout the island and formulate a plan to escape.

Leaping into action, she returned to the dinner tray. She removed the metal cover, ignoring the tempting rice and seafood, along with a mouthwatering side dish of fried plantains. Instead, she zeroed in on the utensils—a butter knife and fork. *Too dull.*

She checked the minibar and came up empty, then scanned the rest of the room. Her gaze landed on a vase filled with tropical flowers, and she rushed over and picked it up. Taking it into the bathroom, she eyed the stone bathtub with gilded feet, the troughlike vessel sink, the marble shower with its dizzying array of controls.

The tub. It would contain the damage best. Leaning over, she dropped the vase, and the glass shattered into jagged shards. She picked up a sliver and held her breath, then made a quick, shallow gash on her left arm. Hissing at the pain, she wrapped it in a hand towel and headed for the cottage door.

"I cut myself," she told the guard outside. "The flower vase slipped and broke. I need to go to the hospital right away." She held up her arm. Blood seeped through the towel, providing proof.

The guard frowned. "Close the door and stay inside. I'll radio for an escort."

"Hurry. I'm losing a lot of blood."

Satisfied, she closed the door. Then she took a seat at the table. Still plotting her plan of action, she dug into her dinner and prepared to wait.

The knock came fifteen minutes later.

Swallowing the last bite of her dinner, she hurried

over and opened the door. She caught sight of the tall
man filling the door frame, and her breath came out
in a rush. *Rasheed.* She gripped the door, a wild surge
of emotions careening inside her, threatening to turn
her knees to mush.

His hair was damp from a recent shower. He'd
combed it back, and the dark strands grazed the col-
lar of his clean black T-shirt, drawing her gaze to his
corded throat. He'd shaved the beard stubble from his
face, and she curled her hands, yearning to reach up
and stroke the enticing smoothness of his tanned jaw.
The faint woodsy aroma of his aftershave mingled with
the fresh, soapy scent of his skin.

Her gaze drifted lower, over the jeans slung low on
his hips to his battered hiking boots. He wore a shoulder holster over his T-shirt, emphasizing his flat belly
and muscled chest. The gun added to his ruthless look.

Her eyes rose to his, the sensual heat in them a jolt
to her nerves. And despite knowing that he couldn't
help her, that he had to stay in his abductor role, she
suddenly felt less alone.

But then he frowned. "What happened?" His voice
was rough, abrupt, a clear warning to watch her step.
She shifted her gaze to the guard standing behind him,
taking in his flat eyes and stony face, the snake tattoo
climbing up his thick neck. A cartel member. That tattoo had to be their sign.

She tempered her response, not wanting to tip him
off. But as Rasheed's hot black eyes devoured her, it
was all she could do to keep from launching herself
into his arms.

She cleared her throat. "My hands were wet, and I
dropped a vase in the bathroom. I was cleaning it up

when I got cut. I need to bandage the wound, maybe even suture it if I can."

Rasheed's gaze dropped to her arm. A crease furrowed his brow, concern shadowing his dark eyes. Then he turned to the other guard. "I'll take her to the clinic and bring her back. It shouldn't take long."

"I'll go with you."

"That's not necessary. I know the way."

"My instructions are to stay with her."

Rasheed shrugged. "Fine, but I'm telling you there's no need."

With one hand gripping the bloody towel, Nadine stepped outside into the night. Rasheed's warm scent instantly swamped her, mingling with the aroma of the island's flowers. She walked beside him down the flagstone path, attuned to his every movement, and wanting desperately to speak. But she couldn't do that until they were alone.

Palm fronds rustled in the breeze. The heat had fallen with the setting sun, and the air sang with the calls of insects and the rhythmic pull of the sea. They followed a path leading away from the main residence, a pink coral mansion with beautiful arched porticoes and terraces brimming with flowers. But despite the lanterns marking the way, she couldn't see much beyond the path, certainly not enough to plot her escape. The vegetation was too dense.

Instead, she sneaked a furtive glance at Rasheed. He moved with quiet strides, his obvious strength both reassuring and unbalancing her somehow. And once again, questions tumbled through her mind, that nagging curiosity about him she couldn't quite manage to quell. Why had he started investigating her father?

Why had he spent years living with terrorists, witnessing who-knew-what kind of crimes? Had it just been his job? Was he doing it out of a sense of patriotic duty? Or did he have another reason he hadn't named? And what had caused that terrible anguish she kept seeing in his eyes, that agony he couldn't hide?

Did it matter? She tugged her gaze away. Because frankly, despite the way he'd kissed her, despite his attempts to shield her from harm, she couldn't weave fantasies around this man. He was here on a mission. He had a job to do. He'd made that abundantly clear. She couldn't afford to lose focus, couldn't afford to do anything that would endanger her safety—or his. One inadvertent slipup, one incautious glance and they both could wind up dead.

Suddenly another guard appeared on the path. In one hand he gripped a rifle, in the other a leash attached to a growling German shepherd dog. The man's neck bore the snake tattoo.

"Where are you going?" he asked.

The guard behind them spoke up. "The clinic. The woman cut herself and needs a bandage."

The man shifted his gaze to her. His eyes narrowed on her face, then inched over her body, his blatant sexual appraisal causing a shudder to work up her spine. But thankfully, he stepped aside. "Go ahead."

Grateful for Rasheed's presence, she hurried past. Maybe he couldn't take on the entire drug cartel, but it helped having him at her side. Still, she didn't breathe easier until they reached the clinic, a white, one-story stucco building with cement steps.

"I'll stay here," the guard who'd escorted them announced. He pulled out a cigarette and lit up, then leaned against the side of the building, launching puffs of smoke into the night.

Nadine went up the steps and entered the clinic. She took in the empty receptionist's desk, the vacant chairs lined against the wall, the absolute silence pervading the room. The lights were on, but no one seemed to be around. Just past the desk was a door labeled *Privado.*

She motioned to Rasheed. "Back here." Taking the lead, she entered a short, deserted hallway. She walked to the end, glancing into the empty examination rooms on either side, then passed through another door. It was a small pre-op or recovery area, complete with a chair and bed. Beyond that was the operating theater itself. Once inside, she stopped and glanced around.

She had to admit she was impressed. The room was surprisingly modern with an operating bed and lamps, an autoclave to sterilize equipment and a computer on a small, wheeled desk. A sterile supply cabinet took up one wall. On another was a built-in mass spectrometer and a status indicator for a generator.

She raised a brow. "Whoever built this knew what he was doing. They even have a backup generator."

"They probably need it. Power goes out a lot on an island like this."

Still skimming the room, she gave him a nod. The room was state-of-the-art—testimony to the drug cartel's enormous wealth. If the doctor was any good, Leila would be fine.

Rasheed motioned toward her arm. "So what's really going on?"

She met his eyes. His black hair gleamed in the harsh, artificial light, the white walls and floor tiles making the dark tone of his skin more pronounced.

Trying to keep her mind off the way he made her pulse jump, she sighed. "I wanted to see the clinic. My sister-in-law, Leila, is here. Sultan's wife. She's having surgery tomorrow."

"Here? What kind of surgery?" He sounded as skeptical as she felt.

"Facial reconstruction work." She filled him in on what she'd learned. "It's hard to say what my brother's up to. There might not even be any surgeon." It would be typical of him to make Leila suffer by building up her hopes and then dashing them again.

Rasheed rubbed his jaw, his eyes turning thoughtful now. "Some men just arrived from the mainland on the weekly supply boat. The doctor could be one of them."

"If so, I'd like to find out who he is and where he studied and did his training. Not that it makes much difference. She intends to go through with the surgery no matter what. But I'd like to reassure myself. And I figured this was an excuse to see the island, to try to find a way out."

"Yeah, about that." He speared his hand through his damp hair. "Listen, Nadine. I'm sorry. I didn't mean to put you in this kind of danger. I didn't know your brother was here."

"I know. It's not your fault."

"Sure it is. I asked you to stick around. I promised I'd keep you safe. And instead, I delivered you right into your family's hands. You'd be halfway home by now if it weren't for me."

"I knew there was a risk. And there's no way you could have predicted that he'd be here. So this really isn't your fault."

He shook his head. "Regardless, I've got a plan. The supply boat leaves—"

The rapid thud of approaching footsteps cut him off. Tensing, Nadine spun toward the door as it flew open and banged against the wall. Her brother strode in, carrying a box.

He came to a halt. His eyes narrowed, his gaze skipping to Rasheed, then back. "What are you doing here?"

"I cut my arm." She lifted it up as proof. "I was looking for some bandages and ended up in here."

His eyes still suspicious, he walked over to the sterile storage cabinet and unlocked the door. Then he placed the box inside. "Look in the cupboard over there."

Nodding, she opened another cupboard, and pulled out some sterile gauze. Striving for an offhand tone, she turned around. "I talked to Leila, by the way. I heard she's having surgery tomorrow."

Sultan shrugged. "She needs it. She's getting ugly. Her cheeks are all caved in, so she's having implants to fill them out."

Nadine's face burned. She opened her mouth, then snapped it closed, biting back a nasty reply. She couldn't afford to antagonize him if she wanted to intercede on Leila's behalf.

"Who's doing it?" she asked instead.

"Does it matter?"

"Of course it matters. The surgeon is important. Leila said he's a specialist?"

He snorted. "Now where would she have gotten that idea?" He locked the supply cabinet door with a shrug. "He's a doctor from one of the villages, that's all. He came over on the supply boat tonight. They call him *El Carnicero*. The butcher."

Her jaw dropped. She stared at her despicable brother, outrage robbing her of words. Of course he'd lied to his wife. Later he'd deny that he ever mentioned a specialist, insisting she'd imagined it. He'd even deny that the surgery was his idea. And if the operation went badly, and Leila ended up even more deformed, he'd find a way to blame it on her.

It took all Nadine's effort to moderate her voice. "I'll do it. I'll do the surgery tomorrow."

One black brow lazily rose. *"You?"*

"Why not? I'm a plastic surgeon. I can do a better job than some jungle quack. I take it you have the implants?"

He nodded toward the storage locker. "They're in that container."

"I'll check them out. The other doctor can assist me if he wants and help with the anesthesia, but I'm taking the lead." If nothing else she could minimize the scarring and make sure an infection didn't set in. She shot him a pointed glance. "I assume you want your wife to survive."

"Of course." His lips slid into a smirk. A gleam of barely veiled triumph lit his eyes. "Be here by eight o'clock."

He turned his attention to Rasheed. "Take her back to her room now. The evening patrols have started. The guards have their instructions—shoot first, ask questions later. I'd hate to lose you before your job is done." He spun on his heel and left.

Nadine's stomach seethed. She realized her hands were trembling from the effort it took to keep her anger in check. She despised that man. He deserved to be behind bars. And that's exactly where she intended to put him, before this ordeal was done.

"You know he manipulated you into that," Rasheed said slowly.

She pushed a stray lock of hair from her eyes. "I know."

"Any idea why?"

She made a face. "Who knows? He likes to play mind games with people. It's his way of controlling what they do. Maybe the idea amused him. Or maybe he intended for me to do the surgery all along. I don't know. And honestly, I don't care. I'm more worried about Leila and making sure she gets through this all right."

"There's just one problem."

"What?"

"I met with the other agent, the one I was telling you about who's embedded with the drug cartel. He can sneak you on board the supply boat, but it leaves at dawn. That's the only way we can get you off the island before it's too late."

"But what about the investigation, the attack? I thought you needed information from me."

"I did. I do. But having your brother here changed things. It's too dangerous for you to stay. The supply boat leaves first thing in the morning. We need to get you aboard before then. I'm still ironing out the details, but that's the plan."

Undecided, she chewed her lip. She couldn't deny that she was tempted. Rasheed was offering her the perfect way out, a chance to escape Sultan.

"But what about Leila? I can't abandon her here."

.Not to mention the innocent people who could die in the attack.

"Forget Leila."

"And let some jungle quack massacre her face?"

Rasheed closed the distance between them. He stood directly before her, his eyes holding hers. "You've done what you could. You told me you tried to convince her, but she'd made her choice. You don't owe her more than that."

Didn't she? "Would you leave her if you were in my place?"

He didn't answer. He didn't have to. They both knew he'd stay.

"You still have to go," he finally said, his voice firm.

"But—"

"For God's sake, Nadine. Listen to me. Your life is in danger. This is your only chance to get away."

"It's not just because of Leila." She dragged in a breath, needing him to understand. "She's important, but I need to stay for myself, too. I told you. I can't run anymore. I've been hiding from my family for fifteen years. You have no idea what it's like living under a death threat—always worrying that they'll find me, always having to run. They're always there in the back of my mind, shadowing everything I do.

"I have to escape them, Rasheed. I have to end this thing for good, no matter how it turns out. It's my only chance to lead a normal life. I can't keep living like this, with this constant paranoia weighing on my mind. They're like ghosts trapped inside my head."

His jaw worked. His eyes darkened even more. And all of a sudden, she saw it again, that flash of remembered pain.

"You're wrong," he said, his voice stripped bare. "I know exactly what that's like."

Her heart rolled, the anguish in his voice sparking something inside her, the deep-seated need to pull this wounded man close and soothe his pain.

Instead, he turned away. Trembling, shaken by the misery he'd revealed, she gathered up several more supplies and followed him to the door. And suddenly, she was sure of one thing. Maybe this wasn't the right time. Maybe he wasn't ready to confide in her.

But before this ordeal was over, she intended to find out what haunted this lonely man.

Chapter 8

Nadine stepped out of the clinic late the following morning, then blinked in the brilliant sunshine, feeling vaguely disoriented after operating on her sister-in-law. Her back ached. Her leg muscles quivered from fatigue. The two-hour operation had sapped her of all her energy, the acute focus it demanded now spiraling toward a major crash. It hadn't helped to have her brother hovering over her shoulder, watching every move—or worse, having to keep her eye on the jungle doctor so he didn't overdose Leila with anesthesia and cause her even more harm.

Her ever-present guard emerged from the clinic's shadow. Resigned to the constant surveillance, she massaged her gritty eyes with a sigh and started down the steps. Then she caught sight of Rasheed leaning against a palm tree beside the path, and her pulse ramped up. He straightened and padded toward her, the raw angles of his face, the power in his fluid strides causing every part of her to spring back to life.

Lord, but he was attractive. There was something about him that thoroughly demolished her senses, appealing to her in a decidedly primal way. His gaze connected with hers, the quick punch of heat generating an avalanche of sensual impressions, flashbacks of his touch and taste and smell.

He shifted his gaze to the guard. "I'm supposed to take over here. They want you to go to the airstrip and help unload a plane."

"That's not what I was told."

Rasheed shrugged. "Then call them and check."

Frowning, the guard pulled out his radio. After a brief conversation, he nodded to Rasheed and walked away.

"How did you manage that?" she asked when the guard was out of earshot.

"Lucky timing," he said, his low-pitched voice rumbling through her chest. "A big shipment of paste is coming in, and they're shorthanded. Since I speak English, Manzoor suggested I stay with you."

Shaking her head at his effect on her, she walked with him down the flagstone path. Just one penetrating look, one husky word, and memories of that kiss kept swirling through her, making it impossible not to react.

"So how did the operation go?" he asked.

"Good. She's in recovery now."

He tilted his head, his perceptive eyes studying her. "Are you all right? You look tired."

"I am tired." Although the infusion of adrenaline

she'd experienced at the sight of him had given her another boost. "I always feel drained after surgery."

His gaze held hers for another heartbeat. Then he motioned toward another path. "Come on. I know a place on the beach where we can sit and talk without being heard."

"Are you sure?" She spotted a guard patrolling the pathway behind the clinic and frowned. "Won't the others notice if we're gone?"

"Not right away. I think we can spare a few minutes. And I don't want to risk using your cottage until we sweep it for bugs."

She hadn't thought of that. "All right."

"This way." Moving quickly, he led her down an overgrown path between the trees. A bird took flight as they hurried by. A gecko ran across the dirt and darted into a patch of ferns. Nadine pushed aside a branch obstructing her way, her thoughts still lingering on Rasheed. And she had to admit that it wasn't only his looks that appealed to her, although they definitely played a part. Every time he entered her vicinity, her composure became unhinged.

But what intrigued her even more was the fierce intelligence in his black eyes, those glimpses of inner pain, his absolute determination to stop the terrorists, no matter what the personal toll. He both fascinated and disturbed her, making her yearn to know more.

"So what did you do for Leila?" he asked as the path widened and they walked abreast again.

Not enough. Forcing her thoughts back to the surgery, she released a sigh. "I ended up using a combination implant, one that covers the malar and submalar areas." She pointed to her face to explain. "That way I could give her cheekbones projection and correct the sunken look in her midface. I couldn't do anything about the nerve damage, though. She needs to see a neurologist about that. But she'll look a little better, at least for now."

"Won't the implants last?"

"They should. But if Sultan hits her again…" She shrugged. "All I can do is correct her physical problems. I can't change her life."

He shot her an assessing gaze. "That must get discouraging."

She couldn't deny that. It broke her heart when the victims returned to their abusers, and the cycle started again. "Sometimes it seems pointless," she admitted. "But I still have to do what I can."

Trying not to dwell on that depressing thought, she tugged in a breath, filling her lungs with the fresh sea air. The sound of the waves began to grow louder as they neared the beach.

"So why did Leila marry your brother if he treats her like that?" Rasheed asked after a moment.

"She didn't have any choice. The marriage was arranged. She was an orphan, and her guardian owed my father money, I think. I don't remember the details exactly." She'd had her own problems to deal with back then. "But I think the marriage was part of the arrangement they made to pay off the loan."

"That sounds barbaric."

"It *is* barbaric. Women are property to men like him. And Leila was pretty. She had those typical Persian cheekbones." Or at least she did before Sultan ruined her face.

Rasheed turned his head. "That's unusual, isn't it—an Iranian marrying a Jaziirastani?"

"Not really." But she knew what he meant. Jaziirastan and Iran were ancient enemies, neighboring countries whose border was in perpetual dispute. Even now they were political rivals, both vying for dominance in the Middle East.

"Intermarriage isn't that uncommon in the border areas. Not as much as you'd think. And I doubt my brother cared where she came from. She was pretty, and he needed a wife."

The path came to an end in a grove of casuarina pine trees. Beyond the trees was the sandy beach. "Over here." Taking the lead again, he walked to a wooden bench in the shade of the wispy pines.

She settled on the bench beside him, fallen needles carpeting the sand beneath her feet. Then she gazed out at the turquoise water, the electric greens and blues dazzling her eyes. The beach wound along the shore, a blinding white streak against the azure sky, a true tropical paradise.

And for the first time since her ordeal began, the tension knotting her shoulders began to unwind. She'd been so incredibly scared during the kidnapping, so worried about helping Henry, so terrified at facing her brother again that it felt good to relax for once—no matter how brief the respite.

Rasheed bent down and picked up a tiny pinecone, then tossed it across the sand. "So what's next for Leila?"

She turned her mind to her sister-in-law again. "She's not out of danger yet. I'll go back after lunch to check on her. I have to watch for bleeding and infection, at least for the first few days. She'll be uncomfortable for about a week after that, until the swelling goes down."

"So the surgery's painful?"

"It's not fun—not something I'd go through to please a monster like Sultan." She made a face. "Of course, it's not just battered women who have cosmetic surgery. It always amazes me the lengths people will go to just to look a certain way."

"That's easy for you to say. You're already beautiful."

She laughed at that. "Hardly."

He raised a brow. "Oh, come on. You must know how you look."

Her face warmed. She knew she had nice, symmetrical features. And her unusual eye color made her stand out. "I guess I'm okay."

"Okay?" His gaze traveled over her face, the intensity in his eyes making her belly do a somersault. "You're a hell of a lot more than just *okay*."

The gravel in his voice made her pulse leap. The heat in his gaze held her immobile, making it impossible to draw a breath. Her heart thundering, she skimmed the beard shadow emerging on his jaw, the slight fullness of his lower lip, the craggy hollows of his lean face. And the memory of his kiss came back in a crazy rush—the heat, the delirium, the need.

Her pulse going haywire, she looked away. She was glad that he found her attractive. God knew, she was having a terrible time resisting him. But even if they wanted to take this maddening need to another level, they couldn't risk it. They had way too much at stake.

"I don't put much stock in physical beauty," she explained. "It's more a handicap than an asset."

"How do you figure that?"

"Because if you're pretty, that's all men see. Beautiful women are objects to them, something they want to acquire. If I'd been plainer, if I'd had a different nose or eyes, my father wouldn't have cared so much about marrying me off. But he saw me as a commodity, an object he could trade to increase his power."

"Nadine, nobody who knows you could think you're only a pretty face."

Her heart tumbled again, his words loosening something inside her, a need she'd repressed for years. *The deep-down need to connect.* "My father and brother do."

"Yeah, well, they're Neanderthals." A smile slashed his face, and everything inside her stilled. Grim-faced, he made her pulse race. But when he smiled…the crinkle of his dark eyes, the flash of his white teeth against his swarthy skin, the wicked slant of his sexy grin made every feminine part of her burst to life.

"I'm surprised you became a plastic surgeon," he continued. "Considering what you think about beauty."

Still slightly breathless, she tore her gaze away. "I know. It's complicated." As complicated as her feelings for him.

Determined to compose herself, she fastened her gaze on the gorgeous sea. Seagulls swooped and dived for fish. The small waves curled and boomed to shore, a million drops of water sparkling in the midday sun. A container ship dotted the horizon, sailing north toward the United States. "My mother had a lot to do with it."

"You two were close?" he guessed.

Nodding, she closed her eyes. The sun warmed her

face and arms. The breeze whispered offshore, tousling her hair. Sitting beside Rasheed, with his hard arm brushing hers, and the rhythmic pull of the waves filling the air, it was so darned tempting to forget the world, forget the evil men lurking nearby, forget the violence of her dreadful past. But she could never escape the harsh reality of her life. The fact that her father had found her proved that.

"I never would have become a doctor if it weren't for my mom. She knew it was my dream. And she knew my father would never let me go to medical school, that I'd eventually have to escape. So she put away money for me. When I found out…it really tore me up at first." She'd been a total mess inside, plagued by the worst kind of guilt. "If she hadn't saved that money for me, if she'd spent it on her medical care instead, maybe she would have survived."

"You don't know that. And even if it's true, she made that choice. Parents who love their kids sacrifice for them. That's what they do."

"I know." It had taken her a while, but she'd finally reconciled herself to her mother's choice. "But I still felt that I owed it to her to fulfill my potential. I didn't want to waste her sacrifice."

"And that's why you help others now."

She glanced down the beach. A guard had begun walking toward them, but he was still a hundred yards off. She lifted her gaze to Rasheed's. "What was your childhood like?"

"Normal, I guess. My parents were Jaziirastani immigrants, and I was their only child. They were linguists. They both taught at the Defense Language Institute in Monterey. That's where I grew up—in California. They worked hard and were grateful to live in the States. They taught me to appreciate the freedom we have."

"But you felt safe."

"Sure."

"Well, I didn't. I grew up in an abusive family. You can't imagine how bad that is. I watched my father beat my mother. We were terrified and always on edge. And the constant threat of violence, the hyperalertness you live with in a house like that…you never really overcome it. It affects how you think, who you are, what you do.

"I was too young to help my mother. And I couldn't stop my brother from mistreating his wife. But I still wanted to fight back. These women…these victims of domestic abuse…the surgery isn't really about beauty. It's about restoring their self-esteem. I figure if I can ease their suffering, if I can help restore their appearance and feelings of self-worth, maybe it'll encourage them to take charge of their lives."

He picked up her hand. He threaded his fingers through hers, the rough warmth of his skin a balm to her soul. He gave her hand a squeeze, the spontaneous gesture more soothing than any words could ever be.

"And that's why you changed your name?"

Impressed that he understood, she met his eyes. "Nadira brings back too many bad memories. I'm not that helpless child anymore. I've left that repressive lifestyle for good."

For a minute neither spoke. Then Rasheed released her hand and looked away. She tipped her face toward the sun again, delighting in the warmth on her skin. And suddenly she realized why Rasheed had brought her to this spot. He'd noticed her exhaustion and wanted to help her relax.

She slipped him a sideways glance, thrown abruptly off balance again. Who was this enigmatic man? How could someone so violent be so compassionate, too? How could he be willing to fight Amir one moment and show her tenderness the next? He kept poking holes in her preconceptions, forcing her to constantly reassess her opinion of him.

She'd always divided men into two distinct camps—good and bad, gentle and violent. Those who lived peaceful lives and those who attacked. And by most measures, Rasheed fell in the latter group.

Except...he wasn't bad. Despite his violent lifestyle, he kept protecting her. He kept blurring those rigid lines, muddling the black-and-white world she'd constructed to keep herself safe, turning her impression of men on end.

"So what happened when you ran away?" he asked.

She met his gaze again. She never talked about those days. The threat of discovery had always been too high. Once she'd become Nadine Seymour, she'd left every trace of her former life behind.

But Rasheed already knew who she was. He'd revealed his undercover work to her. And she knew he'd understand.

"It was scary," she admitted. "I was only seventeen."

"Where did you go?"

"Baltimore. It was the closest big city to D.C., which is where we lived. I figured I could disappear there. But life on the streets..." Goose bumps rose on her skin despite the heat. "It was awful. Terrifying, really." The criminals, the drug addicts, the predators preying on unsuspecting girls.

"I got lucky, though. I met up with two other girls right away, the ones I told you about. Haley and Brynn.

We became best friends. They're a few years younger than I am, so I was the leader of our little group."

"You watched out for them."

"I guess. Some guardian I turned out to be, though. I didn't have a clue about how to survive. But neither did they. We muddled along together, figuring things out."

"You said you witnessed a murder?"

She nodded, the memories of that horrific day rushing back. "Brynn did. She'd gone into an abandoned warehouse to take some photos. She wanted to be a photographer, so she was always taking pictures of people and things. Haley and I went with her, but we were too scared to go inside. There was a gang that hung around there, the City of the Dead, and we were afraid they'd be inside. So we waited for her on the street.

"It turned out that we were right. They were in the warehouse, executing a man. Brynn caught the shooting on film. The killer chased her. He chased us all." She hugged her arms, remembering the terror of their escape, the awful paranoia that had plagued them for years. "He's been after us ever since."

She shook her head. "Ironic, isn't it? I left home to escape the violence, but what I found on the streets was even worse."

A wave crashed over the beach. A sandpiper lifted his leg, waiting stoically as the water swirled around him and raced back into the sea.

"Anyhow," she continued, "we stayed on the move after that. After enough years went by, we started setting down roots. I went to medical school and moved to New York. Haley opened a shelter for pregnant teens in Washington, D.C. Brynn became a photographer, a famous one, actually. She lives in Alexandria, Virginia now."

"You weren't afraid the killer would find you?"

"We figured he was probably dead by then. Gang members tend to die young. But we've been careful. Even if he's not around, we all have other reasons to hide." The same reasons that had caused them to run away from home.

"And that's why you need to contact them?"

She nodded. "I need to warn them, just in case."

He pulled a piece of paper and pen from his pocket, and handed them to her. "Write down their phone numbers, and I'll pass them to my contacts. I've already asked them to check on Henry, too."

Grateful, she jotted down the numbers, then gave the paper back. He tucked it into his pocket, but his gaze lingered on hers. Uncomfortable with his inspection, she tipped her head. "What?"

"You take care of everyone—Henry, Leila, your friends. The battered women you help. I just wondered who looks out for you."

For a moment, she couldn't speak. She gazed into his inky eyes, the dark potency luring her in. And without warning, she had the strongest urge to curl up in his muscled arms, to take refuge in his embrace, and let him shelter her from harm.

Startled, she looked away. What was wrong with her? She couldn't depend on Rasheed. No matter who he was, no matter how much she wished life could be different, that was a risk she couldn't take. She knew darned well that only the strong in this world survived.

"No one," she said. "I don't need anyone looking out for me." Rising, she nodded toward the guard closing in on them. "We'd better go. We're about to have company."

And they still had a terror plot to foil.

Not waiting for an answer, she led the way down the jungle path. A dragonfly buzzed past. Birds flitted through the trees, their plumage as bright as the tropical flowers peeking through the leaves. But the scene didn't seem as peaceful now.

Because the truth was, the temptation to lean on Rasheed had left her shaken. It had opened the door on a yearning she'd buried for years—the need to have a partner in her life, the hunger to find a man who would share the burdens and joys and pains.

The cottage came into view, its fuchsia bougainvillea spilling over the clay tile roof. Rasheed pulled her to a stop. "I'll come back later this afternoon with the agent I told you about. He wants to talk to you."

"All right."

"I've been assigned to guard you again tonight. Not that it matters. Everyone on the island is loyal to the cartel. If you try to escape, no one will help you leave."

"I figured that." And she was used to relying on herself.

But as Rasheed strode away, a wistful feeling seeped through her heart. Because for the first time, she *wanted* to lean on him.

And that was the scariest thought of all.

He was in trouble.

Rasheed knocked on the cottage door several hours later, a drum of anticipation making his muscles taut. He'd tried to convince himself that this was all about the case, that the restlessness gripping his nerves was due to the urgency of the upcoming attack, but even he wasn't buying the excuse. His feelings toward Nadine were growing personal. Sexual. He was having a hard time thinking of her as anything except a woman he desired. And the longer he hung around her, the more he learned about this amazing woman, the worse the craving got.

And that was wrong on too many levels to count. He had a job to do. He couldn't get involved with a woman he had to protect. And even if he wanted to ignore that reality, Nadine wasn't the casual-sex type—and he wasn't a long-term man.

She swung open the cottage door. He drank in the amazing sight of her—her smooth, tawny skin, her slumberous green eyes, the alluring fullness of her soft lips—and his good intentions crumpled to dust. Her snug T-shirt hugged her breasts to perfection. Her loose, drawstring pants rode low on her hips, emphasizing the curve of her slender waist. Her black braid shimmered in the light, and a small crease crossed one cheek, as if she'd just awakened from a nap. Her eyes were heavy lidded, adding to the sleepy look.

Lust arrowed through him, the sudden image of her lying naked beneath him directing all his blood straight south. With difficulty, he tamped back the surge of arousal, determined to keep his mind in line.

The answering heat in her eyes didn't help.

Suddenly remembering the agent standing behind him, he cleared his throat. "Can we come in?"

"Of course." She stepped back, and he brushed past her, trying not to inhale her enticing scent. He signaled for her to stay quiet as the CIA agent followed him through the door, carrying a leather bag.

Disguised as one of the island's gardeners, his fellow operative wore a grimy ball cap, a dirt-stained, sleeveless T-shirt and baggy jeans. But unlike the other gardeners, he kept a pouch filled with high-tech equipment hidden in his wheelbarrow beneath his tools. Opening it, he pulled out several gadgets, then methodically scoured the room, sweeping it for cameras and electronic bugs. Several minutes later, he stopped.

"The room's clean," he announced. "No one is listening or watching that I can tell."

Nadine frowned. "You're sure?"

Rasheed spoke up. "Don't worry. He knows what he's doing. This is Felipe Ochoa, by the way, the agent I was telling you about."

Ochoa, a Hispanic man of medium height in his thirties, walked over and shook her hand. Nadine gestured to the table, and they all took their seats.

"So how much has Rasheed told you about the upcoming attack?" Ochoa asked her.

"Not much, just that you think my family's involved."

"That's right." He glanced at Rasheed, and he nodded for him to take the lead.

"To be honest, we don't have a lot of information right now," Ochoa said. "Rasheed is keeping watch on the terrorists. We've got people monitoring the internet chat rooms, teams dedicated to looking for clues, but we haven't been able to learn that much. All our informants have suddenly clammed up."

"Why don't you arrest my brother? If he's here on the island, doesn't that prove that he's involved?"

"Not necessarily. In fact, we think that's why he brought his wife here for surgery. It provides him with an excuse to be on the island. He can claim he didn't know the other men would be here, that it was a coincidence. We can't prove otherwise."

"We can't arrest the others, either," Rasheed told her.

"Why not? If you know they're going to do something dangerous—"

"They might not be the only cell involved. Or there could be a contingency plan if these guys fail. We can't make a move until we're sure. And we don't want to blow our covers too soon, either. We still need to work out the money trail. If we can stop the flow of money, we can shut the entire group down for good."

Her lips pursing, she seemed to process that. "I still don't see how I can help."

Ochoa leaned across the table toward her. "For starters, we need your insight into how they think. We don't even know why they're planning this attack. The easy answer is that the U.S. is a popular target, and the Rising Light is an extremist group. So on the face of it, it makes sense.

"But the U.S. and Jaziirastan are allies. If they bomb us, and if we can tie the attack to high-level people like your father, our government's going to rethink those ties. And Jaziirastan has a lot to lose if we do."

Rasheed stirred in his seat, drawing her gaze. "Do you know Senator Riggs?"

Frowning, she shook her head. "Not personally. Why? Should I?"

"Your father contributes to his campaign. He also acts as a liaison between the senator and some American Islamic groups. In return, the senator does a lot of favors for Jaziirastan, like brokering weapons deals between them and companies in the U.S.

"Right now, Jaziirastan is lobbying for the right to buy E-13's. That's an experimental weapon that isn't on the market yet. Walker Avionics makes it. You might have seen some of the drug cartel members carrying them around."

"Not really. But how did they get them if they aren't on the market yet?"

"A shipment got stolen last month. It was supposed to go to the army for testing, but it went to the drug cartel instead. It was a payment, part of the deal they made to bring this terror cell into the States.

"The point is that Senator Riggs is on the Senate Arms Committee. As soon as these weapons go on the market, he can influence which foreign governments are allowed to buy them. And if Jaziirastan is linked to this attack…"

"They don't get the guns."

"Right. Everything changes. Senator Riggs's influence won't help them anymore. So Jaziirastan has a lot to lose."

She nibbled her lip, her green eyes troubled now. "I can't explain it, either. I know he's a fanatic, but my father likes living in the U.S. I don't think he wants to go back to Jaziirastan again, at least not permanently. He doesn't have as much status there."

"I thought he was a member of the royal family."

"He is. But he's a minor one. That's why he tried to marry me off. The marriage would have increased his standing, strengthening his connection to a powerful man. But in the States, he's more important than he is back home. I can't see him doing anything that would jeopardize that, like financing this attack."

Rasheed slumped back in his chair. "And yet, here we are."

Still frowning, she rose and went to the minibar. "Does anyone want water?" she asked. When they both declined, she poured herself a glass, then returned to the table.

Rasheed watched her drink, following the movement of her slender throat, noting the sheen of moisture forming on her tempting lips. Trying to keep his thoughts from wandering down that distracting track, he pulled his gaze away.

"So what *do* you know about my father so far?" she asked.

"Not that much about him personally, but we've amassed quite a bit of data about his bank. We've been investigating it for years."

The edge of her mouth tipped up. "Give me the cheat sheet version, then."

He nodded back. "All right, the gist of it is this. Your father is one of the primary shareholders in a bank holding company, the Royal Jaziirastani Holding Group. So is his good friend, the ambassador."

"The man he wanted me to marry."

"Right. We think he invited your father in. The holding group owns several banks, including Jannah Capital. I told you that we started detecting suspicious transactions there years ago, and that a lot of that activity involved a bank called First Bangladesh.

"I was a financial analyst at the time. I went to their main branch in Dhaka to investigate. My job was to track the money coming in from those Jannah Capital accounts and figure out where it went. The problem was, it went all over, to multiple accounts in different banks all over the world. First Bangladesh is only its first stop. But we think the money eventually ends up at a charity, the Islamic Foundation of Jaziirastan. They're the ones funneling it to the Rising Light terrorists. The charity's name, and your father's, keep coming up in our interrogations. But we can't make the link to shut them down."

"Do you know anything about his bank?" Ochoa asked her.

"Not at all. I told you, I haven't been around him in years. And even when I lived there, he never discussed business with me."

Ochoa leaned forward, his expression suddenly intent. "Is there any chance he keeps bank records in his house?"

She shrugged, causing her thick braid to slither over her arm. "I don't know. He used to run his *hawala* out of his home office, so he might still do business there."

Rasheed blinked. "Wait a minute. Your father's a *hawaladar?*"

"He used to be. But he shut that down a long time ago, when I was still in elementary school."

Rasheed exchanged a glance with Ochoa, the agent's obvious excitement echoing his own. *Hawalas* were ancient financial remittance systems common in a lot of countries, particularly in the Muslim world. They operated parallel to the banks—not exactly underground, but off the record and exempt from government control. Funds were transferred without formal documents, based on personal connections and trust.

And if Nadine's father was a *hawaladar,* a former broker…it explained why the CIA hadn't made any headway. They were looking in the wrong place. And it explained why al Kahtani was part of a high-powered holding group, despite his low status in the royal clan. He'd have extensive contacts—family, friends, former clients—he could call on to move the Rising Light's funds through the current banks.

"Do you think you could find the records?" Ochoa asked.

Rasheed's head jerked up as Ochoa's words sank in. "Forget it. She's not doing it."

"Why not? They're delivering her to her father. They'll never suspect anything. It's the perfect opportunity to get someone inside."

"*Someone,* sure, but not her. Her father intends to kill her. She's not taking that kind of chance."

"What kind of chance?" Nadine asked, looking confused.

"We've tried to get someone inside his house before," Ochoa explained. "But security's too tight. We need access to his files."

"She's not doing it," Rasheed repeated. "She's not going near that house."

Ochoa threw up his hands. "She's our only hope. Hell, you know that. We've tried everything else. And if al Kahtani was a *hawaladar,* he'll have records, lists of his contacts. It could be the break we need."

"No, absolutely not." Rasheed shoved away from the table and paced across the room to the window, his agitation increasing with every step. "That was never part of the bargain. The deal was that she'd talk to us—that's all. She's not going back to the States."

Bad enough that he'd exposed her to her brother. There wasn't a chance on earth he'd risk letting her near her father, too. "We'll have to use a decoy."

"But—"

"It's nonnegotiable, Ochoa."

The agent sighed. "Fine. I'll see if I can bring in another agent, a woman who can play her part. She can go on the plane in her place."

Nadine wrinkled her nose. "How would that work? They'll know it isn't me."

"Not if she wears a burka," Rasheed said. "Could you train her, teach her what she needs to know to act like you?"

"I don't know." She looked even more skeptical now. "She'd have to speak Jaziirastani. And what about her voice? The minute she speaks they'll know it isn't me."

"We'll work something out. We just need to get her into the house. She can take it from there."

Ochoa gathered his surveillance detectors and stood. "I'll get right on it. We don't have much time, though, just a few days at most."

"A few days? To teach her how to act like me? I need more time than that."

Ochoa shrugged. "We'll try to delay the flight, maybe come up with a mechanical problem that might buy you a day or two, but you'd better plan on working fast."

Still looking doubtful, she sat back and crossed her arms. But then her gaze turned inward, taking on an expression he'd seen once before—in the village before she'd gone searching for that coca pit.

And suddenly, he sensed where her thoughts were heading. She didn't intend to train that decoy. She was planning to get on that plane and search her father's house herself.

"I'll be in touch," Ochoa told her, heading toward the door. "I'll bring the agent by as soon as she arrives." He opened the door and slipped outside.

"I'll be right back," Rasheed told her. Hurrying,

he followed on Ochoa's heels. "She's not doing it," he warned him again when he got outside. "I don't care what she says. She's a civilian. She's not getting involved in this."

Ochoa tossed his satchel in the wheelbarrow, then shot him an assessing gaze. "We've used civilians before. Any reason this one's different?"

Good question. One he didn't care to answer now. Scowling, he planted his hands on his hips. "The reason doesn't matter. She's not getting on that plane."

"Fine. We'll use the decoy."

"Damn right we will." Now he just had to convince Nadine.

Chapter 9

His jaw set, Rasheed swung open the cottage door and strode inside. No matter how stubborn Nadine was, no matter how convinced she was that only she could get inside her family's compound, he had to persuade her to listen to sense. It was bad enough that he'd brought her to this island, putting her under her brother's control. But entering her family's house would be suicidal. She'd never make it out alive.

He tugged the door closed behind him, then started across the room. She stood facing the window, silhouetted by the waning light. She turned at his approach, her dark-lashed eyes filled with resolve. And before he could block it, a jumble of emotions swarmed inside him—admiration, respect, desire.

He ruthlessly shut them down. He couldn't let her beauty confuse his thinking. He couldn't let her impressive spirit influence him to change his mind. No matter what she believed, entering her father's house would be far too dangerous. He'd never be able to keep her safe.

"I meant what I said." He closed the distance between them. "You aren't getting on that plane."

She leaned back against the window and crossed her arms. "Don't you think I should decide that?"

"No. This isn't your job."

"Maybe not, but it's my family. I'm not exactly a disinterested bystander. And I know how dangerous they are."

The hell she did. He came to stop close beside her, forcing her to tip her head back to meet his eyes. "They're going to kill you. You told me that yourself."

"Right. But they aren't going to do it the minute I walk in the door."

"Which is exactly why we're sending in a decoy, a trained operative, a professional who can search the compound, then get away before they figure out who she is."

"You'll never pull it off. He'll insist on making sure it's me. There's no way it's going to work."

It had to. He could *not* let her risk her life. Frustrated, he braced his forearm against the window and glanced outside, trying to think of a way to get through. A palm frond scratched the glass. The late-afternoon sun had dipped toward the horizon, lengthening the shadows across the path. A sudden movement caught his eye, a cat prowling past on the hunt. Beyond the cluster of cottages, the mansion's security lights winked on.

Unable to come up with a persuasive argument, he

shook his head. "You'll just have to believe me. We can't take the risk."

"But—"

"For God's sake, Nadine, look at what happened here. I thought I could protect you. I thought I could get you off the island before anything went wrong. And your brother showed up. We're going to have a hell of a time getting you away as it is. And we'd have even less control at your father's house. Anything could happen to you once you go inside. By the time we mounted a rescue, it could be too late."

For a moment, she didn't answer. Her arms stayed crossed. Her stubborn gaze challenged his. But then she slanted her head, her eyes turning thoughtful, her brows gathering into a frown.

"This isn't only about me, is it?" she asked slowly. "There's another reason you don't want me to do this, something you haven't told me about."

His jaw tensed. He cut his gaze back to the window encased in the wrought-iron bars. She was right. There'd once been another woman, another hapless victim he'd failed to protect. But he didn't want to tell her that.

"What is it?" she asked. "What's really going on here? I think I deserve to know."

Her gentle voice rippled through him, drawing his gaze. And for several long moments he simply looked at her, her unflagging courage, her fierce determination to help mistreated women impressing him so damned much. He couldn't bear the thought of her being harmed.

"You're right," he admitted, dragging the words out. He never spoke about the past. He never discussed the horror of that attack, or his role in the affair. But something about this woman compelled him to tell her the truth of the harm he'd caused. Turning back to the window, he focused on a thin crack snaking across the glass, then fracturing into a dozen lines. "I told you I went overseas to investigate a bank, First Bangladesh. I got hired as a midlevel manager, nothing important, nothing that would attract any attention, but it gave me the access I needed to the accounts I wanted to check.

"My contact, the CIA station chief, worked at the embassy. I met with him about once a month and passed him anything important I'd learned. We varied our locations each time for security reasons. Terrorism in Bangladesh had been heating up."

He worked his jaw, dread rising inside him at the memories, but he forced himself to go on. She had to understand exactly how monstrous these men were. "I'd just made a discovery. I'd tracked some of the funds coming from your father's bank, Jannah Capital, to a third account in A'lam Financial, a Saudi Arabian bank. It's notorious for its terrorist ties. I needed to tell him what I'd found. So we arranged to meet.

"My wife, Sarah... I took her to Bangladesh with me. She hadn't adapted to life there too well. She'd had to quit her job when we moved, and she wasn't happy about that. She'd worked for a marketing firm back in the States and had a great career. She was bored in Bangladesh. It wasn't safe for her to go out alone, so she was cooped up in the house a lot. And I was never around." Thanks to the ungodly hours he'd put in, trying to crack the case.

"She was desperate to get out of the house, so I arranged to meet my station chief at a mall, a place where a lot of foreigners shopped. I figured Sarah would provide me with the perfect cover. I'd be the long-suffering husband waiting by the food court while his wife browsed in the shops."

The pressure in his chest increased. He closed his eyes and inhaled, the terrible memories piling in on him, making it hard to breathe. "She'd just found out that she was pregnant. We'd decided it was a good time to start a family since she couldn't work."

But instead of providing comfort, the pregnancy had made her even lonelier. She'd missed her mother, her girlfriends from college, the extended family who should have shared her joy. "There was a maternity store at the mall, so that's why I suggested we go there."

He turned his head, meeting Nadine's gaze straight on. "What I didn't know was that your father was onto me. One of his men, a Bangladeshi national who worked in the embassy, had already discovered the station chief's identity. He'd been monitoring his activities to find out who he was contacting at the bank. Another of their contacts, a guy who worked at the bank, figured out that it was me. So they followed us to the mall."

"Oh, God." Horror filled her voice. "They didn't…"

He nodded. "They saw us meet. But they didn't go after me right away. They went after Sarah instead. They shot her as she came out of a store. They wanted me to see her die."

He had seen it, all right, in excruciating detail. He still saw it every damned time he closed his eyes. He saw Sarah smiling as she hurried toward him, her blond ponytail swinging, her beautiful blue eyes sparkling, lugging a mountain of shopping bags. He saw the spring in her steps, the flush on her pretty cheeks, the way her eyes lit up when she spotted him across the room. It had been the happiest she'd looked in weeks.

And with one quick shot, she was dead.

Nadine pressed her hand to her lips. Moisture shimmered in her eyes. "Oh, Rasheed, I'm so sorry."

"They came after me, too," he continued, his voice faltering. His belly knotted, an awful feeling of desolation welling deep inside him, but he needed to tell her the rest. "But the other agent got us away. We eventually crossed the border into India and then flew home." Sarah's body had followed later under heavy guard.

"I'd been using my real name in Bangladesh. My banking background was legit—it was just the CIA part I concealed. When I came back to the States, the CIA faked my death, giving me a new background and another name."

And as the shock of Sarah's death wore off, the need for vengeance took root inside him, turning into full-blown rage. He'd vowed to bring down the murderers who'd killed her, no matter how many years it took.

"That's when I asked for permission to infiltrate the Rising Light. I grew up speaking the language. I knew I could pull it off. And my parents had died by then. I didn't have any family left, nothing that could trip me up.

"I started attending a mosque we'd been investigating in Northern Virginia, one where we thought the imam was promoting jihad. Most of the members were from Jaziirastan. I earned their trust, pretended to let them radicalize me.

"They eventually sent me to Jaziirastan. I stayed with the right people and proved my loyalty. It took a while, but they finally admitted me into the training camps. That's where I've been ever since." Working step by step through the organization, insinuating himself into the top tier of Rising Light terrorists.

Seeking revenge.

Nadine's gaze held his. "Your wife's death wasn't your fault."

"The hell it wasn't. She'd quit her job because of me. She moved halfway around the world because of me—because I was sure I could track those funds. I knew she was miserable there. I knew she missed her friends and family, but I ignored it. I didn't want to see it. I kept working longer hours, leaving her more alone.

"It was even my idea to start a family. She wanted to wait until she'd established her career. But I thought it would keep her busy, help cure the loneliness. Instead, it got her killed."

He hauled in a breath, disgusted at what he'd done. He'd been her husband, the man who'd vowed to cherish and protect her, but he'd failed her in every way. And there wasn't a damned thing he could do to change that now. He couldn't redo the past. He couldn't go back and die in her place.

And he couldn't escape the haunting image of her execution, the constant, horrific memory that plagued him every time he closed his eyes—reminding him exactly how badly he'd screwed up.

And he refused to fail another woman again.

"We learned later that your father had ordered the hit."

Her face turned ashen. "Are you sure?"

"We heard it from several informants."

This time she turned away. Silence fell between

them as she gazed out at the gathering night and hugged her slender arms. "And that's why you're trying to prove the link to him. You've got a personal reason to bring him down."

"I know what he's capable of. I can't let him hurt anyone else." *Especially you.*

Her gaze swung back to his. Compassion mingled with pain in her eyes. "I'm so sorry, Rasheed. I'm so sorry about your wife. My father…he's a despicable man."

"Then you understand why I can't send you in there? It's too dangerous."

"I'm already in danger. He's been trying to kill me for years."

"It's not the same. You'll be at his mercy. Trapped. We need to send in someone who's trained for this."

"But she'll be in danger, too. As soon as he realizes it isn't me—"

"We'll take precautions. We'll figure out a way to make it work."

"But—"

"Promise me, Nadine. I don't want you to take the risk."

She didn't answer. For an eternity, she just watched him, her soft gaze searching his. Then she cupped his jaw with her hand, the light touch arrowing straight to his heart.

"I'm not your wife, Rasheed. I know the risks. I'd be going into this with my eyes wide-open."

She wasn't his wife, all right. But she was another beautiful woman he couldn't bear to see hurt. A woman he was beginning to care about in ways he couldn't afford.

"I can't let anything happen to you," he confessed.

Her gaze remained on his. His pulse ticked up a notch. And suddenly, he was hyperaware of every detail about her—the curve of her slender throat, the flowery scent of her shiny hair, the perfect fullness of her lush lips.

His heart began to thud. The compassion in her eyes held him motionless, awakening something dormant inside him, a part of him he'd thought was dead. Longings, dreams he'd buried with his dead wife, feelings he'd had to crush to survive.

She slid her hand to his neck. Somehow, she'd shifted closer, and her breasts now brushed his chest. She pressed her other palm against his breastbone, and her mouth came nearer yet.

His muscles turned taut. His blood began to pound his skull. And God help him, but he couldn't resist her. He needed her too damned much.

He splayed his hand over her jaw. He tilted her face toward his, his gaze devouring her mouth. And then he lowered his head and kissed her, inhaling her like his dying breath.

Her soft moan lanced his heart. Her smooth lips parted, the moist welcome firing his nerves. Her velvety warmth both soothed and aroused him, tempting him to take refuge in sexual oblivion, urging him toward the desperate need to *forget*.

The kiss lengthened and merged with another. He plunged his hands through her satiny hair. His mind dimmed, the reasons this was wrong rapidly fading as more primitive urges mounted inside him, the desire for comfort giving way to lust.

But even as his heart started flaying his rib cage,

even as his body began to throb with that age-old need, he knew this was more than just sexual hunger, more than a basic, human need for warmth. There was something different about Nadine, something different than what he'd felt for his beloved wife.

She was the product of a violent childhood. She'd been terrorized by her family, experiencing even more fear during her years on the streets. But instead of cowering, instead of seeking the protection she rightly deserved, she dedicated her life to fighting back. Even now, with her father determined to kill her, she refused to run away. She was courageous, incredible.

The kind of woman he could love.

Shocked by the realization, he broke off the kiss. His hands trembled. His stunned gaze went to hers. He took in her deliciously blurred eyes, the rosy flush to her creamy skin, the temptation of her swollen lips. And the need she'd awakened thundered inside him, threatening the remaining vestiges of his self-control.

He had to resist. Calling on all his willpower, he pulled away. But he was vibrantly aware of every detail about her—the smoothness of her skin, the silky hair tumbling around her face, the heavenly taste of her mouth.

"Promise me," he said, his voice rough. "Promise you'll train the agent."

Her eyes began to clear. "All right. I'll train the agent for you."

Still feeling off-kilter, he released a breath. "Good." Needing to put some space between them, he shoved a hand through his hair. He'd sort through her effect on him later, when she wasn't around to fog his brain.

"Look, I'd better go. I need to touch base with Man-zoor so he doesn't suspect anything."

Her cheeks still flushed, she gave him a nod. "I need to check on Leila again. I want to make sure she's set-tled down for the night."

"I'll walk you over." He stood back while she gath-ered her supplies.

But as he watched her move around the room, her black hair shining in the lamplight, he realized some-thing had changed over the past few days. When he closed his eyes now, he didn't see his murdered wife. He saw Nadine.

And if he wasn't careful, he'd fail her, too.

"That's enough," Leila protested as Nadine plumped the pillow behind her head in the clinic's small recov-ery room. "I don't need it any higher."

"You're sure? You need to elevate your head. It'll help keep the swelling down."

"I'm fine, really. You've done enough."

Nadine slanted her head, inspecting her sister-in-law's face in the fluorescent light. The implants looked intact. Her temperature and blood pressure were nor-mal. No bruises were forming yet. As long as she took the antibiotics, as long as she followed Nadine's orders to rest, Leila would be fine.

She wished she could say the same for her heart.

"I'll get you a fresh ice pack," she told her. "Keep it on until you're ready to sleep."

She walked over to the supply cabinet, activated another ice pack and brought it back. But even as she made sure Leila was comfortable for the night—filling her cup with water and adjusting the height on the hospital bed—thoughts of Rasheed kept swirling in her head.

It wasn't only his kiss that had destroyed her equilibrium this time—although that had shaken her to the core. She'd never felt such a blaze of passion, such a riot of instant need. Even now little quivers kept coursing through her bloodstream, making her body thrum. But what had completely blasted through her resistance was his revelation about his wife.

She gave Leila's blanket a final tweak. "Now rest," she ordered. "If you need anything, anything at all, just let the guard know, and I'll come back."

"I will." Closing her eyes, she placed the ice pack against her cheek.

Reassured that her patient would manage, Nadine dimmed the lights, closed the door to the recovery room and went back down the hall. Rasheed's story had affected her deeply. She couldn't imagine the horror he'd experienced watching his pregnant wife die. To lose someone he loved that profoundly, along with his unborn child, and then to feel responsible for their deaths… She didn't know how he'd recovered from that.

It accounted for the guilt she'd glimpsed, that terrible bleakness that haunted his eyes. It also explained why he'd gone undercover, exiling himself both physically and emotionally, not only infiltrating the enemy, but making himself become one of them, cutting himself off from all civilized behavior to get revenge.

But while she understood it, while she respected and admired his determination, she also couldn't fool herself. A loss that staggering had changed him. Her instincts about him had been right. Living with cold-blooded men, doing who-knew-what dreadful acts to prove he was one of them…he hadn't escaped that ordeal unscathed.

Sighing, she exited the clinic, then paused on the cement steps. His story had made one thing abundantly clear. He was still completely wrong for her. Maybe he jerked on her heartstrings. Maybe he made her yearn to heal his pain. But that still didn't change the facts. They had no future together—and no matter how much he tempted her, she had to remember that.

A puff of cigarette smoke drew her gaze to the side of the building. Realizing her guard wasn't watching, she took advantage of his inattention and started down the path toward the cottage alone. Not that she could flee anywhere. The island was too secure. But even if the reprieve was fleeting, it felt good to be on her own for once, without some hulking guard dogging her heels.

Night creatures rustled in the jungle. Spotlights peeked from the low-growing ferns, casting a glow on the smooth stone path. In the distance, unseen waves pushed and pulled against the shore, their rhythm as old as time.

She was still trying not to think about Rasheed when she arrived at a clearing. In the center was a tall stone fountain, its water burbling in the peaceful night. She stopped and glanced around, unsure which path to take. The jungle looked different in the dark.

Then a man's deep voice reached her ears. Her pulse took a leap, the precariousness of her position suddenly hitting home. She didn't have Rasheed to protect her. She was utterly alone, at the mercy of whoever was heading her way. Scared now, she spun on her heels to hide.

But two men appeared on the path. Realizing it was futile to run, and that any sign of weakness would only make things worse, she forced herself to stand her ground. Both men wore checkered, kaffiyeh scarves. One was medium height, about her brother's age, with angular features and a full beard. She frowned, something about him prodding a memory, although she couldn't imagine what.

Then the other man looked up, and her heart abruptly stopped. *Amir.*

Panic mushroomed inside her. She struggled to swallow, but failed. Unwilling to let Amir know he scared her, she forced herself to stand steadfast, but her knees quivered so badly, they could barely support her weight.

"We'll talk later," the other man murmured in Jaziirastani. He turned down the opposite path and disappeared into the night, leaving her alone with Amir.

The fountain continued to trickle. The terrorist's gaze held hers, the hatred in them chilling her gut. Memories of his fist plowing into her jaw made her insides chill, and it was all she could do not to bolt.

His silver tooth flashed as he came closer. "Where's your lover? Isn't he around to defend you now?"

Lover? Her heart raced. Had Amir seen them kiss? But how could he have? Unless he'd been looking through the cottage window…

"I don't know what you're talking about." Deciding to brazen it out, she started walking toward the closest path, suddenly hoping the guard she'd evaded caught up—and saved her from Amir.

But he lunged over and barred her way. She took a quick step back, the involuntary motion betraying her fear.

Amir smiled, a terrible glee filling his eyes. "Not so fast. We have unfinished business."

Her mind sped frantically through options. A fight was out of the question. He was too big, too fast, too strong. And she'd made a fool of him in the town, tricking him into letting her out of that shed. He was bent on reprisal now.

Seizing her only recourse, she whipped around and ran—straight into a human wall. She stumbled back, her heart beating triple time, but then her panic morphed into relief. *Rasheed.*

"Get behind me." His voice was deadly still. His gaze stayed locked on Amir's. Too grateful to argue, she darted behind him, then peered over his shoulder at Amir.

"I warned you to leave her alone," Rasheed said.

"And I warned you to watch your back." Without warning, a blade appeared in the terrorist's hand, its lethal edge catching the light. Shocked, Nadine ceased to breathe.

No one moved. The tension crackling between them cranked up to a fevered pitch. "It's time to end this," Amir said.

"Agreed. We'll settle this right now."

"Knives only," Amir added. "They're quieter. I don't want anyone interfering in this."

"Your choice." To her horror, Rasheed set aside his holster and gun. Following Amir's example, he stripped off his T-shirt and wrapped it around his forearm to serve as a makeshift shield. Then he bent down, reached into a sheath strapped to his ankle, and withdrew a knife.

Her heart began to quake. Oh, God. She couldn't let him do this. What if he got hurt?

But he'd already stepped away. The men squared off beside the fountain. Their wicked blades flashed in the light. The water gurgled and splashed, its cheerful sound incongruous with the tension pulsating in the night. Somewhere in the darkness, an owl made a savage cry.

Rasheed was taller, leaner, younger. But Amir had at least thirty pounds of muscle on him—and probably more experience, given his lifestyle and age. He'd also removed his shirt, exposing his thick, powerful neck and bare shoulders glistening with sweat. He gripped his knife in his giant fist.

The two men began to circle. Their feet crunched on the gravel, their bodies poised for attack. Horrified, Nadine stood motionless beyond the fountain, too terrified to make a peep.

Suddenly, Amir charged. Rasheed feinted and danced away. The terrorist whirled around, his expression growing even more thunderous, and attacked again.

But Rasheed didn't dodge him this time. Their bodies slammed together, the sickening thud making her flinch. And then they fought—lunging, parrying, their arms swinging and steel blades flashing so fast that all she could do was gape.

Amir made a slash at Rasheed. Crouching slightly, Rasheed moved to the center, as if to meet the thrust. Instead, he sprang sideways, shooting his blade upward toward Amir's eye. The terrorist barely jerked back in time.

Nadine watched in terror, cringing as they stabbed and deflected, unable to tell who had the upper hand. They never stopped, never paused. Their bodies blurred in the constant motion, their harsh rasps filling the night.

She'd seen men fight before, but never like this. Never with this savage hatred. Never with such furious speed. Never with the dreadful certainty that moments from now, one of them would die.

Rasheed dodged a crossing stab. Sweat streamed down his face, the tendons standing out in his arms. Then Amir rushed him again.

They fell to the ground with a heavy thud. They rolled in the gravel around the fountain, each one grappling for supremacy, twisting and tumbling in a heart-stopping flurry of arms and legs.

Then Amir pinned Rasheed. He plunged his knife downward, and Nadine choked back a cry. And for one agonizing moment, the blade hovered over his vulnerable throat, the terrorist's arm shaking visibly as he strained to drive it home.

Rasheed struggled to hold him off. The veins stood out in his face. Nadine rushed over and picked up his gun, determined to stop Amir at any cost. But miraculously, Rasheed heaved him away. He leaped to his feet, and they instantly collided again.

The two men continued to circle, their breathing ragged and harsh. Amir lunged again, and Rasheed jumped back, but a dark line formed on his chest.

Nadine nearly cried out. *He'd been stabbed.*

Amir's tooth gleamed. He clearly had the advantage

now. Rasheed backed up, seeming to falter, and his attacker drew closer, victory at hand.

But in an instant, everything changed. Rasheed went on the offensive, and in a series of moves too fast to follow, he flipped the terrorist onto the ground, knocked his weapon away and held his own knife under his jaw.

And Nadine realized in that moment that he'd been toying with Amir. Rasheed was a highly skilled, highly trained, highly dangerous man.

Tension-fraught seconds ticked past. Dead silence gripped the air as she waited for the final thrust. Would he kill him? Unable to watch it, she closed her eyes.

"Yield," Rasheed ordered instead. "From now on you'll leave Nadine alone."

The terrorist didn't answer. Pure hatred blazed in his eyes.

"I said to yield," Rasheed repeated, his voice hard.

"All right. She's yours."

Rasheed waited another heartbeat. Then he rose, his eyes still clamped on the terrorist lying at his feet. Finally, he turned on his heel and headed toward her. Relief barreled through her, so intense her knees went weak.

Still breathing hard, he reached her side. Sweat glistened on his craggy face. Blood dripped down his washboard abs. His eyes burned black, the smell of testosterone and adrenaline evoking a swarm of feelings she couldn't control. He looked terrifying, violent, primitive.

But for the first time in her life, she wasn't afraid.

Chapter 10

Nadine paced around her cottage a short time later, the sound of the shower in her bathroom adding to the tumult inside her nerves. She was grateful to Rasheed. She owed him more than she could ever repay for saving her life *again*. And she couldn't bear to think what might have happened if he hadn't won that fight. Just the thought of it made her sick.

But now, with the adrenaline beginning to wear off, the shocking brutality was sinking in. That knife fight had appalled her. The sight of them wielding those weapons had confirmed what she most feared about men—that violence ruled their lives. And Rasheed had just proven that he wasn't that different. Whether he was on her side or not, whether he made her feel safe at the moment or not, he was the most lethal fighter she'd ever seen.

The shower abruptly cut off. Her composure completely shattered, she took refuge behind the table and started rearranging her first aid supplies. A moment later the bathroom door swung open and Rasheed strolled out, wearing nothing but a pair of jeans.

Her gaze flew to his sculpted shoulders, traveled over the impressive contours of his biceps, and her heart skittered a beat. His hair was wet, and stray droplets slithered loose, gliding down his unshaven jaw. He raised his arm, using a hand towel to mop the moisture from his face, his flat belly rippling as he moved. Blood still welled from the slice on his chest.

Tearing her eyes away, she cleared her suddenly thick throat. She set down the roll of gauze she was mangling, then picked up the cotton balls and antiseptic she'd brought over from the clinic when she cut her arm.

Trying hard not to stare at his body, she joined him near the sink. "Let me look at that cut."

"It's not serious."

She shifted closer to see. The slash began near his heart and crossed his sternum, slicing down the rock-hard planes of his abs. Her gaze crept to the thick tendons padding his shoulders, the massive swells of his powerful biceps, the taut sinews cording his arms. Crisp, dark hair dusted his chest beneath his clavicle, tapering down to the waistband of his jeans.

Feeling her face flush, she looked away. Determined to keep her mind in check, she gave herself a mental shake. Rasheed was a patient, a man she needed to treat, even if he did have an amazing physique. He scooted closer, and she struggled not to notice the heat rising from his muscled frame, the rogue drop of water forging a track down his chest, the scent of his shaggy, damp hair.

Uncapping the antiseptic, she risked a close-up glance at his face. His hot, black eyes collided with hers, the impact scattering her thoughts. Every time she looked at him, he grew more appealing, with his straight, black brows; his high-bridged, noble nose; that wickedly sensual mouth. He looked like an ancient warrior, all dark, sexy angles and feral planes. More water dripped off his midnight hair, running through the heavy beard stubble coating his jaw, adding to his virile look.

And she was ogling him like an idiot while his cut was beginning to bleed.

Her face turned even hotter. She moistened a pad with the antiseptic, then leaned toward him again. Bracing herself for the rush of awareness, she met his gaze again. "This might sting."

Crinkles fanned his eyes. The edge of his mouth kicked up, causing a riot inside her chest. "Is that doctorspeak for *it's going to hurt like hell?*"

She couldn't help but smile back. "I guess we'll find out."

She applied the pad to his wound. His muscles contracted, and he sucked in a hissing breath.

"Sorry," she murmured. This close, she inhaled the musky scent of his skin, caught the gleam of his wet hair as he bent his head toward hers.

Still struggling to maintain her equilibrium, she slid the pad down his granite abs, across his rock-hard stomach to the edge of his jeans. Then she paused. His belly went tight, a sudden movement behind his zipper drawing her gaze. She jerked her eyes to his, his blatant sexual interest wicking every remaining drop of moisture from her throat.

She yanked her hand away. "You don't need stitches. The wound is superficial." She sounded breathless.

"I thought so." His voice came out low and deep.

A maelstrom swirling inside her, she turned back to the table, trying to hide his effect on her. Hoping distance would help, she picked up the antibiotic ointment and held it out. "Here. Put this on. We need to keep the wound from getting infected. I'll wrap gauze around it when you're done."

Thankfully, he didn't argue. While he dabbed ointment on the gash, she unwrapped several sterile pads. But he had a primitive male beauty, a battle-honed strength she was finding increasingly hard to ignore.

She waited for him to finish, then placed the sterile pads over the gash, and pulled out the roll of gauze. "We need to wrap that, just for a day or two until the wound starts to heal."

While he held one end, she made several circuits around him, trying vainly not to touch his skin. She cut off the gauze and secured it, tucking the end against his chest. "That's good." Relieved, she stepped away.

But Rasheed grabbed hold of her wrist and pulled her back. Her pulse tripped. His iron grip held her immobile, trapping her palm against his chest. Startled, she tipped her head back to meet his eyes.

They burned.

Her heart made a crazy thud, then took off at a maniacal pace. She couldn't mistake his hunger—or her own desire rooting her in place.

It was probably the adrenaline from the fight. It was probably their isolation and the danger they were in that made her respond this way. God knew, he was all wrong for her, exactly the kind of man she'd always feared. But standing in his embrace with the warm, male scent of him swamping her senses, she couldn't seem to make herself care.

He tugged her closer against him. Then he released her wrist and encompassed her jaw with his rough hands. Her entire body going haywire, she dropped the forgotten roll of gauze and wrapped her arms around his back.

And then his mouth was on hers, the amazing feel of him like gasoline on a wildfire, igniting every nerve ending she possessed. His hard thighs pressed against hers. His back muscles went rigid beneath her palms. His kiss was hard, relentless, demanding, the unshackled sensations pulling her under in a sensual onslaught she couldn't withstand.

A faint moan filled the air. She heard it from a distance, vaguely aware it had come from her. He felt so good—the thrilling roughness of his jaw, the dizzying feel of his lips on hers, the latent power in his massive frame.

She knew that he was violent. She knew he was capable of repugnant deeds. And she knew that if Amir hadn't conceded, Rasheed would have killed him in a heartbeat to keep her safe.

But at the moment, none of that seemed to matter. With his mouth gliding down her neck, sending pleasure spinning through her veins, any objections seemed to disappear.

With a groan, she pulled him closer. He slid his hands under her shirt. Her nipples tightened, her body aching for his touch. Thrills shuddered through her, the delirious feel of his callused hands on her skin drugging her senseless. Needing him closer, she urged his mouth back to hers.

The kisses grew hotter and deeper. Her womb moistened and pulsed. She plunged her hand through his damp, shaggy hair, lost in the glorious sensations, knowing she'd go crazy if he tried to stop.

Panting hard, he broke away. He rested his forehead against hers, his hoarse breath dueling with hers. Her lungs heaved and sawed, her heart pattering in frenzied beats, her entire body on fire for this man.

"If we're going to stop, it has to be soon," he ground out.

She struggled to think. A hazy warning arose that this wasn't wise, that there was too much danger around them, that they still had a terror attack to thwart.

And he was wrong for her. A man who lived in a savage world.

But just for this moment she wanted to forget the case, forget the family trying to kill her, forget the fear that had dogged her all her life. For once she wanted to throw caution to the wind, lose herself in this sensual madness and surrender to her body's demands.

"I don't want to stop," she admitted in a whisper.

His dark eyes flared. Before she realized what he intended, he scooped her off her feet, then carried her across the cottage to the king-size bed.

"Wait," she protested. "Your cut. It'll start bleeding again."

"Let it." He set her on the bed, and in one quick motion, stripped off his jeans.

Her throat went bone dry. Riveted, she devoured every bunched sinew and angle of his fabulous frame—

his impressively roped thighs, the silver scars webbing his skin, the blatant male part of him pulsing with life. He was a warrior from head to toe—battle-scarred, potent, tough—his sheer potency overwhelming.

But instead of making her want to flee, she found his power exciting. More arousing than she'd ever dreamed.

He followed her onto the bed. She slipped to one side and tugged off her shirt, the heat in his eyes as he watched her tempting her to draw the action out.

She dropped her pants and kicked them aside. His gaze went to her legs, his blatant approval spurring her on. Encouraged, she unclasped her bra and slid it off, thrilled when a muscle jumped in his jaw. She peeled off the rest of her clothes.

His Adam's apple bobbed. His eyes turned molten, his breath suddenly harsh. She returned to the bed, and he swept her beneath him in one swift move, his fiery gaze scorching her skin. Then he braced himself above her and with excruciating thoroughness ran his hand over her breasts and belly and legs, exploring every sensitive inch of her, trailing a riot of heat in its wake.

"You're so beautiful."

So was he. His black eyes held her spellbound. His face looked chiseled from stone. The skin tightened over his high cheekbones, shadows pooling in the hollows, emphasizing the taut cords roping his throat.

And a swarm of emotions welled up from deep inside her—tenderness, lust and something she'd never felt before, as if her heart could no longer fit in her chest.

Then his mouth claimed hers again—and this time he didn't hold back. This kiss was insistent, possessive, urgent, touching off a restlessness deep inside her. She grew frantic, desperate, consumed with a craving so delirious it brought her close to the breaking point.

But once again he stopped. His rough hands framed her face. His eyes captured hers. "You're sure about this?" His voice was guttural, hoarse.

She swallowed hard. She wasn't a virgin. She'd dated occasionally over the years, and sometimes those dates had led to sex. But she'd always chosen gentle, cerebral men, men who didn't incite this out-of-control feeling, who didn't make her teeter on the edge of insanity.

Men who were safe.

But Rasheed…he was ruthless, violent, driven. He was exactly what she shouldn't want. And yet, she arched against him, wanting to rub herself against every part of his masculine body, knowing she'd never desired anyone more in her life.

"I'll probably kill you if you stop," she admitted.

With a growl, he reclaimed her mouth. She plunged her hand through his damp hair, drowning in the hunger of his kiss. And then he entered her in one hard thrust, the feeling so exquisite that she cried out. Not pausing, he moved against her, driving the pleasure higher and tighter, the tension nearly making her scream.

And then she exploded inside, the sensation so intense her entire world seemed to dissolve. Rasheed joined her a second later, his throaty sounds mingling with hers.

For an eternity, she couldn't move. It was impossible to catch her breath. Rasheed had collapsed against her, his weight pinning her to the mattress, his uneven breath rasping against her ear.

Long minutes passed. Feeling completely boneless, she closed her eyes and drifted, gliding gradually down to earth.

But making love to Rasheed had changed her. The feelings he elicited were mind-boggling, unlike anything she'd ever experienced in her life. Those other encounters now seemed insipid, a mere parody of the ecstasy he'd evoked.

But as she ran her hand up his muscled arm, tracing his powerful shoulders, questions formed in her mind. Why him? Why now? And where did they go from here? She frowned slightly, skirting the bandage on his chest, then slid her hand through his still-damp hair. Obviously they couldn't go backward. They couldn't pretend this had never happened when every wonderfully sated part of her knew it had.

But even if he didn't lead a dangerous lifestyle, even if he wasn't damaged from his traumatic past, she still didn't have a future with this man. Because no matter how safe he seemed right now, no matter if he'd risked his life to protect her from Amir, she could never predict how he would act.

He could suddenly erupt in violence. He could physically or emotionally abuse her to keep her under his control. She'd seen it too many times growing up, witnessed too many publicly charming men turn into monsters behind closed doors. Even now, she saw the pain those men inflicted every time she performed surgery, repairing a battered woman's face.

She knew not all men were abusers. She knew there were plenty of decent guys in the world—

compassionate, gentle men who adored their children and protected their wives. And maybe Rasheed was one. But how could she ever be sure?

She released a sigh. She couldn't. So no matter how much Rasheed rocked her world, no matter how deeply his sad past resonated with her heart, she had to keep an emotional distance from him. She definitely couldn't fall in love with him.

But as he began stirring against her, his wicked mouth scorching a path down her throat to her breast, she hoped she could remember that.

Rasheed woke up with a start. He jerked open his eyes, oddly disoriented, not sure where he was. Then the night came back in a rush, a kaleidoscope of memories bringing him to full alertness—the threat, the fight...

The sex.

The cottage was still and dark. A hint of dawn peeked around the shutters, a slight shade lighter than the surrounding room. He heard Nadine's soft, rhythmic breath, felt the heat of her lying beside him, the scent of their lovemaking still strong in the air.

And his heart dove. The night had been a mistake. He'd made a huge error in judgment succumbing to the hunger she provoked—because nothing had really changed. She was still a woman under his protection. She was still a vulnerable civilian caught up in a deadly affair. And she was still the kind of woman who needed a man who could love and protect her—a man his past failures proved he could never be.

Shoving his hair from his face, he expelled a sigh. He'd made a mistake, all right. He'd surrendered to their mind-boggling chemistry, resulting in the best damned sex of his life. And then he'd compounded the problem by staying the night—a blunder that could have gotten them killed. If one of the terrorists had missed him, if the cartel had checked to make sure he was on duty outside, they'd both be dead.

But somehow, lying next to her on the quilted mattress, with her soft hair caressing his shoulder, her tempting body within easy reach, he couldn't seem to care. He turned his head, just able to make out her profile—the entrancing curve of her lips, the dark sweep of her lashes against her pale cheeks, her long, black hair streaming over her shoulders and spilling across the bed. The sheet had slipped, baring one tantalizing breast to his gaze. His body instantly hardened, and he shook his head, amazed he had any energy left after the night they'd shared. By rights he should be exhausted. Instead, every part of him surged to life again.

Unable to resist, he stroked her hair, winding several glossy strands around his finger, then inhaling the erotic scent. God, she smelled good—her hair, her skin. Enthralled, he traced the slope of her breast, marveling over its perfect shape. Her nipple peaked in response, prompting a corresponding throb in his groin.

Her beauty overwhelmed him. He was hard-pressed to find a single flaw. Her face had a rare kind of symmetry, each feature coming together to create a marvel of nature—that straight, feminine nose, the delicate flare of her winged brows, the elegant angle of her fine-boned jaw. And that mouth...his blood went hot, the memory of how those lips had looked doing any number of erotic things during the past several hours making his body turn rock-hard.

He flopped onto his back and groaned. Calling this the most fantastic night of his life was an understatement. And he was raring for another round.

But he couldn't ignore the future—or lack of one. Neither of them had wanted to discuss it. They'd been too caught up in the tornado exploding between them to stop and reason things out. But now...

"What's wrong?" she murmured, her voice scratchy with sleep.

"Nothing."

She rose on one elbow, her hair spilling over her naked shoulders and breasts. His breath stalled, the arousing sight rendering him incapable of speech. And without warning, a feeling of possessiveness took root inside him, the urge to claim this woman as his— something he had no damned right to feel.

She angled her head, her green eyes dark in the shadowy room. "Listen, Rasheed. Just for the record, I'm not... I don't have any expectations after this. This was just something that happened, not anything we expected or planned. So don't start worrying that I want more."

"You deserve more." Regrets pulled at his voice.

"Maybe. And maybe not. In any case, I don't want it. You, me... It just can't work."

He agreed. But hearing her say it bothered him more than he would have believed. Frowning, he tucked his hand behind his head and stared up at the shadowed ceiling, the paddle fan standing idle in the dark.

"I'm not the man I used to be," he admitted. "Living with terrorists, the things I had to do in the training camps...it changed me. I don't have relationships anymore. It's just not in me now."

And even if it were, he couldn't do it. He bore the burden of his past failure. He could never escape the reality of what he'd done. He'd been so determined to take down the terrorists, so sure that he'd prevail, that he'd overlooked the threat to his wife. And he refused to ever hold the fate of another defenseless woman in his hands.

Nadine placed her hand on his arm, the soft touch twining around his heart. "I'm serious, Rasheed. This really isn't necessary. I don't have relationships, either, definitely not anything long-term. So let's just leave it at that, okay? A night we both enjoyed."

Enjoyed? That pale word didn't come close to describing the mind-altering sex they'd shared. Still, he knew he should feel relieved. She was offering him the perfect way out. And normally, at this point, he couldn't wait to hit the door. The last thing he'd ever wanted was a woman begging him to stay.

But damned if he didn't *want* to stay this time.

Startled, he sat up. "I need to go before anyone comes by."

"Do you think Amir's going to be a problem?" Worry laced her voice.

"It's hard to say. I think I convinced him to leave us alone. But he's pretty thick. We need to stay on guard."

She nibbled her lip, a small line forming between her brows. "I forgot to tell you. There was a man with him last night. Another Arab. I saw him just before you showed up. He had a long beard, a thin face, medium height."

"I met him. He arrived right after we did."

"So he's a terrorist?"

"Yeah. His name is Abu Jabril."

"That doesn't sound like his real name."

"No, it's a nom de guerre." Most terrorists assumed fake names to hide their identities. "I'm not sure why he's here, though. I've been trying to find out."

"He looked familiar."

He shot her a glance. "You know him?"

She grimaced. "I don't know. I could be wrong. He has a pretty generic face."

But if they could link him to the upcoming plot… "If you remember anything, let me know. We need all the clues we can get."

"I will." She sat up. Her hair fell back, baring her glorious breasts. His gaze dropped, the sight banishing any thoughts of terrorists from his mind. His blood thickened, his good intentions evaporating like rain in the desert sand.

With a groan, he gave up and kissed her. A distant part of him knew he should worry, that he was getting in way over his head.

But then instincts took over, and he didn't think again for a long time.

Chapter 11

By rights he should feel pleased. Nadine's decoy had arrived on the island. The mission was going according to plan. They had a new lead in the investigation— al Kahtani's old *hawala* connections—along with a mysterious newcomer who might provide a clue. With luck, they'd soon get the breakthrough they needed to dismantle the Rising Light network and stop the upcoming attack.

And to top it off, he'd just experienced the most exhilarating sex of his life. He should feel sated, satisfied, relieved the end was finally in sight.

So why did he want to start another knife fight or hurl his coffee cup across the beach?

Perched on a boulder in a hidden cove, he scowled at the sparkling sea. The midday sun beat on his scalp. Sweat beaded his forehead and pasted his shirt to his back. A flock of seagulls screeched as they dive-bombed a fishing boat trawling offshore, their raucous shrieks reverberating through his skull.

"Are you listening to me?" Ochoa asked.

"Yeah, I'm listening." He downed a slug of the sludgelike coffee, then dragged his gaze back to the agent standing beneath a pine tree, loading pine needles into his wheelbarrow to use as mulch.

"She speaks Jaziirastani," Ochoa continued. "She's Nadine's height and weight, and has the same general appearance, so as long as no one looks at her too closely, we're good to go. She's sharp, too, a real quick study. It won't take her long to get up to speed."

Rasheed choked down another swallow of coffee. Ochoa had made good on his promise. Patricia Ramirez, the agent who would serve as Nadine's decoy, had arrived first thing that morning on the nearby fishing boat. She'd scuba dived to shore and was now ensconced in the clinic with Nadine, posing as a maid while she learned her role.

He should be glad. He *was* glad, damn it. For once everything was going the way they'd planned.

And they had to use a decoy. He had to remove Nadine from her family's reach. Just because they'd had earth-moving sex didn't change that fact. It didn't matter if she'd touched something inside him. It didn't matter if a barrage of erotic memories kept derailing his thoughts—the heavenly taste of her skin, the sultry feel of her amazing mouth, the incredible pleasure of her throbbing around him as he'd hurtled into oblivion time after time…. And it didn't matter if he had the worst kind of need to haul her into his arms, run with her to somewhere safe and forever shelter her from harm.

He wasn't that kind of man anymore. He knew it.

She knew it. His experiences had changed him in a fundamental way, tainting him too badly to ever lead a normal life. Now, for her sake, he had to step away.

"Get her on the next supply boat," Ochoa was saying. "She'll have to hide in the maintenance shed until then."

Rasheed tossed back another gulp of coffee, needing the infusion of caffeine to clear his head. Luckily, Ochoa was too busy talking to notice his foul mood.

A mood which made no sense. Because this was exactly what he wanted—Nadine gone. Safe. Out of his life for good.

Ochoa walked over and leaned on his rake. "What's going on?"

He frowned. "What?"

Ochoa jerked his head toward the fishing boat. "You look like you're planning to shoot someone on that boat."

Rasheed sighed. So maybe Ochoa had noticed his crummy mood. He rubbed his eyes again. "Sorry. I didn't get much sleep, that's all. I was guarding her cottage all night."

Ochoa tipped back the brim of his ball cap. His astute eyes studied his. "Aw, Christ. So that's what this is about."

"What?"

"You're sleeping with her. That's why you don't want her on that plane."

His face burned, but he knew it was futile to deny the truth. Ochoa wasn't blind, and Rasheed probably had "great sex" tattooed on his face. But it was none of the agent's business what he and Nadine did. "You got a problem with that?"

"Yeah, I've got a problem with that. She could get into that house for us. This is the perfect chance. But instead, you're letting your damned di—"

"Shut up, Ochoa. The answer's still no."

Ochoa's face flushed. He took off his ball cap, slammed it against his thigh and shoved it back on his head. "You're not thinking straight."

He was right. The idea of Nadine in danger completely unnerved him, making it impossible to stay detached. And the worst of it was that this possessiveness was totally baseless. She wasn't his. She could never be his. He had no right to dictate what she did.

"Forget it," he repeated. "She's not going in there. It's not even up for discussion. Now what else do I need to know?"

Scowling, Ochoa stomped back to the pine tree, then jabbed his rake at the ground. "Just one thing. They were loading the plane this morning."

His heart skipped hard. "You think we're taking off soon?"

"It looks that way. I tried to get at the engine, but they had it under guard, so I couldn't create a delay." He shot him a glare. "Which is all the more reason to send the real woman in."

Rasheed stared back until Ochoa raised his hands in defeat. "All right, fine. We'll stick with the decoy."

Damn right they would. "Any news about that new guy, Abu Jabril?"

"Not yet. We're still looking into it." Ochoa ducked his head. "Don't look now, but we've got a guard coming our way."

And he had a terrorist to check out. He slid off the

rock, then paused. "You'll get her off the island when the time comes, right?"

Ochoa scooped up a pile of pine needles and loaded them into the wheelbarrow. "Don't worry. I've got it arranged. She'll get away fine."

"Good." That was all that mattered, keeping Nadine safe.

No matter what the cost to his heart.

"The study's in the main wing off the dining room." Nadine bent over the drawing she'd made of her family's compound and labeled the last two rooms. "The fastest way to get there is through the kitchen. I used to spend a lot of time talking to the cook, so no one will be surprised to see you there. And the study's just down the hall."

She drew an arrow on the map, then pushed it across the table to Patricia Ramirez, the woman who would play her part.

The agent studied the map. "When's the safest time to avoid the cook?"

She sighed. "It's hard to say—it's been so many years. It used to be early, before five-thirty. Or after the men had their breakfast, and the cook had time to clean up, around eight. I'll check with Leila to make sure their schedule hasn't changed."

Patricia folded the map, then stuffed it in her pocket, along with the other notes they'd made. "I think I've got it. You can quiz me tomorrow."

Nodding, Nadine rose. She had to hand it to the CIA; Patricia was good. She spoke fluent Arabic and Jaziirastsani. Her memory was beyond compare. She even bore an uncanny resemblance to Nadine, her long black wig and green contact lenses adding to the effect. And she'd attacked this project with an intensity Nadine admired. She'd insisted on working through lunch, making do with a hurried bowl of *ceviche* so they'd have more time to train.

As a result, she could now credibly mimic Nadine's gestures. She knew the family dynamics and could "reminisce" about various events. She'd even devised a plan for Nadine to come down with "laryngitis," minimizing her need to talk.

Of course, she had a good reason for that kind of drive. The price for failure was huge. And there was still so much that could go wrong, so many family and cultural land mines that could trip her up—and expose her for a fraud.

Nadine blocked off her doubts. This would work. The CIA was busy behind the scenes in Virginia, doing their part to help pull it off. They were even manufacturing a crisis at her father's bank, a critical problem that would draw him away from the house at the moment Patricia arrived. They just needed to get her inside the compound, fooling the staff long enough to unearth those files.

"I'll meet you here first thing in the morning," Patricia promised.

"Bring the floor plan with you. We'll go over it in more detail after I talk to Leila and make some contingency plans, depending on where they lock you up."

"I will." The agent picked up her bucket of cleaning supplies and left the room.

Alone now, Nadine walked across the exam room to the window and looked outside. A few seconds later,

Patricia appeared on the path, then disappeared into the jungle, heading toward her unknown hiding place.

Stifling a yawn, Nadine rested her forehead against the glass, unable to avoid the reality she'd tried to block out all day. Her ordeal was almost over. In a few short days, Patricia would get on that plane with her brother, and Ochoa would spirit her safely away. She could finally check on her friends and see Henry. She could return to her normal life.

Hopefully, Rasheed would halt the attack. Patricia would find the information they needed to put her family under arrest. And she'd finally put an end to the fear and death threats that had plagued her all her life.

But instead of feeling relieved, her stomach churned. The thought of not seeing Rasheed again filled her with an awful dread. And it wasn't only because she was worried about his safety. She didn't want to leave *him*. Somehow he'd breached her defenses over the past few days. Somehow he'd gotten to her. And for the first time in her life, she was in danger of falling in love.

Which was absurd. Rasheed didn't want a future with her; he'd made that abundantly clear. And that was fine. She didn't want anything long-term with him! So what if he confused her? So what if he challenged everything she'd once believed about men? She was a realist. This rogue kind of wistfulness had to stop. She just had to enjoy their time together, however brief it was.

And keep a tight leash on her traitorous heart.

Just then her brother appeared on the path. She instinctively recoiled, his slick good looks filling her with distaste. Jerked abruptly back to reality—and the charade she had to help pull off—she darted into the recovery room and grabbed a pillow then raced to the bathroom down the hall. She quickly shut the door, then buried her face in the pillow and screamed with all her might, trying to make herself hoarse. She paused, unwrapped the slice of lemon she'd saved from the *ceviche* and squeezed some drops into her throat, and screamed into the pillow again.

Coughing, she exited the bathroom. She returned to Leila's room and started bustling around, still hacking into her sleeve.

"What's wrong with you?" Sultan asked, striding through the door a moment later.

"I'm coming down with a cold. I think I'm losing my voice." Thankfully, she sounded raspy enough to back that up.

Grimacing, he stepped away. "Don't breathe on me."

"I'll try not to." She coughed again, trying to prolong the hoarseness as she trailed him to Leila's side.

"Oh, Sultan," Leila said, looking up. "What do you think about my cheeks? Nadira did a good job, didn't she?"

He tossed the sport bag he was carrying into an empty armchair and glanced at his wife. "You don't look any better to me."

Leila's face fell. She bit her lip and blinked, her eyes shiny with tears.

Nadine clenched her jaw. Damn Sultan! Did he always have to be so cruel? "She's doing great. She has a bit of swelling, that's all. It's normal. She'll look better every day. In another week she's going to be gorgeous."

"She'd better. I'd hate to think this was all a waste."

Leila studied her hands, obviously trying not to cry. Nadine shot Sultan a glare, wishing she could convince her sister-in-law to leave him, that she'd be better off on her own.

But they'd been through this before, and Leila would never agree. She felt bound to her husband by the vows she'd made. And pathetic or not, twisted as it was, she loved Sultan. She would never divorce him, never do anything that could be construed as disloyal—such as helping Nadine escape.

He motioned to the sport bag on the chair. "I brought your things. We're leaving in half an hour."

"What?" Nadine jerked up her head. "Leaving for where?"

"Home."

"Back to the States?"

"Where else?"

"But she can't fly yet. She just had surgery."

"She doesn't have a choice. It's time to go." He checked his watch. "Both of you stay here. I'll be back in half an hour with the car." Not waiting for an answer, he strode back into the hall.

Panicked, Nadine went in pursuit. They *couldn't* leave yet. She hadn't finished training her decoy. There was too much Patricia didn't know. And flying this soon after surgery could endanger Leila's health. "Stop," she called.

Sultan paused at the end of the hallway and glanced her way. "What do you want now?"

"She can't do it, Sultan. It's only been a day since the surgery. She's still in the postoperative phase."

"So?"

"So she needs to rest." She struggled to reason with him. "Look, any kind of activity right now is bad, even walking. Movement increases her blood flow. That causes bruising, swelling. It prolongs her healing time.

"And a higher heart rate means higher blood pressure. She could have complications, like internal bleeding. She's even at greater risk for blood clots, and I'm sure you've heard how deadly they can be. She needs to stay put for at least a few more days."

Sultan shrugged. "You'll just have to watch her to make sure nothing happens. Now go help her get dressed." He made a show of glancing at his watch again. "I'll be back in twenty minutes."

Twenty minutes? Dumbfounded, she watched him leave. But his insensitivity was typical. She could hardly expect her self-centered brother to show compassion toward his wife. Heaven forbid that he thought about anyone besides himself. And frankly, she had a much bigger problem right now. She urgently needed to find Patricia—and she had no idea where to look.

She stuck her head into Leila's room. "Can you get dressed by yourself? I need to run an errand."

Leila stood beside the cot, unzipping the bag. "Sultan said to wait here."

"Don't worry. I'll be right back." Her thoughts whirling, she ran outside. She stopped in front of the clinic and glanced around, but had no idea where to go. She didn't even know how to contact Rasheed. And if she tried to return to her cottage, she'd alert the guards.

And really, what good would it do? Even if Rasheed got hold of Patricia, even if the decoy got here in time to take her place, she wasn't ready to play her part. Maybe in a few more days she could pull it off, but not yet. It was way too soon. And they couldn't take a chance on failing with so many lives at stake.

Still trying to come up with a solution, she went back inside the clinic and returned to Leila's room. Spotting her sister-in-law struggling to slip a burka over her head, she rushed over to grab it away. "You can't wear that."

"Why not?"

"You shouldn't put anything on your face yet. The pressure isn't good for it. You could cause it to bleed."

"But I have to wear it. I can't go outside uncovered. There'll be other men on the plane."

"That doesn't matter."

"Of course it matters. I'd shame my family."

Just as she had. The accusation hung between them in the quiet room. And for the first time, Leila's eyes revealed a hint of steel.

Nadine blinked. She'd always pitied her sister-in-law. She'd never understood how she could put up with Sultan's abuse. She'd blamed it on Leila's upbringing, her brother's intimidation or even a character flaw.

But she'd misjudged her. Leila took pride in her obedience to her husband. She garnered strength playing a backseat role to him. Upholding her family's honor gave her life meaning and made her feel worthwhile.

And who was she to object? Leila had as much right to live her life the way she wanted as Nadine did—even if she didn't approve of her choice.

But that sense of honor also had a dark side, a side that affected *her.* "You know my father's going to kill me."

Silence hovered between them. Nadine had just given voice to the unspeakable, the issue they'd both been dancing around. Would her sister-in-law defend the violence or denounce it and help her escape?

"I don't believe that," Leila said. "You just need to ask for forgiveness. Show him that you've changed, that you accept his decision about what's best for you. I'm sure he'll understand."

"I insulted his honor. You know as well as I do that he'll never forgive that."

Leila bit her lip. She picked at the burka, her eyes revealing her distress. "You have to submit to his will, sister. He will decide what's best."

Right. Her heart sank, any hopes that Leila might help her vanishing for good. She would never defy her husband. Her role was too ingrained. She probably wouldn't even believe her if she told her about the upcoming terrorist attack. Instead, she'd go to Sultan, tipping him off that the CIA was onto them and possibly endanger Rasheed.

Rasheed. She closed her eyes, a sudden, visceral memory crashing through her of his dark, sexy face, his hard muscles gleaming in the lamplight, the passion burning in his eyes....

She couldn't fail him. He was depending on her to make this mission a success. He'd dedicated his life to it, sacrificing everything he held dear to fight these evil men. Now she had to do her part.

Opening her eyes, she walked over to the bag. "Do you have another burka in here?"

"Of course." Leila dug through the sport bag and pulled one out. "I'm glad you're seeing sense. This will help show your father you've changed."

Her father wasn't that dumb, but she wasn't about to argue the point. Making a face, she slipped it on. It had been years since she'd donned the traditional garment. Even at home she'd only worn one under extreme duress. But now, shrouded in the heavy black fabric, the awful memories came rushing back. Her hands trembling, she put on the head covering and flipped the fabric over her face.

Her vision blurred behind the small mesh patch. Heat instantly infused her, sweat pooling beneath her breasts. She dragged at air, trying not to hyperventilate in the stifling darkness, but she felt suffocated, claustrophobic, trapped.

Her breath came shallow and fast. A frantic feeling erupted inside her, the desperate need to rip the damned thing off. She wanted to run screaming down the beach. She wanted to glory in the sunshine and fill her lungs with the fresh sea air. She wanted to live and laugh and luxuriate in her freedom. Instead, she was caged beneath yards of cloth, her movements restricted, her identity deleted, a prisoner of the family who wanted her dead.

The door opened, and Sultan strode into the room. He paused, obviously taken aback to see her covered head to toe. "Good. You're both ready. It's time to go."

He picked up the bag and left. Leila instantly trailed him out the door. Nadine brought up the rear, struggling not to trip on the swirling fabric, but she couldn't see her feet. She stumbled down the hallway, then staggered into the sunshine, feeling dizzy in the blast of heat.

A car was waiting outside. She stopped on the steps and swallowed hard. This was it—her last chance to bolt for freedom, her last chance to break free of her family and escape.

Sultan bundled Leila into the car. He turned and met her gaze, the crazed zeal in his eyes solidifying her resolve. She had to do this. She was the only one who could stop these monsters. She couldn't let them succeed.

And even if she died trying to do it, she refused to abandon Rasheed.

Rasheed sat aboard the sleek, forty-foot Gulfstream jet, frowning out his window at the sun-drenched tarmac. Amir and Manzoor occupied the seats behind him. The pilots were busy in the cockpit, conducting their requisite preflight check. The cabin door hung open, the stairs still in place as they waited for their final passengers to arrive.

A bad feeling swirling inside him, he kept his gaze on the runway baking in the afternoon heat. This had happened too damned fast. One minute he was meeting with Manzoor, the next they were boarding the plane. There'd been no chance to contact Ochoa, no chance to coordinate plans with the decoy.

No chance to tell Nadine goodbye.

A black sedan sped toward them across the tarmac. He watched it approach, his misgivings growing stronger now. He knew he didn't need to worry about the mission. The decoy was reputedly smart, and Ochoa had assured him she could play her role. Their people in D.C. were working every possible angle to unravel the plot, keeping every suspect under surveillance, minimizing the chances that anything would go wrong.

And so what if he missed Nadine? This was what he'd wanted. This was the way it had to be.

And it was better to end it like this—with no prolonged farewell, no awkward excuses or scrambling over what to say. No promises neither one would keep. Just a clean, swift break.

The sedan pulled to a stop by the stairs. Sultan climbed out and handed a waiting worker several bags. Two faceless women followed on his heels, their black burkas fluttering in the afternoon breeze. His mind still on Nadine, Rasheed watched them board.

Sultan took a seat in front. "Go to the back," he told the women, and they filed ghostlike down the aisle.

The first woman drifted past Rasheed. The second one followed more slowly, as if finding it hard to walk. He studied her as she drew near, unable to see her features behind the heavy veil, but there was something about the angle of her head…

He went stock-still, the sudden sensation that it was Nadine causing his heart to thud. But she continued past, and he shook his head, convinced he was imagining things. *Ochoa had promised.* He was getting her to safety as planned.

And he had to stop thinking about her. His mission had entered a critical phase. He had to focus on finishing his job, not indulge in a distraction that could get him killed.

Determined, he sat upright and buckled his seat belt. A second later the workers wheeled the stairs away. The flight attendant closed the cabin door, and the plane started to roll down the runway, steadily picking up speed.

He shifted his gaze to the window and eyed the scenery zipping past—the line of whitewashed hangars, the palm trees bordering the runway, the wind sock blowing in the breeze. Nadine was out there somewhere. A wave of loneliness caught him square in the gut.

And for the first time, he wished that he were different. He wished that he could offer her the kind of life she deserved. But the terrorists had taken more than the lives of his wife and child that day in Dhaka; they had stolen his future from him.

Now he intended to rob them of theirs.

Seven hours later, they touched down at the Manassas Regional Airport in Virginia, an hour southwest of Washington, D.C. Dragging himself from sleep, Rasheed opened his eyes and peered out the window at the night. The jet's engines screamed, shapes whipping by in the darkness as they taxied down the runway and stopped.

Stretching his arms, he rose, stooping slightly so he wouldn't bump his head. He took out his passport to get it stamped, a mere formality. The drug cartel's contact was working the airport's desk, enabling them to bypass the usual customs and immigration checks. As far as the cartel was concerned, this was a regular drug flight. The cocaine in the cargo hold was real.

A few minutes later, the flight attendant opened the cabin door, allowing in a blast of frigid air. Determined to play his part, Rasheed ignored the two women standing in the aisle behind him and followed the men outside, his breath making puffs of frost in the December air. He stuffed his hands into his jacket pockets to keep them warm.

Several cars waited beyond the chain-link fence, their motors running, their headlights illuminating a cluster of waiting men. A thick-set man in his sixties separated from the group and strode toward them, his status obvious by his sure strides. He greeted Sultan warmly, then turned to the other men, and Rasheed caught sight of his face. Yousef al Kahtani. Nadine's father.

The man who'd killed his wife.

Rage scorched a path inside him, the burning need for vengeance making his breath come fast and hard. But he knew he had to bide his time. He had to focus on the bigger goal, bringing the entire Rising Light network down. He'd get his revenge in time.

Besides, he had a bigger crisis on his hands right now. Al Kahtani wasn't supposed to be here. The CIA had promised to create a diversion, keeping him away from the family compound so the decoy could get inside.

So what the hell had gone wrong?

The women came down the steps. The taller one stopped and helped the person behind her. It was a nice touch, he had to admit, exactly the kind of thing Nadine would do. Now if she could just keep up the act and fool al Kahtani until she'd gained access to the house…

The women drew close. The decoy tripped on her hem, then recovered, the tilt of her head as she straightened so like Nadine's that everything inside him froze.

Hell. That wasn't a decoy. It was Nadine. And she was heading straight into her family's compound—and certain death.

Chapter 12

Nadine had left home on a late winter's day when the weak afternoon sunlight was coaxing crocuses from the ground and melting the lingering patches of snow into slush.

She'd come back in the dead of night.

Walking through her bedroom door had been like entering a time warp, prompting a swarm of emotions she'd fought for years to forget—longing for her courageous mother, terror of her vicious father, resentment at the abuse she'd had to endure. And yet, her room had completely changed—the carpet, the drapes, the furniture. Even the paint color on the walls was new. Her father had redecorated after she'd run away, stripping away every trace of her existence here.

Now he intended to eliminate *her*.

And Rasheed—if he tried to rescue her.

Trying her hardest not to panic, to ignore the emotions swarming inside her and *think,* she crossed the suite to the window and gazed out at the moonless night. Her room overlooked the pool, winterized now, its silver mesh cover gleaming in the outdoor lights. The tennis courts lay behind the pool house. Past that was the compound's wall. She shifted her gaze to the acres of unlit woodland extending beyond her father's property to the Potomac River, the freedom it offered so tantalizingly close.

The house itself was ridiculously huge, more like a gaudy palace than a family home. Its features were over-the-top enough to suit her ambitious father—an indoor pool and theatre, an elevator leading to the fifteen-car underground garage. There was an entire wing built for entertaining, including a ballroom that rivaled Versailles.

But escaping from it was going to be hard. Security cameras monitored the grounds. An electric fence ran parallel to the compound's ten-foot-high stone walls. And if that weren't deterrent enough, armed guards patrolled outside, men specially chosen by her father for their loyalty. She'd spent her teenage years probing for flaws in the system without success. The security would be even tighter now.

But somehow, she had to succeed. She'd seen the horror in Rasheed's eyes, his shock as he'd recognized her leaving the plane. And she knew what he was going to do. He was going to try to intervene. He'd done it too many times already for her to have any doubts.

And she absolutely couldn't let that happen. Her family would kill him if he tried. She had to hurry and do what she'd come for—find the information they needed to tie her family to the Rising Light—and then leave before Rasheed showed up. He'd already risked his life enough.

A sharp rap on the door made her jump. Her heart beating chaotically, she whipped around. The door swung open, and her father strolled in. He crossed the room and stopped.

Blood pounded her skull. Frissons of panic seized hold of her nerves, and it took all her willpower to stay in place. She'd caught a glimpse of him at the airport, but not this close. Not alone. Not when she was at his mercy and unable to escape.

His hair was threaded with gray now. His short, salt-and-pepper beard was expertly trimmed. He still dressed impeccably, his custom charcoal suit and hand-made leather shoes befitting the royal status he tried to exude. His silver signet ring flashed in the light.

He was handsome despite his age, an older version of Sultan. And like her brother, his face bore the stamp of cruelty, his eyes lacking human warmth. And as she stared into those black, expressionless eyes, the last remaining flicker of hope inside her died.

This man was a stranger. She felt no surge of familial love, no dormant trace of any fondness, no whisper of loyalty. He hadn't taken her on family outings. He hadn't engaged in father-daughter chats. He hadn't sung to her, read to her, or played with her while she'd been growing up. For the most part, he'd been mercifully absent, an explosive man she'd learned early on to avoid. A man who'd been completely disinterested in her—until the summer she'd turned fourteen.

She stared into his unflinching eyes, that moment flashing back with utter clarity, that moment that had changed her life. It had been a sizzling summer day, the sweltering Washington humidity making her sweat. She'd been lying around the pool, studying for the PSAT test she intended to ace, already dreaming of medical school. She'd decided to take a swim, and was just coming out of the water when her father had walked outside. He'd stopped in his tracks, his shocked appraisal startling, making her feel dirty and exposed. Railing that she was immodest, that her conservative, one-piece tank suit was shameful, he'd struck her across the face. That night she'd worn her first burka at his command, her battered face hidden beneath the veil.

She'd vowed it would be her last.

She'd been wrong. There had been other burkas, other blows before she'd fled from home, just as there had been plenty of beatings before that time. But that moment had been a turning point in her life, driving home the stark realization that this man intended to control her, and she'd have to escape to survive.

And now she was back, face-to-face with the man who'd vowed to see her dead.

The clock on the mantel ticked. The flames in the fireplace snapped, but she shivered, despite their warmth. Her father continued to watch her with a hunter's cold alertness as the silence between them stretched.

She realized that it was a strategy, that he expected her to buckle and beg. But instead of terror over her predicament, she felt disgust. She was no longer a frightened child. She refused to cooperate with his twisted script.

He was nothing but a deluded and pathetic man,

a hate-filled, insecure tyrant who bolstered his self-esteem by abusing the weak. A man lacking basic compassion, who had an emptiness inside him. A man she intended to see locked behind bars.

A sudden surge of sadness washed through her, regret that her mother had suffered through a marriage to this man. She understood why her mother stayed; she'd sacrificed her own chance at happiness to protect her daughter from harm. And now, for her brave mother's sake, she had to bring this evil man down.

"You operated on Leila," he finally said.

Thrown off balance by his choice of topics, she sharpened her gaze. "That's right."

"I'm holding a reception in the ballroom tomorrow night. I want her made presentable. You and Leila will both attend."

Startled, she cocked her head. This had to be a trick. He rarely included women in his events. And she didn't trust his suspiciously civil tone. He was holding her prisoner after threatening to kill her, and now he wanted her to play hostess at a formal event?

"Who's attending the reception?"

"Important people. The vice president. He's receiving an award. Sultan needs his wife there. You'll make sure she acts the right way."

Her frown deepened. Maybe Sultan had political ambitions. Maybe he was trotting Leila out in public so he'd look like a reform-minded Jaziirastani, determined to present the world with a modern face.

Or maybe this had to do with the upcoming attack.

"And if I don't?"

"You will if you want to live. There are gowns in

the closet. Find something suitable to wear." Dismissing her, he walked to the door.

"Wait a minute," she said. "What about Leila? I need to check on her."

"She'll come see you in the morning. I've given her a list of guests to study. You'll help her memorize the names." He opened the door and left. The latch clicked in the sudden silence, locking her in.

Shaken, she sank into the armchair beside the fireplace and struggled to absorb what had occurred. Her father had ordered her to attend a reception. Not only was that bizarre, but it made no sense. He had to know that she'd try to escape, that she'd approach the first American she saw and plead for help. So why would he take that risk?

She didn't believe for a minute that he'd changed his mind and intended to let her live. That was even more far-fetched. He wouldn't have kidnapped her in the first place if that had been his plan.

No, he had something up his sleeve, some ulterior motive for wanting her at that reception the following night. But what?

Unable to come up with an answer, she rose. Then she leaned against the fireplace mantel and stared into the dancing flames. And before she could stop it, her mind wandered back to another fire, another night, another time she'd been held in captivity—that storm-ravaged night she'd met Rasheed.

And suddenly, a terrible ache filled her chest, a longing so acute it stole her breath. She missed him. She missed everything about him—his intelligence, his courage, his strength. How safe and cherished he'd made her feel. She'd never dreamed that she would come to care so deeply about him in such a brief expanse of time.

The flames wavered and curled, bathing her face with heat. She closed her eyes, images rising in rapid succession—the flash of his sexy smile, the hunger in his onyx eyes, the fierce pain racking his face when he'd told her how he'd failed his wife, how he no longer had it in him to love.

He was wrong.

He was a hero. A protector. A brave and selfless man who'd do anything, no matter how suicidal, to keep her safe.

A man who intended to infiltrate this compound, sacrificing his life to get her out.

She couldn't let him.

It was time *she* protected *him*.

"What do you mean, I can't go in there?" Rasheed stared at his boss sitting across from him in the crowded fast-food restaurant just off M Street, unable to believe his ears. "We can't just abandon her. She wouldn't be here if it weren't for us."

His CIA chief, a middle-aged bald man named Dennis Caldwell, shrugged. "We're not abandoning her. We just have to wait until tomorrow night. We'll use the reception as cover to search the house."

Rasheed clamped down hard on a curse, knowing a blowup wouldn't help his cause. But damn it! They couldn't leave her in that house. "That's a day from now. Nearly twenty-four hours. She could be dead by then."

"I'm sorry, but there's nothing I can do. We tried

to get a search warrant, but the D.A. wouldn't buy it. He's getting pressured from the top."

"From who? Senator Riggs?"

Caldwell made a face. "Worse. The vice president. He's probably afraid it could cause a backlash, making him look xenophobic, and he's counting on the Muslim vote."

Which left them screwed. Rasheed slumped back in his seat and hissed. He knew the drill. Every time they'd gotten a lead in this damned investigation, some ambitious politician kept tying their hands.

And the political climate was getting worse. The president had maxed out his term limit. The vice president was a shoo-in to win the next election, assuming he didn't tick off too many voters before then. And rumor had it that Senator Riggs was aiming to be his running mate.

"The veep built his career on Middle East outreach," Caldwell added. "Now he's getting this award. He needs it to go off without a hitch. He can't do anything to look bad."

"I don't care how he looks. I care about Nadine. I told you, her life's at stake."

"You don't know that."

"The hell I don't. She told me her father's going to kill her."

"You can't prove that. You can't," he insisted, when Rasheed opened his mouth to argue. "At this point, it's hearsay. You can't prove that he's made any threats."

"He kidnapped her."

"Actually, *you* kidnapped her. He'll deny any involvement in that."

"What about the terrorist angle, his connection to

the Rising Light? We should at least be able to do a sneak and peek based on that." The Patriot Act authorized secret warrants in cases involving national security. "Al Kahtani would never have to know we were there."

"It's too risky. He contributes to too many campaigns. No one's going to take a chance on doing something that potentially explosive without more proof.

"And besides, she's an adult. She got on the plane of her own free will. She had an opportunity to escape at the airport, and she didn't try to get away. No one held a gun to her head."

Rasheed shoved his hand through his hair. "She thought she could do this."

"Maybe she can." When Rasheed growled, Caldwell raised his hand, his gold watchband gleaming in the fluorescent light. "I told you. There's nothing we can do right now. We can't just storm in there without a warrant. We have to follow the rules."

"Because of politics." His voice came out flat.

Caldwell shrugged again. "We'll have people at the reception. They can conduct a secret search then."

"Assuming she's still alive."

Frustrated, he blew out his breath. He had to get her out. There wasn't a chance in hell he was leaving her in there alone, no matter what his boss said.

But this case was unraveling fast. Everything had gone totally haywire in the past twelve hours. Nadine had boarded the plane instead of the decoy. Sultan had taken her to the family compound where no one could get at her. And if that weren't bad enough, the terrorists had changed their plans, checking into a hotel in Washington, D.C.—ten lousy miles from McLean.

He didn't know why they'd altered their plans. He worried that Amir had alerted Manzoor, who'd somehow caught on to him. And to add to the mess, it appeared the CIA now believed that the *president* was the target of the upcoming attack. His boss was insisting that Rasheed forget al Kahtani and stay embedded with the terrorists to track their moves.

"This thing stinks," Rasheed muttered. "Al Kahtani's in this up to his eyeballs."

"We intercepted those messages, Rasheed. All signs point to an attack on the commander in chief at one of his holiday events."

"I still don't believe it. The timing of this is wrong."

Caldwell sighed. "Look. We've told the vice president our concerns. We tried to convince him to bow out of the reception, to be on the safe side, but he wouldn't agree. He insists the security is tight enough."

It was tight, all right. They were sweeping the reception area for bombs. Dogs would be on-site. There'd be metal detectors, snipers on the roof, military firepower patrolling the air—not to mention the on-ground secret service detail watching his back.

"They get security threats all the time," Caldwell added. "That's part of their life. They deal with it."

"But what if the messages are a ruse? What if they're trying to lead us away from the real threat at the reception?"

Caldwell rose. "Go get some sleep, Rasheed. Keep your eye on the terrorists and leave the al Kahtani woman to us. Like I said, the security team will do a sweep. They'll try to make contact with her tomorrow night. If she wants out, we'll get her out. That's the best we can do."

It wasn't enough.

Scowling, Rasheed watched his boss work his way past a cluster of patrons and exit the restaurant. He had his orders. He needed to go back to the hotel and continue watching Amir and Manzoor.

Rising, he tossed his soda cup in the trash bin, then followed his boss into the night. He had his orders, all right. But he'd already failed one woman with deadly results. And he refused to do it twice.

Nadine's mother hadn't only been a courageous woman, she'd been a smart one. And now her intelligence might help save Rasheed's life.

Nadine stuffed another pillow under her bed covers and bunched up the bedspread, then took a final glance around her room. The fire in the fireplace had died. The mantel clock struck three, its lilting chime loud in the silent night.

She knew she was taking a gamble. Her mother's secret door led straight through her father's bedroom where he was asleep. But she couldn't afford to wait. She might not have another chance to get out. And the odds that Rasheed would try something dangerous mounted with every hour that passed.

Hurrying now, she crossed the room to the walk-in closet built into the common wall between the suites. She flicked on the light, grateful her father's renovations hadn't extended to the closet—or the small shelving unit that doubled as a hidden door. Her mother had named it *Bab irr* after a gate in ancient Aden, a gate the townspeople had opened only in emergencies. She'd used it to visit Nadine, bringing her food when she'd been punished, textbooks when her father had insisted that she stop studying and prepare for marriage instead.

Fighting back the memories, she found the key taped beneath the bottom shelf and unlocked the door, revealing the matching shelving unit on the opposite side. Even more cautious now, she cracked it open and listened hard.

The closet on her father's side was the former nursery. When she'd gotten older, her mother had converted it into an elaborate dressing room. Unbeknownst to her father, she'd also installed the secret door. After her death, the maids had disposed of her shoes and clothes, using the huge space to store extra bedding instead. The door had remained concealed.

Sending her mother her silent thanks, Nadine crawled through the opening, then hurried through the dressing room to her father's suite. The sound of snoring reached her ears, proof that he was still asleep. *So far, so good.*

Praying that he wouldn't hear her, she raced across the bedroom to the hallway door. The floorboards creaked. The snoring abruptly stopped, and she froze, terrified that he'd wake up. But after a second, the snores resumed. Her pulse going berserk now, she unlocked the door with a quiet snick and slipped outside into the hall.

She was free, thank God.

But she couldn't breathe easy yet. She had to find the files Rasheed needed first. And she didn't have much time. Careful to muffle her footsteps, she bolted down the hall to the back staircase and descended to the bottom floor. From there she cut through several rooms to the main block between the wings.

Several minutes later, she entered the study and closed the door. Still breathing hard, she made a beeline to the window and closed the blinds. Convinced that no one could see her, she snapped on a table lamp.

The low light pooled across the room. The study was a man's domain with dark paneling, dark furniture and a dark-toned Persian rug. Dozens of photos of her father shaking hands with various dignitaries hung on the walls.

She set the timer on her watch and got to work, starting at his executive-size desk. A search of the drawers came up empty, which was no surprise. Her father was smart. He wasn't going to make this easy by leaving an incriminating file lying around.

She turned on the computer next, but a password prompt came up. After trying various possibilities, she gave up and turned it off. Someone with computer expertise would have to tackle that. But she pocketed a dozen thumb drives on the off chance that they held a clue.

Rising, she studied the room, the quantity of built-in cabinets and cupboards daunting, given her lack of time. But Rasheed was depending on her to find evidence. Resolute, she worked her way clockwise around the room, searching the various drawers and shelves. An hour later, only the antique file cabinet remained.

Her heart sank when she opened the top drawer. There were hundreds of files, crammed together so tightly she could hardly pry one loose. It would take hours to check them all, far more time than she could spare.

Still, she thumbed through a couple of drawers before admitting defeat. She didn't even know what to look for. And the chance of finding a folder conveniently labeled *hawala network* was nil.

But there was a file marked *Leila* in the bottom drawer. Curious, she yanked it free, then took it over to her father's desk and spread it out.

The file contained various documents—Leila's birth certificate, marriage certificate and social security card—fairly typical stuff. There was also what appeared to be a travelogue or itinerary of sorts. Surprised, she studied the list—places Leila had visited, bus and train rides she'd taken, hotels that she'd stayed in. But the more Nadine read, the odder the whole thing seemed. *They were all in Iran.*

Was Sultan or her father having Leila followed? But that was ridiculous. Leila never went anywhere alone—let alone to Iran.

She opened a manila envelope next and leafed through the photographs inside. Some were photos of places—villages at the foot of mountains, a dry, high-altitude plateau. Others showed Leila shopping at a local bazaar and standing with people near village huts. The last item in the file was her passport—with entry and exit stamps from Iran.

Totally perplexed now, Nadine lowered herself into the nearest chair. What did this mean? It was true she hadn't been around Leila in fifteen years, but her sister-in-law hadn't changed that much. And she couldn't imagine her traveling without Sultan—especially to Iran. And yet, Sultan didn't appear in any of the photos. He wasn't mentioned in the file. There weren't any ticket stubs belonging to him.

Incredulous, she leaned back, trying to make sense of what she'd found. Leila had been born in Iran. She was an orphan, raised by a legal guardian, the same man who'd owed her father money and arranged the marriage to Sultan. Maybe these were her relatives. Maybe she'd made a trip to find her birth family. She could have been curious about her heritage or wanted to see her old guardian again.

Nadine took another look at the photos, but there was no family resemblance that she could see. And something else struck her as wrong. Leila wasn't wearing a burka—and she was traveling in public, standing beside various men.

Stunned, she shuffled through the pictures again, the *wrongness* leaping out at her this time. These pictures couldn't be real. There wasn't a chance on earth Leila would have gone traipsing through a village in the Middle East, exposing her face to public view. Anyone who'd ever met her knew that.

Were these photos fakes? If so, they were high-quality work, for sure. She doubted even an expert could find a flaw. But she knew better than anyone what money could buy. She'd shelled out thousands of dollars for documentation to support her own fabricated past. And both her father and brother had money. They could definitely afford the best.

But why would they bother? Why fake these photographs? If Nadine was reading the reports right, they'd gone to considerable trouble, creating an elaborate itinerary to make it appear that Leila had visited Iran.

But what was the point? Could it be related to the attack? She couldn't see how; her sister-in-law might be married to a fanatic, but she wasn't an activist herself.

Her watch beeped. Glancing at it, she rose. She'd have to mull it over later. Her time had just run out.

She needed to get over to the ballroom and hide before anyone in the house woke up. As soon as the workers arrived to prepare for the reception, she'd use the commotion surrounding the preparations for the reception to make her escape, then somehow track down Rasheed.

She straightened the blotter on the desk, erasing any evidence that she'd searched the room. Then, taking Leila's mysterious file with her, she turned off the lamp, returned to the window and opened the blinds again. She doubted her father would notice the position of the slats, but she couldn't afford to take the chance.

Without warning, a shout came from outside. She ducked, her heart suddenly sprinting, afraid that she'd been seen. She crept to the corner of the window, pushed aside the edge of the bottom slat and braved a quick peek out.

Several guards stood near the building. They weren't looking her way, thank God. They seemed to be grappling with someone on the ground, wrestling him into submission. Then they handcuffed him and stepped away.

The prisoner rose awkwardly to his feet. He staggered and turned, his face coming into the light. Her heart stopped dead.

Rasheed.

Chapter 13

Nadine had experienced plenty of desperate moments as a runaway teenager. She'd been attacked and robbed at gunpoint, chased by a gang executioner determined to kill her, and had suffered more cold nights and hungry days than anyone deserved.

But she'd never felt this all-consuming panic, this awful, relentless fear. Her father had captured Rasheed. He was holding him prisoner somewhere on the estate. *And it was all her fault.*

She angled the blow-dryer over Leila's hair, trying hard not to fall apart. She'd been so sure she could pull this off. She'd thought she could sneak into her father's study and get the information the CIA needed before anyone in her family caught on.

Instead, she'd failed miserably. Not only hadn't she discovered anything about the *hawala* network that could connect her father to the Rising Light terrorists, but they'd caught Rasheed trying to rescue her. And she had no idea where to find him, no idea how to set him free.

Assuming he wasn't already dead.

Blanching at that terrible thought, she turned off the blow-dryer, then started twisting Leila's long hair into a chignon. She'd had no choice but to return to her bedroom after the guards had captured him. She didn't dare attempt her own escape until she'd figured out how to free Rasheed.

But his presence in the compound had tipped her father off. He'd instantly stepped up his security, posting armed men in the hallway outside her room. She'd had no way to summon help—no computer or cell phone, no old landline to use. And sneaking out again was pointless, assuming she could skirt the guards. Her father's security people swarmed the grounds.

"What's the matter?" Leila asked. "You seem worried."

She *was* worried. She was on the verge of total panic over the disaster she'd caused Rasheed.

She met her sister-in-law's eyes in the mirror, wishing again that she could confide in her. But Leila would only tell Sultan. "I'm just tired."

"So am I."

Shifting forward, Nadine scrutinized Leila's face. The swelling was down, but her eyes showed signs of strain. "Are you all right?"

"My head's a little woozy. I think I studied too hard."

Frowning, she placed her hand on Leila's forehead.

Her skin was flushed and warm, sparking her concern. "You're still taking the antibiotics, aren't you?"

"Yes."

"You have to take the entire course."

"I am. And I'm sure I'm fine. I just spent a long time memorizing that list of names, that's all."

Still not convinced, Nadine continued to study her face. Could she have developed a delayed infection? She didn't see any nodules or lumps. "Do your cheeks hurt?"

"Maybe a little."

"We might have to change the antibiotic." Get her on something systemic. "Let me know if you start feeling any worse."

Leila's forehead creased. "You really think something's wrong?"

Not wanting to worry her unduly, she managed a smile. "I doubt it. Infections are pretty rare after implants. Maybe you just need a vacation—a real one this time."

Leila shot her a lopsided smile. "Sultan's always too busy working to take a break."

Nadine nodded, her mind swerving back to the itinerary in that file. When she wasn't worrying about Rasheed, she'd spent the day poring over every detail, and was more convinced than ever that Leila was being framed. But she had no idea what for.

"I've thought about visiting Jaziirastan again someday if I get a chance," she said, deciding to probe. "You know, to see the family homeland."

"That's a great idea."

"Have you ever gone back to Iran?"

"No."

"Really? I thought Sultan said you'd gone there recently to visit your old guardian."

Leila shook her head. "No, I haven't been back since I married Sultan. My life is with my husband now." She blushed, her voice dropping to a whisper. "We're trying to start a family. I'd like to have children before it's too late."

Nadine nodded, even more confused. Leila sounded sincere—which meant the documents in that file were fake. It also explained Leila's willingness to undergo surgery. It was a desperate attempt to interest Sultan so she could have the children she desired.

But why would anyone bother forging those documents? For the life of her she couldn't imagine the point. Leila wasn't interested in politics. She would never engage in criminal activities or plot to do anyone harm. And the motive couldn't be personal. If Sultan wanted to divorce her, he could do it easily enough. He didn't have to fabricate a cause.

Still struggling to make sense of the forged papers, she put the last pins in Leila's hair. She had to show them to Rasheed. Maybe he, or his CIA cohorts, could figure out what they meant. But first she had to discover where her father had taken him.

"That looks great," Leila said, peering in the mirror at her hair.

Nadine stepped back to admire her handiwork. She was right. Leila's hair had turned out lovely. And her face looked better than she'd expected, the swelling too slight to see. Her makeup would cover the faint bruising beneath her eyes.

"Do you need help putting on your makeup?"

"No, I'll be careful. But if you want to drill me on

the guest list again, that would be great. I don't want to make any mistakes."

"Sure."

While Leila started applying her makeup, Nadine retrieved the pages from the table and perched in a nearby chair. She had little in common with her sister-in-law. She disagreed with her about marriage and a woman's role in life. But it was hard to dislike her when she tried so hard to please everyone.

"All right," she said, eyeing the list. "Where do you want to start?"

"The businesspeople. I have the hardest time keeping them straight."

Nodding, Nadine worked her way down the list, quizzing her on the names. Leila had definitely studied. She could connect nearly every guest with the right business, an impressive feat.

"That's great," she said when they were done. "I circled the ones you missed."

"Oh, good. I was so afraid I'd mess up."

"You did a lot better than I could have." She rose and handed her back the list. The guests were typical of the people her father usually invited to his events—business executives, politicians, foreign diplomats—Washington's elite.

But while the guest list didn't surprise her, the timing of the reception did. Could it have any relation to their planned attack? The idea seemed far-fetched. No matter what jihadist nonsense they espoused, neither her father nor her brother wanted to die. They wouldn't mount an attack in their own home, where they could cause themselves harm. And both the vice president and Senator Riggs—two of Jaziirastan's biggest advocates—would be attending the reception tonight. What was the point in hurting them?

Unable to come up with an answer, she went to her closet and slipped on her gown. Her dress was a lot like Leila's with a high neckline, long sleeves, and a hemline that reached the floor. Not an inch of her skin was exposed. But the silk was a gorgeous lilac, the quality and fit superb.

"Will you help me with my scarf?" Leila asked.

"Sure." Picking up the gauzy fabric, she rejoined her at the dressing table. She draped it carefully over her head, then stepped back to take a look.

"You look beautiful," she said truthfully. The dark kohl brought out her lovely brown eyes. Her pale yellow dress made her skin tone glow. And thanks to the implants, her cheeks were symmetrical and pronounced, giving her a more youthful look. She'd never be the beauty she once was, and the nerve damage still marred her smile, but with the subtle lighting in the ballroom, she would do her husband proud.

"Thank you," Leila whispered, her eyes brimming with tears. She reached out and squeezed her hand. "I appreciate what you did for me."

"I was glad to do it. I wish I could have done more."

The clock on the mantel chimed six. The reception was about to begin. Nadine hesitated, knowing she was taking a risk involving Leila, but she was fast running out of time.

"Maybe you could do something for me," she said slowly.

"Of course."

"I just need you to answer a question. Did you notice any odd activity today? I don't mean the preparations for the reception, or the Secret Service guys. I mean the guards, the men working for my father. Were they doing anything unusual, like patrolling in a place they don't usually go?"

Leila's gaze bounced away. She rose quickly and went to the window, looking out toward the inky night.

"Leila?"

"I haven't really paid attention. I've been in my room studying that list." She shot her a glance over her shoulder, a hint of fear in her eyes.

"I know." Nadine joined her at the window. "I'm not asking you to share any secrets or do anything disloyal. It's just… I thought maybe if you saw something a little unusual…you'd do me a favor and tell me where it was, that's all."

Leila nibbled her lip. Several more minutes stretched past. "The pool house," she finally said. She nodded toward the white fairy lights decorating the patio around the pool. "I've seen… There've been a lot of guards out there today, going inside and coming back out."

Nadine sagged against the wall in relief. "Thank you." She knew it was still a long shot. Their movements might not have anything to do with Rasheed. But it was a place to start.

"There's Sultan," Leila said, peering out the window again.

"Where?"

"Down there."

Nadine moved closer to see. Two men walked along the path between the wings, their heads bent close as they talked. Then they stopped, and the man with Sultan lit a cigarette, his face turned toward the light. Her heart missed a beat as she glimpsed his face.

Abu Jabril. The man she'd seen on the island. What was he doing here?

"Who's that man with him?" she asked, trying to sound casual. "Do you know?"

"Yes. That's Kamil al Bitar. His friend from college."

His old college roommate. *Of course.* No wonder he'd looked familiar. He'd visited the house a few times when she'd lived at home.

She hadn't paid much attention to him back then. He was Sultan's age, six years older than she was, and not the least bit interested in her. And she'd been absorbed in her own problems, trying to figure out how to apply to medical school. Then her mother had died, and her world had come crashing apart.

Alert now, she took a closer look. He was older, and not as lanky. His full beard partially covered his face. But now that Leila had confirmed it, she could tell it was definitely him. "Why is he here?"

"He's probably going to attend the reception."

She gave Leila a sharp glance. "He wasn't on the list."

"He wouldn't need to be. He's practically one of the family. He and Sultan spend a lot of time together when he's in town."

That made sense. He was wearing a tuxedo like Sultan. And inviting him seemed natural enough. Why wouldn't Sultan include his close friend?

But warning bells were going off in her head. He'd shown up on the drug cartel's private island with the terrorists. He used a nom de guerre. And now he was here—at the house of the man presumed to finance the Rising Light's terror attacks—when rumors of a plot were high.

Could the terror attack be taking place tonight? Ice filled her veins at the thought. But would they really risk the lives of their closest American allies—and in their own house, no less?

And even assuming they were willing to do it, *how* could they pull it off? She hadn't missed the extensive security preparations, even with the limited view from her room. There was no way anyone could get a gun or bomb within a mile of the estate.

Still, Abu Jabril's presence couldn't be a coincidence. These men were up to something big.

"Leila…" She swallowed hard, knowing she had to take the chance. "Listen…I found something I want to show you."

She hurried over to the dresser and picked up her evening bag, a large, vintage piece she'd found stashed in the dressing room. She couldn't fit the entire file inside, but she'd crammed in as many pages and photos as she could to show Rasheed.

Carrying it, she started back across the room toward Leila. But then a knock sounded on the bedroom door. Leila opened it before she could stop her, and her nerves suffered another hit. Two men stood in the hallway, their black paratrooper-type uniforms and weapons marking them as her father's guards.

"It's time to go to the ballroom," the taller guard said.

Nadine didn't move. She wasn't ready. She needed more time with Leila. What if the attack was tonight and she failed to stop it in time?

Suddenly, Leila wobbled on her feet. She clutched a

nearby chair, swaying so badly that Nadine feared she was going to fall. She rushed over to steady her arm. "What's wrong?"

"I'm just dizzy. I think I stood up too fast."

"You were standing at the window, not sitting down." Even more alarmed now, she peered at her sister-in-law's face. The dress color hadn't caused that glow; she was feverish—and getting worse with every minute that passed. "You need to go back to bed."

"What? Don't be silly. I'm not sick."

"You've got a fever, Leila. You need to rest."

"I'll rest later."

"But—"

"I can't miss the reception. Sultan's depending on me to do my part."

Nadine swallowed her reply. Her sister-in-law wanted to do this. She couldn't deny her this moment of glory, no matter how ill-advised.

"All right. But if you get any weaker, you're going to leave." Even Sultan couldn't force her to stay if she collapsed. She caught the tall guard's eye. "Hold on." She grabbed a water bottle from the dressing table and gave it to her to drink. "You need to keep hydrated. Drink this on the way."

Leila obediently took a sip, then preceded her into the hall. The short guard fell in behind them, preempting any attempt to escape. They padded down the hall, their slippers soundless on the plush oriental carpet, Nadine's nerves winding tighter with every step.

The night had turned into a disaster. Everything was going wrong. Not only was Rasheed being held prisoner, but now Leila was getting ill. And for all she knew, they could be waltzing straight into a trap.

Struggling against a tide of panic, she tried desperately to think this through. Sultan's roommate had to be here for a reason. The timing was too suspect.

Her brother had met Kamil al Bitar their freshman year of college. They'd instantly hit it off, rooming together for all four years. Her brother had studied business and finance. His roommate had studied engineering, graduating near the top of his class.

"Leila, what did Kamil do after college?"

Leila paused to sip her water. "He went to graduate school at M.I.T. We visited him once in Boston after we were married. Then he went back to Jaziirastan."

"So he's an engineer?"

Leila started walking again. "I think so. I'm not sure where he works…maybe at a research group? I don't really know."

Her thoughts whirled. Maybe Kamil was the Rising Light's bomb maker. With his engineering background, it made sense. Maybe he'd come here tonight to deliver an explosive device—assuming he could sneak it past the massive security presence swarming the grounds.

But then why had he been on the island? How did Leila's forged file fit into all this? Or did it? Maybe she was trying too hard to connect a bunch of unrelated dots and missing a more obvious clue.

They made it to the main floor, then followed another hallway to the adjacent wing, the same route Nadine had taken before dawn. Leila slowed and continued to stagger, and Nadine took her arm, struggling to support her weight. Her sister-in-law was burning up. Whatever this infection was, it was gaining strength fast.

And that wasn't a good sign. She had to get her to

a hospital. She needed to put her on an antibiotic drip right away. And if the drugs didn't kick in quickly, she had to do a culture to find out what they were dealing with.

Sultan was waiting for them at the ballroom door. He gave his wife a once-over, something that almost resembled approval in his eyes. Leila beamed.

"Leila isn't well," Nadine announced flatly. She hated to burst Leila's bubble, but she had to consider her health. "She has a bad infection. She needs to get to a hospital right away."

Sultan scowled. "She can't. She has to attend the reception."

"She's feverish. She can hardly stand up."

Leila swung around in alarm. "Nadira, no. I'm fine, really. I want to be here. I promise you, I'm all right."

Sultan gave his wife a nod. "Good. I want you there." He shifted his gaze to Nadine. "Stay right beside her. You can help her if she feels too weak."

"But that's ridiculous. She's burning up. Feel her face. You can see yourself that she's too sick. I can greet the people. She doesn't have to—"

"You'll do as I say. She needs to be here. This reception is important."

"More important than your wife?"

Anger flared in Sultan's eyes. "You'll stand in the receiving line beside her and make sure she doesn't make any mistakes. Once everyone has entered the reception, she can leave. But not before I give the word."

Nadine stared at her brother, at a loss for words. What was so important about this reception that he'd risk his wife's health?

"And, Nadira?"

"What?" she asked, still incredulous.

He held up a two-way radio. "If you try to contact anyone, or if you leave Leila's side even for a second—your CIA friend will pay the price."

Her blood went cold. Her head felt suddenly light. He'd just admitted that Rasheed was his prisoner. *He knew who he really was.*

And now Sultan would be keeping his eye on her, making sure she didn't sneak off to rescue him. And if she disobeyed his order, if she slipped away during the reception to try to find him, Rasheed would die.

Sucking in a reedy breath, she struggled to form a plan, but any hope she had of rescuing Rasheed skittered away. For his safety, she had to stay at the reception. She couldn't risk causing him any harm. But what if Sultan was toying with her? What if he intended to kill Rasheed regardless of what she did? Was it better to take the chance?

Her brother gave the guards a signal. They hustled Leila and her through the walkway connecting the wings. Feeling dazed, she glanced through the windows at the guests milling around outside, oblivious to the danger playing out before their eyes.

She followed Leila through a metal detector at the entrance to the ballroom. A stern-faced guard searched her purse. A bomb-sniffing dog checked her over while she stood there woodenly, too worried about Rasheed to make a peep.

Why had he come? Why couldn't he have waited a day before taking such a terrible risk? Sick with worry, she trailed Leila into the lavish ballroom and took her place in the receiving line.

Chandeliers glittered overhead. A string quartet

played in the background, its muted strains sounding far away. Waiters slipped through the gathering crowd, serving champagne and gourmet hors d'oeuvres.

She ignored it all, her mind in a total uproar, stray thoughts circling like an endless carousel. *The island. The surgery. The terrorists. Leila's mysterious file.* She knew she was missing something. Something important. Something to do with Sultan's roommate, the engineer who might have built a bomb.

"Biomedical engineering!" The thought sliced at her out of nowhere, the clue she'd been trying to recall.

Standing next to her, Leila gave her a funny look. "What?"

"Biomedical engineering. That's what Sultan's roommate studied."

"Yes, that's right. He interned in a hospital for a while."

And biomedical engineers designed things—imaging equipment, replacement joints, prostheses. *Surgical implants.*

Oh, good God. Horror congealed inside her as everything began to fall in place. Maybe that's what he was doing on the island—delivering Leila's implants. Sultan had brought the package to the clinic that night.

And if he was a bomb maker…could the implants contain a bomb? *A bomb that she installed?*

Nausea roiled inside her. She clamped her hand to her mouth, the absolute horror of it making her want to retch. But she knew that it was possible. Drug cartels and prisoners had smuggled contraband via body cavities for years. And terrorists had tried to implant bombs before; they'd done it in Saudi Arabia not long ago. That plot had failed. They'd had problems with the detonation, a design flaw they'd needed to fix.

But Kamil was smart. He'd graduated at the top of his class, then done his grad work at M.I.T. And if he'd perfected the design…

She shuddered, convinced now that she was right. It explained Sultan's insistence that Leila have surgery. It explained why they'd done it on the island, where they could escape scrutiny from the U.S. authorities. It even explained Leila's infection. The explosive material inside the casings could be leaking out.

The plan was diabolical, yet brilliant. The bomb-sniffing dogs would never detect them. The scanner would have picked them up, but they wouldn't have raised any concerns. Half the women in attendance probably sported implants of various sorts—breasts, buttocks, cheeks. Even the vice president had supposedly undergone surgery to enhance his chin. All her brother would need was a detonating device, probably a cell phone he could depress as soon as the target approached.

And they'd be dead.

Her hands began to shake. Her head whirled as unsuspecting guests greeted her warmly, then continued by. The target was probably the vice president. He was the most important dignitary here.

But *why* would her brother do it? It was too obvious. The reception was at his house. Why would he risk taking the blame?

He wouldn't have to. She gasped as the final clue slid into place. *Leila's forged documents.* They were making her look like a rogue agent, a suicide bomber working on behalf of Iran. No one outside the family knew her. No one knew how ludicrous that idea was. They'd only see that she came from Iran, that her marriage to Sultan was an unhappy one, and assume she wanted revenge.

And the forged documents would back up that claim. Knowing her father, he'd probably even hired someone who looked like Leila to make the trip. Witnesses in Iran would identify Leila as the one they'd seen, lending the story even more credibility.

The attack would be cataclysmic. The vice president would die. Her father and brother would play the shocked allies, horrified that someone they were close to had masterminded such an evil plan. The blame would shift to Iran, an enemy of both Jaziirastan and the United States.

The U.S. government would have to retaliate. They couldn't let a brazen assassination go unpunished, especially one of this magnitude. They'd probably bomb Iran, Jaziirastan's ancient enemy, sparking a war in the Middle East.

Jaziirastan had a lot to gain. As a U.S. ally, they'd receive money and arms to assist the fight, bolstering their power in the Middle East. And with the vice president dead, Jaziirastan's closest political ally, Senator Riggs, would run for president—increasing their influence even more.

Horrified, she stared at Leila, the awful irony sinking in. She'd fled home to become a doctor. She'd risked her life repeatedly, going through years of hell to attain her dream. And then she'd dedicated her life to healing others, to helping battered women regain their dignity.

Now her family had used those very skills, turning them against her to carry out their warped plans.

No wonder Sultan had manipulated her into performing the surgery. How amused he must have been when she implanted the bomb. She would even cause her own death, avenging their honor! She'd played right into his twisted hands.

Shocked beyond reason, she closed her eyes. *She* was going to cause Leila's death. *She* was going to assassinate the vice president. *She* would spark a conflagration that could turn into World War Three.

No. She had to stop this. No matter what the obstacles, no matter how impossible the chance for victory now seemed, she could not let these evil men win. She snapped her gaze to the ballroom entrance. She caught Sultan watching her, a sick half smile on his handsome face.

If she bolted now, Rasheed would die. If she waited, Sultan would detonate the bomb.

And for the first time in her life, she couldn't see a clear way out.

Chapter 14

Rasheed had always prided himself on his patience. He'd spent years working his way through the Rising Light's training camps. He'd spent years forging the right connections and earning the terrorists' trust. And he'd spent more years than he could remember sifting painstakingly through bank documents, tenaciously piecing together their financial network so he could destroy the bloodthirsty group. He'd persevered with cold calculation, tamping back his raging need for vengeance, biding his time as he worked single-mindedly toward the greater goal.

But now that patience was shot. Knowing Nadine was being held captive somewhere in the compound had done away with his self-control.

He closed his eyes and inhaled, reminding himself for the hundredth time that he had to wait. Then he trained his gaze on the guard yawning in his armchair near the pool house door. Sitting idly by while she was in danger was the hardest thing he'd ever done. But this wasn't just a battle, it was a war. Giving away his hand too quickly would destroy any chance he had of getting her out alive.

He grimaced, the slight motion making his swollen eye throb. The endless hours he'd spent curbing his frustration had taught him one thing. He was no longer dead inside. Ever since he'd met Nadine, the emotions he'd thought he'd buried with Sarah's death had come blazing back to life full force. She'd opened the lid and let them out, resurrecting needs and feelings he could no longer ignore.

He felt emotions, all right—fury, frustration. *And fear.* The gut-wrenching terror that he'd arrived too late to save her life.

Voices arose just outside the pool house. His pulse began to thud, but the voices faded away. The guard slumped lower in his seat, his head lolling forward, his eyes drooping closed. But then he jerked them open and pulled himself upright in an effort to stay awake.

Rasheed inhaled through his teeth. The reception was in full swing now. His chance to mount a rescue was nearly gone. While he sat huddled on the pool house floor, waiting for the damned guard to fall asleep, Nadine's time was running out.

At least the long hours he'd spent twiddling his thumbs had done one good thing—they'd given him time to figure out where he'd gone wrong. He never should have let Amir live. He'd humiliated and enraged him, increasing his desire for revenge. To retaliate, Amir had undoubtedly gone to their leader, Manzoor, and reported his suspicions about him. And Manzoor wasn't dumb. Already paranoid, and with a vital mission to carry off, he wouldn't want to take a chance of having a traitor in their midst.

So they'd set him up. They'd checked in to a hotel. They'd separated him from Nadine to see if he'd make a move. And they'd alerted al Kahtani, who'd been watching for him—letting him sneak inside the compound while he set his trap.

Why al Kahtani hadn't shot him outright, he didn't know. Maybe he intended to interrogate him later. Maybe he didn't want to risk a gunshot with the vice president's security detail so close. Or maybe he wanted to torture him by forcing him to watch Nadine die—just as they'd done with his wife.

But al Kahtani had made a mistake. He should have executed him while he'd had the chance. Because now *he* was the one who would die.

The guard's eyes closed again. Rasheed fingered the cord binding his wrists, preparing to break it loose. He'd spent the entire day sawing away, millimeter by excruciating millimeter on the edge of the metal air vent cover on the floor. It was like wearing down a stone with water, spending hours leaning at an awkward angle, the pressure chafing his wrists into bloody pulps. But it had worked. The tiny ripple in the metal had provided the edge he needed to weaken the cord. Now one strong jerk and he'd be free.

The guard's mouth turned slack, his breathing slowing and growing deeper. Even more alert now, Rasheed leaned forward, his gaze fastened on the dozing man. The guards had rotated throughout the day, working in pairs. This guard's partner was posted outside.

The guard began to snore. Seizing the opportunity, Rasheed gritted his teeth, bracing himself for the jolt of pain. Then in one swift move, he snapped the weakened cord.

Ignoring his stinging wrists, he untied his feet, and removed the ropes. Then he rose and crept behind the sleeping guard. Moving quickly, he slid one arm beneath his jaw, the other behind his head in a rear naked choke hold. Then he pulled his shoulders back, applying pressure to his throat, squeezing down hard on the arteries to cut off his blood supply. Seconds later, the guard passed out.

Rasheed lowered him to the floor. He removed his radio and sidearm and stripped him of his shirt. Taking an extension cord from the nearby lamp, he secured the guard's hands behind his back, and used a towel to gag his mouth. Finally, he dragged him behind the couch, out of sight from anyone coming through the door.

Rising, he tugged the guard's shirt on over his own. He strapped on his pistol and pocketed the radio, making sure he turned the volume down. Then he crossed the pool house to the window, inched aside the drape and glanced out.

The second guard leaned against the pillar supporting the overhang, just a few yards from the door. Frowning, Rasheed dropped the drape and scanned the room, needing a diversion to lure him inside.

He headed to the kitchenette. A quick search of the cupboards netted him a barbecue lighter and some magazines. He chose a spot on the floor kitty-corner to the entrance, out of the guard's direct line of sight, then set the magazines on fire. Wisps of smoke curled up, the stench from the glossy pages filling the air.

Slowly, the flames began swirling higher—not exactly creating a bonfire, but generating enough smoke to draw the guard.

Satisfied, he cracked open the door. "Hey!" he called to the guard. "Come here a minute. Help me put this out."

"What happened?" The guard ran in. Rasheed kicked the door shut behind him, then sprang forward and took him down. Hurrying, he yanked off the cord from the blinds to secure him and confiscated his gun. Finally, he stomped out the fire, coughing as the smoke dispersed.

His heart racing, he inched open the door and glanced outside. No one was in the immediate vicinity. The activity was centered on the ballroom where the vice president was scheduled to appear. He set the lock on the door and closed it, doubting it would buy much time. But every second counted now. His head high, trying to exude the impression that he belonged in the compound, he started walking toward the wing where the reception was being held.

He had no idea where they were holding Nadine prisoner. The grounds were too extensive, the mansion itself at least twenty thousand square feet in size. He'd never be able to search it by himself—not with al Kahtani's guards on watch. They'd only capture him again if he tried.

His only option was to get inside the reception. He could alert the CIA people embedded with the vice president's security detail and get them to mount a search. He just hoped to hell they could find her before she died.

Catching the sound of approaching voices, he

slowed, then ducked into the shadows of the main building, tensing as several guards strolled up. The replacement shift? Silently swearing, knowing they could sound the alarm at any moment, he waited as they went past.

Then he raced past the central hall to the wing that held the ballroom. Sticking to the shadows, he peered through the giant windows at the people inside. They were decked out in formal clothes, laughing as they drank champagne beneath the enormous chandeliers. Somewhere out of sight, musicians played.

He couldn't go in the main entrance. He'd never get past all those guards without detection, especially with his swollen eye.

He'd have to sneak through the back, pretending to be a guest. Summoning what little remained of his fractured patience, he settled in the shadows to wait. The wind turned cold. The lights strung around the patio swayed.

Then a side door opened, and laughter spilled out—along with a lone guest. Heavyset and wearing a tuxedo, the man walked to the edge of the patio and lit a cigarette. He stood facing the fountains, his shoulders hunched against the cold—a Washington bigwig relegated to refugee status, smoking furtively in the dark.

Rasheed was about to ruin that bigwig's night. But he couldn't help that now. He had to rescue Nadine.

And this man was his ticket in.

Nadine stood in the reception line beside her sister-in-law, a macabre sense of unreality gripping her nerves. Any minute now, they were going to die—Leila, the vice president, all these unsuspecting people…even Rasheed, unless she found a way to thwart the attack right now.

But she still didn't have a plan.

The newcomers kept strolling through the entrance. They joined the long line snaking toward her—women and men, diplomats and businessmen. They smiled and laughed, a myriad of languages filling the air— English, Spanish, Chinese…. Behind her, in the main part of the ballroom, people were sipping champagne and eating hors d'oeuvres as if at any normal Washington event. The quartet continued to play in the background, the sophisticated music jarring given the brutal savagery that was about to occur.

Anxiety built to a crescendo inside her. She gripped Leila's arm with one hand to hold her up, using the other to greet the guests. Abu Jabril, her brother's old roommate, stood across from her near the entrance, leaning against the wall, his studiously casual posture at odds with the alertness in his cold eyes. *So he was going to watch his handiwork.* But he was a coward, positioning himself clear of the blast.

She shifted her gaze to Sultan. He stood beside their father at the start of the receiving line, a short distance from Leila and her—which was clever. He'd effectively created two receiving lines, separated by a dozen yards. This way, he could keep her in his sights, making sure she didn't try to rescue Rasheed. He could also guarantee that she would stay by Leila's side until the bomb went off. And as soon as he greeted the vice president, he could quickly move away and avoid getting hurt by the bomb.

Her gaze went from her father's cruel face to Sultan's crafty smile, and fury edged out her fear. That they could plot something this sinister against their own family, that they could justify killing her because of some stone age code of honor disgusted her beyond belief. And worse, they intended to kill Rasheed, a man who had more *honor* than they would ever have.

Rasheed. Her heart stumbled hard, a torrent of emotions ripping through her chest. He was brave, honorable, heroic. And she prayed that he would survive. She closed her eyes, battling back the panic clawing at her nerves at the thought that such an amazing man could die.

Beside her, Leila swayed. Nadine moved closer to hold her upright and shot her a worried glance. Her cheeks were flushed, her feverish face beaming as she greeted the guests by name.

And the dread inside her grew. She'd failed her sister-in-law badly. She'd never be able to save her now. The minute she tried, if she made even the slightest move, Sultan would detonate that bomb.

But she refused to abandon her. She'd installed that bomb, and now she would stick by her side. Even if she couldn't save her, even if she couldn't stop the attack, she could try to minimize the results. If all else failed, she would knock Leila down and cover her with her body, muffling the bomb's impact. Leila and she would die, but maybe they could spare some lives.

But what about Rasheed? She studied the men crowding the entrance, distinguishing the secret service agents from her father's guards by their black suits. Would they believe her if she asked for help? Could she convince them to look for him? And how could she do it without alerting Sultan?

Then a commotion drew her attention, and she

glanced at the door again. All of a sudden the vice president strode inside, surrounded by dozens of massive men, their wary eyes roving the room.

Her throat squeezed shut. This was it. In minutes, the vice president would work his way through the line to her. And as soon as he got within range, the bomb would explode. But who held the detonator? Her brother? Abu Jabril? Her father? Or someone she didn't even know? And how many unsuspecting people would die?

A Japanese couple went by in the line. She greeted them by rote, a smile pasted on her face, while inside, her senses screamed. She wanted to rail at them to leave, to beg them to help Rasheed, to plead with them to get everyone away *right now*. She darted a frantic glance at Sultan, but his eyes were glued on her, and her hopes for a rescue died. She'd never felt more vulnerable or helpless in her life.

Feeling nauseous, she cast another desperate gaze around the room. Then suddenly, her eyes stalled on a tall man standing beside a waiter, his black hair disheveled, his tuxedo tie hanging askew. She did a double take as he turned his head, and his gaze collided with hers. It was Rasheed.

For a moment she couldn't breathe. She stared at him, completely staggered, taking in his grim, black eyes—one all puffy and discolored—the stark lines of his angry face. His jaw was bruised. He wore a poorly fitting tuxedo jacket, the sleeves too short, the shirt buttoned wrong, as if he'd thrown it on in the dark. And a barrage of emotions rushed through her with the force of a tsunami—relief that he was alive, terror that he'd try something risky, horror that he'd watch her die.

But at least he was still alive. And Sultan couldn't make good on his threat to kill him—as long as she didn't tip him off.

Her heart racing, she looked away. Every part of her body trembled, as if she'd just injected a massive dose of adrenaline. She struggled to keep her eyes from Rasheed, trying not to betray his presence to Sultan. If her brother spotted him, he'd set off the bomb at once.

The vice president approached the receiving line. Leila continued smiling and greeting the guests, her feverish eyes reflecting her delight. Unable to bear it, Nadine stole another glance at Rasheed, and spotted him weaving his way toward her through the crowd. Panic burgeoned inside her like a primal shriek.

She'd thought her worst nightmare was being in her family's power. She'd been wrong.

Watching Rasheed approach his death was worse.

Rasheed elbowed his way through the ballroom, his instincts jangling hard. Something was wrong with Nadine, something besides the obvious fact that her murderous family had her under their control. He could see the terror in her eyes, feel the unseen menace vibrating the air, the sixth sense he had for danger warning him that something big was about to go down.

Desperate to get closer, he shouldered his way through the crowd. He twisted and swerved, ignoring the startled looks his battered face evoked. Whatever was happening, he had to get her out. Her family might try to stop him, but he wasn't about to let her stay. Not with all hell about to break loose.

He skirted a cluster of people and caught a clearer view of her this time. She stood beside Leila in the receiving line, looking outwardly calm and graceful, and drop-dead gorgeous in a formfitting purple dress. But her face was unnaturally pasty, her eyes terrified when she met his gaze.

She gave her head a little shake. He paused a beat, realizing that she was warning him off. But why?

She raised her hand to her cheek and glanced away. Then she made little fluttering motions with her fingers, and cut her gaze back to him. Frowning, he tried to figure out her message as she greeted another guest. That motion with her fingers…

Growing more confused now, he ducked his head. He grabbed a glass of champagne from a passing waiter so he'd blend in. Then he studied the people around her—her father at the head of the line. Sultan standing beside him, watching Nadine with a strange intensity. Leila smiling and shaking hands as the guests paraded by.

Nadine jerked her head toward her sister-in-law. She wanted him to notice Leila, but why? She made the flutter with her fingers again, pointing clearly at her face.

It was definitely a signal. She was trying to tell him something about Leila's cheeks—possibly the implants. But that bursting motion she was making with her fingers…

A bomb? Inside Leila? *She had a bomb inside her cheeks?*

Incredulous, he gaped at her. For a moment, he couldn't breathe, the idea too shocking to absorb. But it was just heinous enough to be true.

He shot a stunned glance at Nadine's father. He was smiling broadly and clasping the vice president's hands, as if they were the best of friends. Nadine caught his gaze again. She made a pressing motion this time. *The detonator.*

Right. He had to find it. But who the hell had it?

The vice president moved to Sultan. His pulse turning frantic, Rasheed motioned for Nadine to get away. But she shook her head, and suddenly, he realized what she was going to do. She was going to protect the vice president. She intended to throw herself over Leila and sacrifice herself when the bomb went off.

His head felt light. He stared at her, and in that horrendous moment, his image of her sharpened. Her external beauty peeled away, revealing the essence of the woman inside. And all the emotions he'd held at bay came crashing back—admiration, respect, love.

He loved her.

He'd loved everything about her from the moment he'd met her—the feisty way she'd protected Henry. The way she'd refused to back down from Amir. The way she'd volunteered to help him defeat her family, risking her own life for the greater good. She was more than a survivor; she was a warrior.

And now, she was preparing to make the ultimate sacrifice.

She angled her head high. Her eyes turned even more desperate, but she didn't budge. Even in this moment, she wasn't thinking of herself. She was trying to protect him and warn him away.

And suddenly, a flurry of memories flashed through his mind, of another woman, another innocent victim who'd been about to lose her life. He'd watched his wife die. He hadn't been able to reach her in time.

Now history was going to repeat itself.

The hell it was. He wasn't going to let her die.

The vice president was nearing Leila. He'd never reach him in time.

But he could reach Sultan.

His gaze homed in on Nadine's brother. Resolved now, he rushed toward him, hoping to hell he hadn't guessed wrong. But any creep who could put bombs inside his wife would surely want to detonate them himself.

Sultan veered away from the line. He walked briskly toward the door—and then a cell phone appeared in his hand. *The detonator.*

Rasheed shoved through the crowd to his side. "Bomb!" he shouted and took a flying leap. He slammed into Sultan, knocking the phone from his hand. It fell and skittered away.

They rolled across the floor. Rasheed punched and fought with a vengeance, knowing he had to prevail. Around them pandemonium broke out—people running, shouting, pushing. He smashed his fist into Sultan's face, feeling the bones crack, determined to save Nadine's life.

A gunshot rang out. Around him, women screamed. Then more shots barked out in quick succession. People trampled him in their haste to flee.

He rammed his knee into Sultan's groin. Then he dived for the cell phone and scooped it up just as the Secret Service descended on them.

"I'm CIA," he shouted. "He has a weapon."

They hauled Sultan up and snapped on some cuffs. Rasheed jumped to his feet and whipped around. Security guards were barking into radios and swarming the ballroom. The security detail had hustled the ice president away. Nadine's father was on the floor, ying facedown, a gun in his limp hand, blood puddled around his body. *Dead.*

Breathing hard, Rasheed searched the crowd. Then a splash of purple on the floor caught his eye, and everything inside him froze.

Nadine. People knelt and huddled around her, rendering first aid. He stared at the pool of blood, too terrified to think. Then he rushed over and shoved them out of his way. "Nadine!"

Her face looked like wax. Blood stained her silk gown black. Her eyes were closed, her chest unmoving, and his heart stopped cold.

He'd failed again.

Chapter 15

Rasheed paced up and down the hospital corridor, going steadily out of his mind. The sun had risen hours ago. Nadine had made it through surgery, spent several hours in the recovery room and was now in a private room under heavy guard. The nurses had gone through their second shift change since he'd arrived, but every one parroted the same refrain. He wasn't a relative. She was sedated. They couldn't let him in to see her yet.

He wasn't budging from this hallway until they did.

He pivoted on his heel, his shoes making a squeak on the shiny tile, and strode past an open lounge. Another visitor, huddling with a cup of coffee, peered at him with blurry eyes. He knew he looked like hell—his eye swollen shut, dressed in a ridiculously short tuxedo, blood smeared on his once-white shirt.

Nadine's blood.

His steps faltered. He stopped, dragged a hand down his unshaven face, and looked out the window at the grounds below. A catering truck pulled up, unloading food for the cafeteria. A man pushed a patient in a wheelchair toward the door. Nurses and doctors who had just come off shifts filed from the building, then fanned across the parking lot, heading home to their families and lives.

He still couldn't believe Nadine had survived. Hearing those gunshots, seeing her lying in that pool of blood…he closed his eyes, the memory shaking him even now.

But she'd been lucky. The shot hadn't hit anything vital. It had entered the fleshy tissue in her shoulder, missing her major blood vessels and bones. They'd removed the bullet and taken tests, and he knew she'd recover fine. He just needed to see her for himself.

He turned and started pacing again, his thoughts circling back to the past night. Leila had survived, as well. She'd had surgery to remove the bomb and was still in intensive care, battling the infection the explosives caused.

Nadine's father hadn't been as lucky. The Secret Service had taken him out the minute he'd brandished a gun—but he'd managed to shoot his daughter first. The disgusting man had been determined to avenge his so-called honor to his dying breath.

The rest of the terrorists were under arrest, including Nadine's brother, Sultan. And from what his CIA boss had told him, every intelligence and law enforcement agency in the country was at the McLean, Virginia, mansion, poring over it for evidence and clues.

"Mr. Davar?"

Rasheed spun around. A short, middle-aged nurse wearing flowered scrubs walked up, a dour expression on her lined face. "Come with me."

His heart lurched. "What's wrong? Did something happen?" He fell in beside her, his anxiety ramping up again.

"Your boss called my supervisor." She grimaced. "We're authorized to let you in. You can take a peek at her—but just a short one. She needs to rest."

Trying to curb his impatience, he accompanied her down the hall, shortening his strides to hers. Two armed guards stood by the door, their expressions stony as he approached. He waited for them to frisk him, knowing the security was for Nadine's good. They weren't taking any chances on another attack, even though the main terrorists were under arrest.

"Five minutes," the nurse warned.

With a nod, he walked into the room. His gaze went straight to the bed, where Nadine lay asleep. Her black hair spilled over the pillow. Her skin was nearly as chalky as the crisp white sheets. Her eyes were closed, her dark lashes forming crescents on her pale cheeks. Her shoulder was heavily bandaged, her arm hooked to an IV.

An intense rush of emotions consumed him. He loved her. And he'd nearly lost her. He'd nearly failed to keep her safe.

And she looked so fragile, so vulnerable lying there swaddled in bandages, with machines beeping and flashing her vital signs. If he'd arrived even a second later...

He swallowed hard, pushing away the dreadful

thought. She'd survived. She was going to be all right. That's all that mattered now.

And he loved her so damned much. Her courage, her generosity, her passion and intelligence… She'd blasted every scrap of his resistance apart. From the moment he'd spotted her in that mountain camp, his heart had never had a chance.

Stepping even closer, he reached out and touched her hair. Then he stroked his finger along her jaw, tracing the delicate line to her throat.

He'd thought about a lot of things during the past night. There was something about a lonely hospital corridor that encouraged soul-searching and made it hard to evade the truth. And he'd come to the conclusion that most of his resistance to her, the reason he'd convinced himself he couldn't love her was due to fear. He'd been afraid that he would fail her. He'd been afraid that, just like with Sarah, he wouldn't save her when she needed him most.

And most of all, he'd been afraid that he'd lose another woman he loved. He knew he'd never recover from that unbearable pain again.

So he'd tried to avoid getting involved. He'd spent years suppressing his feelings and burying himself in the need for revenge. But even though he'd tried, he hadn't lost the ability to feel. Even though his heart had *seemed* dead for the past five years, Nadine had proven he was still alive.

His heart full, he picked up her slender hand. Then he gazed at the woman he loved, the irony of it suddenly clear. Because even though he loved her, or maybe *because* he loved her, he had to give her up.

In the end, nothing had changed. He still had enemies trying to kill him. The terrorists could still come in pursuit. Even if he didn't work undercover, even if he wanted to lead a normal life, there was still a chance they could come gunning for him—and retaliate against Nadine, just as they did to his pregnant wife.

And that was a risk he couldn't take. After all these years, she was finally free of her family's death threats and the fear that had ruled her life. He couldn't ask her to go on the run again.

His throat thick, he released her hand. He crossed the small room to the door, then paused and took a long look back, feeling as if his heart had been wrenched from his chest. She'd be all right now. She'd survived the gunshot and would recover in a week or two. And she could now live a life free of fear, with the freedom she deserved—but only if he wasn't in her life.

Desolation keening inside him, he left.

The knock on the hospital door jerked her upright. Hope flaring inside her, Nadine snapped her gaze to the door. *Rasheed.* It had to be him this time. She'd been in the hospital for over two days now, and he still hadn't shown up.

"Come in," she called, suddenly breathless.

A gray-haired man poked his head through the door. "Hey. Remember me?"

She blinked, confusion giving way to surprise. "Henry?"

"I can't stay long." His smile widened as he scooted through the door. "I've got to catch a plane. But when I heard you were here, I took a detour. I wanted to see you before I went back to New York."

Incredulous, she studied him as he came toward her.

He looked thinner and his cheeks more hollow, but his skin color had improved. He'd dressed in slacks and a plaid flannel shirt that matched the pale blue of his eyes. His sparse gray hair was combed.

Still not able to believe it, she shook her head. "Are you all right? How's your head? How did get back to the States?"

Laughing, he pulled up a chair beside the bed and sat. "My head's fine. Having a hard skull comes in handy. Either that, or those coca leaves were a miracle cure."

"But what happened? Where did you get off the boat?"

"It was quite a trip, actually. We were halfway to another village by the time the fisherman discovered I was aboard. He wasn't happy, to say the least. I thought he was going to toss me into the river with the piranhas and crocodiles. And I couldn't explain why I'd stowed away. He didn't speak English, and I didn't know enough Spanish to make any sense. I kept trying to pantomime how I'd gotten taken hostage, but he thought I was out of my mind. Anyhow, he forced me to get off in the next village. That was some place, just a little jungle outpost. It was even rougher than Buena Fortuna."

She tried to envision that. "What did you do then?"

"I got lucky. There was an American missionary group passing through. They took me to Tarapoto in their boat. The priest there got me on a plane to Lima, even loaned me money for the trip home. The embassy in Lima had my passport; the rest of our medical team had turned it in. To be honest, the whole thing is kind of a blur now. I was in too much pain to remember a lot of it."

"So the team is all right?"

He nodded. "They made it down the mountain fine. No one was captured or hurt except us."

She reached out and gave him a hug with her good arm. "I'm so glad you made it. I was so worried about you."

"I was worried about you, too." His earnest blue eyes met hers. "But what happened? The guy at the CIA, Dennis Caldwell, told me you'd been shot."

Her brows rose. "How did you meet him?"

"He met my plane at the airport. There was a whole group waiting for me, and they took me to an office to talk. They wanted information about the terrorists. Caldwell told me how the one guy, Rasheed, was undercover. And he told me you were here. That's why I came. I wanted to see you before I flew home."

Her stomach twisted at the thought of Rasheed, but she brushed the pain aside, determined not to dwell on him right now. "I'm glad you did." She took a moment to fill Henry in on the major points of her story, leaving out the intimate parts about Rasheed. "I'm so sorry you got kidnapped," she added.

"It's not your fault."

"Of course it is. My family caused this entire mess."

"Hey, it happened. I'm not worried about who caused it. I'm just glad we both made it through. And it gives me a great story to tell in New York. I can get a lot of mileage out of this. In fact, I know a certain woman in my building who just might show me a little sympathy." He winked.

Nadine smiled back. "Good. You deserve some pampering after that ordeal."

"I'll never forget it, that's for sure. It was the trip of a lifetime...I hope." He glanced at his watch and rose. "I need to go, though. I've got a taxi downstairs waiting to take me to the airport. I'll talk to you again later when you get back to New York."

Her throat thick, she gave him another hug. She was so glad that he'd survived. She couldn't have borne it if he'd suffered any lasting injuries—or died.

But after he left, the melancholy she'd been battling came veering back, settling inside with a vengeance now. She shifted her gaze to the window, watching the gloom usher in the long, December night. And a deep feeling of loneliness hollowed her heart.

Where was Rasheed?

Three days later, it was clear that he wasn't coming. It was equally clear that she had to do something to get him out of her mind.

Nadine sat on the sofa in her friend Brynn's new apartment in Baltimore, wondering for the millionth time why he hadn't shown up. The CIA chief had stopped by the hospital several times. More law enforcement agencies than she'd known existed had come by to interview her. Her two best friends, Brynn and Haley, the former runaways she'd met on the streets all those years ago, had camped out in her room, keeping any pesky journalists at bay. It seemed everyone had beaten a path to her hospital room door, except the one man she wanted most to see.

"Are you all right?" Brynn asked, exiting the kitchen. She grabbed a throw blanket from the back of the sofa, then curled up in an armchair across from her. Still wearing a sling from her own recent ordeal, during which she'd brought down a killer who'd plagued her, she pushed her thick auburn hair off her face.

"I'm fine." Or at least, she should be. Her family was no longer a threat. The gang executioner who'd hounded them had died while she'd been in Peru, thanks to Haley and Brynn. Not only was her life finally back to normal, but for the first time that she could remember, she didn't have any enemies in pursuit.

And yet, she'd never felt worse.

Brynn's gaze stayed on her. "You don't look fine."

"She looks as if her dog died," Haley agreed, entering the room. Cradling a glass of wine left over from dinner, she took a seat beside Nadine on the couch in a graceful move. Thanks to her debutante training, she always managed to look elegant, even wearing a baggy sweatshirt and faded jeans—her usual attire while working in her shelter for runaway teens.

"I'm guessing it's a man problem," Brynn said. The youngest of the three friends, she was now a famous photojournalist who chronicled street life. And like any visual artist, she never missed a detail.

Nadine sighed. She knew it was useless to deny it. Her two best friends could wheedle anything out of her. And they'd spot a lie in a heartbeat. They knew her too well after the years they'd spent together on the streets.

"You're right. It's the guy I met in Peru, Rasheed. The one who was working undercover with the Rising Light. I'm afraid…we got pretty close during the trip to the States."

Haley smiled, her hazel eyes warming with delight. "That's wonderful."

"No, it's not. In case you haven't noticed, he hasn't stopped by to see me. Which is fine. I don't want him to come by. I'm better off alone."

"Obviously," Brynn said, rolling her eyes.

"I am. It's just…the situation was pretty intense, so I miss having him around. That's natural, right, since we were together so much? But it's over. It has to be. There was never a chance that it would be long-term."

Haley frowned. "Why not?"

"*Because.* I don't do long-term relationships."

"None of us did until we met the right guy," Haley pointed out. "Maybe it's your turn to rethink that."

This time Nadine frowned. It was true that both Haley and Brynn had changed in the past few months. They'd overcome their troubled pasts and fallen in love with two incredibly sexy men.

But her friends knew her background. How could they suggest such a thing? "How can I? You know how I grew up. What if he turns out to be abusive? I can't live like that again."

For a moment, no one spoke. A helicopter flew past the high-rise building, rattling the huge glass window overlooking the harbor below.

"Has he done anything to seem abusive?" Brynn finally asked.

"No, of course not." Rasheed had protected her every step of the way. Fighting Amir. Taking down Sultan. Breaking into her family's compound to rescue her. "If anything, he protected me." Even when he wasn't sure who she was.

Haley set her wineglass on the end table, then

propped her arm over the back of the sofa and turned her way. "I'm not getting this. If he protected you, then why are you afraid he's going to be abusive?"

She slumped back and closed her eyes. "Because he's violent. He's spent years living with criminals. And you should have seen him during that knife fight." He'd been incredible, lethal, *glorious*. "I've never seen anyone fight like that. He was deadly, really fast and skilled. He would have killed Amir if he'd had to."

"But he didn't hurt you."

"No," she admitted.

Silence pulsed in the room. Brynn cleared her throat. She shifted forward, her gaze on hers. "Look, Nadine. We all had lousy childhoods."

"No kidding." Haley had fled an emotionally abusive family. Brynn's stepfather had molested her.

"And because of that, our perceptions are a little off. It's hard to know what behavior is normal if you've never seen it at home. We assume that everyone else is as warped as the losers we grew up around.

"But the thing is, men are supposed to protect the women they love. That's what they do. They fight for you. They take care of you. Would you want to be around someone who couldn't do that?"

She frowned. "No, but—"

"It isn't a negative trait, Nadine. Strength is a good thing in a guy. It's only when he's sick and uses it in a bad way that it becomes a problem."

Nadine thought about that. Rasheed was definitely a warrior. He'd exhibited his intelligence and strength at every turn. But he'd also been surprisingly gentle.

And that confused her. All her life, she'd divided men into two distinct camps—good and bad, mild mannered and brutes. But Rasheed had muddled those categories from the get-go, never fitting in either one.

So maybe Brynn was right. Maybe her judgment really was off. Maybe those categories that had helped her survive as a child weren't so useful as an adult. Instead of enabling her to avoid danger, they were now getting in her way, keeping her from seizing the love she deserved.

"But how can you ever be sure? My brother can be charming, and look what he's like. He's a monster inside."

Haley's voice softened. "Are you sure this is about Rasheed? I have a feeling it's more about you, and whether you can give him your trust."

That thought took her aback. "Maybe."

"The thing is…I think you already have."

"How do you figure that?"

"Would you really have slept with him if you didn't trust him?"

Her heart missed a beat. Haley was right. She'd sensed that he was a good guy from the start. "I guess not."

"Do you love him?" Brynn asked.

Did she? She'd never been in love before. But if this aching need to see him, this terrible void he'd left in her heart was any sign… She sighed. "Yeah, I think I do."

"So now you just need to trust yourself," Brynn said.

Nadine swallowed hard. "I'm afraid I'm going to make the wrong choice, and that I'll be trapped. Look at my mother and my sister-in-law. They both made terrible choices, and look how awful that turned out."

"But they didn't really have a choice, did they?"

Brynn asked. "Didn't you say their marriages were arranged?"

She nodded. They'd both been forced to marry men their families had picked.

Brynn leaned forward, her gaze suddenly intent. "Look, Nadine. I'm not trying to minimize this. You're the only one who can decide what's best for you. And with your past, with all our pasts, it's harder than it is for most people. We see the worst-case scenario because of how we grew up. But at some point, you have to let go of the past. You have to stop letting it have power over you."

"Love is always a risk," Haley cut in. "There's never any guarantee that it's going to work out long-term. So what you need to do is figure out if the risk is worth it. Is it better to take the chance or be alone?

"The guys you dated in the past, they were men you couldn't love, men who didn't really excite you that much. They were safe because they never tempted you to make a choice. But now you've found someone who's worthy, and you have to choose."

Risk versus rewards. Trading the status quo for the unknown. "It's scary," she admitted. "And what if I've imagined how he felt? For all I know, he might not even love *me*."

Brynn and Haley both laughed. "He loves you, gorgeous. He'd have to be nuts not to."

"Then why didn't he come to see me in the hospital?"

Haley knitted her brows. "Are you sure he didn't?"

"I think I would have noticed."

"Then he must have had a good reason."

Right. Rising, she made a face. "Like maybe I was just part of the job to him."

"Don't be silly. From everything you've told us, he's head over heels in love." Haley rose and hugged her, careful not to jostle her arm. "Don't worry so much. You'll figure this out. Trust your instincts, and try to keep an open mind. And get some sleep. Things always look better in the morning."

They all smiled. That had been their mantra as runaway teenagers. They'd recited it as if it were a lifeline when their situations got dire. And miraculously, sometimes things had actually improved with the light of day.

"You guys are the best," Nadine whispered.

"Best friends forever," Brynn agreed. She hopped up and gave her a heartfelt hug.

But later that night, as Nadine lay in the spacious guest bed, she continued replaying their conversation in her head. And in the end, she had to admit that her friends were right. Rasheed was nothing like the abusive men she'd grown up with. He didn't even come close. Even though he'd fought Amir, even though he'd done terrible things to infiltrate the Rising Light organization, he had never been the least bit violent with her. He'd never tried to control her, never put his own needs ahead of hers.

On the contrary. He'd proven his trustworthiness multiple times—giving her opportunities to escape, protecting her at his own expense. She could definitely trust her instincts about him.

And he'd truly loved his wife. She'd heard the agony in his voice, sensed the terrible devastation he'd suffered when she had died. And what was it they said—

that a man who had loved once was more likely to love again? And any man willing to go to such extremes to avenge his wife's death had more than proven his fidelity.

But did he love her? That was the big question, the one she'd been trying to avoid in case the answer came out wrong. Closing her eyes, she thought back to the night in her cottage when they'd made love, remembering the heat, the hunger, the need. She envisioned his face as they sat on the beach, the sympathy in his eyes when she'd told him about her life. The stark fear in his eyes when he'd entered the reception and realized the bomb would explode.

He loved her, all right. Maybe he'd never actually said the words, and maybe she'd never seen a man look at her that way before, but she'd recognized it. She'd responded to it. She'd felt it in every kiss.

So why hadn't he come to the hospital?

The heater in the room kicked on. Snuggling deeper into the bedcovers, Nadine started from the beginning, going back over every moment they'd spent together, trying to figure it out. And halfway toward dawn, the answer finally came.

He thought his wife had died because of his mistake. That guilt he felt for failing her had driven him for years. And with his protective nature, he would never want to take the chance that she might suffer the same fate.

The CIA was dismantling the Rising Light network. Her father was dead, and before long they'd have most of the key players under arrest. But Rasheed would still worry—not just that they'd come after him to retaliate, but after her. He would fear exposing her to danger, just as he did to his wife, and with potentially the same results.

And he would sacrifice his happiness to keep her safe.

For the first time in days, her chest grew light. Happiness bubbled inside her, along with a surge of hope. They loved each other. They could make this work. But if she wanted a future with Rasheed, she would have to go after him and convince him that she was willing to take the risk.

Chapter 16

Nadine had never been more nervous in her life.

But then, she'd never had so much at stake.

She stepped into the coffee shop tucked off a McLean, Virginia, side street, a rush of adrenaline making her heart pound as she scanned the room. A toddler wailed from a nearby high chair. A mother hurried past with a wad of napkins, scolding her son for spilling his drink. A trio of teenagers slouched at a table by the door, staring at their cell phones as they scarfed down sandwiches and subs.

Not exactly great ambience, she mused, standing on tiptoe to see through the lunchtime crowd. Not exactly where she'd envisioned baring her soul to the man she loved. But then her eyes landed on Rasheed across the room, and the noisy restaurant faded away, her equilibrium coming undone.

Her heart started to race. Her throat turned completely dry. For what seemed like a lifetime, she stood riveted, soaking in every mesmerizing detail about him—his shaggy black hair, his high cheekbones and stubborn jaw, the thick, dark brows framing his bold face. She skimmed his broad shoulders and corded neck, his lean hands and muscled arms, the width of his sculpted back.

And then his eyes slashed to hers, and the blast of heat they generated scorched straight to her defenseless heart.

"Excuse me," a woman said, pushing past her.

"Sorry." Her face warming, she forced her feet into motion and headed toward the booth. But her gaze stayed locked on his, her stomach doing cartwheels, hoping beyond reason that she could convince him to take a chance on her.

Another man climbed out of the booth as she approached. She tore her gaze from Rasheed, nodding at Dennis Caldwell, the CIA boss she'd met at the hospital.

"Thanks for coming," the older man said. He motioned for her to sit beside him, and she scooted across the bench. She sat directly across the table from Rasheed, and her gaze swerved back to his.

What was he thinking? She was desperate to ask. But she refused to blurt out her feelings in front of his boss. She'd have to hold her tongue until he left, and they were alone.

Caldwell took off his bifocals and cleared his throat to begin. "I have something for you. For both of you, actually. Invitations." He opened a folder he'd placed on the table and pulled out two large, cream-colored envelopes.

Nadine glanced at the one he handed her, and her brows rose. "The White House?"

Caldwell nodded. "It's a special reception. The vice president wants to thank you personally for saving his life."

She ran her hand over the embossed envelope, then opened it and peeked at the invitation inside. It bore the vice president's seal. "That's nice of him, but it really isn't necessary."

"Sure it is. If it weren't for you, he could be dead right now. You put your life on the line for him. You also helped us crack this case. I'd say that warrants a reception, at the very least."

She tucked the invitation back into the envelope and set it aside. "I wanted to bring those terrorists down as much as you did."

Caldwell slipped his glasses on again. "Speaking of that…a bit of news. The ambassador from Jaziirastan has been recalled."

The man her father had wanted her to marry. "That's convenient."

Caldwell made a face. "I'm sure he did it to avoid prosecution. You know, taking advantage of his diplomatic immunity."

"What about the other partners in the holding group?"

Rasheed shifted forward, drawing her gaze. "They've all slunk off like rats abandoning ship. But we'll get them. We hit the jackpot in your father's study. He had all sorts of records on his computer about his *hawala* transactions, going back more than thirty years.

We're still combing through it all, but we're making a real dent in the Rising Light network. We should be able to bring down the key players and implicate several banks before long."

"Your brother was involved in it, too," Caldwell said. "He used his real estate company to help transfer funds. Even without the bomb charges, we've got enough to lock him away for several lifetimes. He's not going to be carrying out any more attacks."

"Good. He deserves to rot after what he did to his wife."

"How is she?" Rasheed asked.

Nadine met his eyes, the usual sizzle buzzing through her veins. She marveled at that, wondering if she would ever get used to his effect on her. "They're releasing her from the hospital tomorrow. They finally got the infection under control. She'll need more surgery later to repair the nerve damage and do some reconstructive work, but not for several more months."

"What is she going to do?"

Nadine leaned back against her seat, careful to protect her injured arm. "I'm not sure exactly. She's going to stay at a shelter for battered women to begin with. The director is Iranian. I think she'll do well there. She'll fit in with the other women. And she has a great lawyer who'll take care of all the legal issues."

Her recovery still wouldn't be easy. Knowing her husband had tried to kill her had forced her to take a long, hard look at her life. But something told her that Leila was stronger than she'd once believed, and would end up pulling through.

Hesitating, she met Caldwell's eyes. "I've been

wondering, though, if you found out how my father found me."

Caldwell shook his head. "Not really. Our best guess is that the old gang leader, the one who led the City of the Dead when you saw that murder, figured out who you were, probably through your friends."

"It couldn't have been easy to find me in Peru, though."

"No, but once they knew who you were, if they knew you volunteered with Medical Help International, they could have looked up your itinerary. We might never know for sure, though. Not unless we get lucky and some of the people in prison talk."

She gave him a nod. "The main point is that they aren't after us anymore."

"No, you're all safe." Caldwell rose, then reached down and shook her hand. "Listen, I've got to go. But you've got my number if you need me, and I'll be in touch. We'll probably have questions as we work through the evidence. I'd like to set up another inter-agency meeting soon. And we'll need your help with your brother down the line when we go to trial."

"Anytime," she said. She'd definitely do her part to lock Sultan away for good.

The CIA boss walked away. Nadine swung her gaze back to Rasheed, her heart beating faster now. People chatted in the booth beside them. A car started up in the parking lot, then backfired as it drove away. She dragged in a breath, but instead of the nerves that had gripped her earlier, a sudden feeling of calmness over-took her, the conviction that this was right.

"I asked Caldwell to bring you here today," she told Rasheed.

His dark brows rose. "Yeah?"

"I figured he owed me a favor. And I wanted to talk to you."

"That's interesting." The corners of his eyes crinkled up. "Because I did the same thing. He was going to mail the invitations to us, but I asked him to deliver them in person so I could see you."

Her breath hitched. Hope pounded inside her, echoing the quick, heavy beats of her heart. "Then why didn't you come to the hospital?"

"You're right. I should have gone back."

"What do you mean by *back?* You were there?"

"That first night. I hung around until the nurses finally took pity on me and let me go in your room. You were asleep."

She stared at him, surprised. "I didn't know."

"I thought it was better for you if I left." He reached out and took her hand. His thumb stroked her wrist, sending quivers racing through her nerves while she waited for him to speak.

His eyes met hers again. His Adam's apple dipped, revealing a hint of nerves. "The truth is that I love you. But I was worried about your safety. I couldn't stand the thought of putting you in danger again."

The blood thundered in her skull. It took her a moment to find her voice. "You love me?"

He held her gaze. "You must know that. I've been nuts about you from the start." His big hand tightened on hers. "But I can't ignore the danger. We're dismantling the Rising Light organization, and most of the key players will probably end up behind bars before too long, but there's always a chance someone could come after me. And I didn't want to expose you to that."

"I'm probably in as much danger as you are now. I helped bring them down, too. And we're probably stronger together than we are alone."

"That's what I finally figured. And I was miserable without you. I missed you so damned much. But I wanted to be sure you're okay with that."

"I'm sure. I'm not going to let them ruin my happiness, Rasheed. I waited too long to find you. I don't want to lose you again."

"You won't. You can't. I'm not going anywhere. I even resigned from the CIA."

"What?"

"I took a job as a private consultant." His mouth slid into a smile. "That's the other thing I've been doing the past few days—taking care of that. Basically it means I'll be doing the same work for a lot more money. But I'll mostly do it from here, from D.C. So I'll be around a lot more. And I can be myself. I don't have to go undercover again."

"I like that." He'd lived that hellish life long enough.

"I needed time to think about Sarah, too." His gaze met hers dead-on, the stark honesty in his expression causing her to swallow hard. "What happened to her... I can never go back and redo the past. I'll always feel a little guilty about her death. But I've finally come to terms with it, that it wasn't completely my fault. Bringing down the Rising Light network has helped."

"I'm glad." He deserved closure after the burden he'd carried for years.

"By the way, I'm sorry about your father, that it ended the way it did."

"Don't be. His death was his own fault. He was so determined to avenge his honor, even at the end. I think he realized I was going to escape, that we were going to defeat the bomb, so he decided to shoot me instead."

"Still…"

"I'm not grieving, Rasheed. I'm not even angry any-more. He was never really a father to me, just a cruel man who wanted to control my life. If anything, I feel pity for him and disgust. He beat out any love I might have had for him early on.

"That's one of the things I wanted to tell you," she continued. "I've been thinking about my job, too. And since I don't have to hide anymore, I've decided to start speaking out about honor killings and abuse. I'll still do my surgical work, but I think there's a need for women who are willing to speak out. Senator Riggs is helping me set something up."

"That sounds perfect."

She smiled. "I'll relocate to D.C. I want to be near my friends, the people I love…including you."

His gaze didn't move from hers. Her heart swelled at the love swarming in his coal-black eyes—the same crazy feeling bursting in her. How could she have had any doubts?

"Nadine, I… Wait a minute." Without warning, he slid out of the booth. "Come on." He reached out his hand and pulled her up. Then, keeping a firm grip on her hand, he tugged her toward the door.

"Where are we going?"

"Outside." He pushed open the door, and pulled her into the parking lot. He angled between two cars, cross-ing to a tree at the edge of the lot, then stopped.

The cold wind blasted her face. Shivering, she squinted in the bright afternoon sunshine shining through the leafless tree. "What are we doing?"

Careful not to bump her sling, he pulled her close. "I didn't want to propose in a restaurant." He glanced around. "Not that the parking lot is much better."

Her heart went wild. "You're proposing?"

His eyes turned somber. His cool hands bracketed her face. "I love you, Nadine. I think I loved you from the moment I saw you in the camp. Whatever you want to do, wherever you want to go, I just want to be with you. Will you marry me? Will you do me the honor of becoming my wife?"

Her eyes turned moist. Her lips trembled, emotions swamping her heart. She reached up and stroked his beloved face, tracing the tiny bristles covering his skin, the bruises fading around his eye, the aggressive angles of his jaw. He had the face of a warrior. A man tested by violence. A man who would always protect her. The man she loved.

She'd run the gamut of extremes. She'd suffered through an abusive childhood. She'd witnessed her mother's painful marriage and the brutality her sister-in-law endured. She'd known vicious men, and gentle, unthreatening men—men she could easily forget.

And then she'd met Rasheed. Her kidnapper. A man who'd tossed her world on end, shaking up her composure and making her feel vibrantly alive. And it turned out that the man she'd thought was so totally wrong for her instead had been perfectly right.

"I'll marry you," she whispered. "I've never wanted anything more in my life."

He tugged her even closer. And then his mouth took hers in a kiss so tender that more tears sprang to her eyes. And she realized he'd chosen the perfect place.

They were outside in the sunlight, a place where the darkness of their pasts would never touch them again. They had emerged from the shadows for good.

Epilogue

"Hurry. Get the champagne."

Nadine stood by the window in her friend Brynn's apartment overlooking Baltimore's Inner Harbor and checked her watch. It was just a few minutes before midnight on New Year's Eve. In mere moments, the old year would give way to the new one, and the biggest fireworks show on the Eastern seaboard would begin.

"Here we go." Brynn bustled around the small group, topping off glasses. "Refills, everyone. Last chance."

"We've got it covered here," Brynn's fiancé, Baltimore Police Detective Parker McCall said from the kitchen, where he stood with the other men. He uncorked another bottle, the loud pop making her smile.

She never would have believed they'd end up so happy. Brynn and Parker. Haley and her hunky ex-soldier fiancé, Sully Turner.

And now Rasheed and her.

Haley came over and hugged her, her face flushed from love and champagne. Brynn joined them a moment later, her eyes dancing as she glanced back at the three handsome men leaning against the kitchen counter, discussing sports. "Did you ever think this would happen to us?" she asked, echoing Nadine's thoughts.

Nadine shook her head. "Never." She glanced down at the festive harbor, her throat suddenly thick with emotions as the significance of the moment sank in. "You know, the place we met wasn't far from here."

"I know." Moving closer, Brynn pressed her hand to the window, her expression somber now. "It was different back then, before they revitalized the downtown."

"We were different. We were so young."

"And scared." Three terrified teenagers, each running from her own nightmarish home life, determined to survive despite the odds.

They'd suffered even more on the streets.

Those years had been far from easy. They'd lived through hell—hunger, cold, muggings and attacks. They'd stayed on the run, moving around the country, concealing their identities and protecting each other from harm. "But we survived."

"We did more than that," Brynn said. "We ended up happier than I would have ever believed."

Haley glanced back at the three men heading toward them, a smile warming her eyes. "Dreams can come true."

"Ours certainly did," Nadine admitted, her gaze going to Rasheed, his dark features sparking the usual flurry of nerves.

They'd come full circle. They were back in the place

they'd started, but this time, they weren't on the run. They'd vanquished their old ghosts for good.

"And this is the perfect night to celebrate." She held up her glass. "I propose a toast.

"Here's to the end of our journeys, the end of being on the run, the end of the time of fear. And to beginnings."

The men came up and joined them. Her heart expanded. Three best friends. Three women in love with three very worthy men. They could now begin their new lives beside the men they loved—lives filled with the happiness and love they deserved.

They clinked their glasses. "To beginnings."

* * * * *